MW00528041

Gilda Trillim: Shepherdess of Rats

Beautifully bizarre! I could not have taken this dizzying journey except for a master hand leading me through the surprising giggles into the even more surprising blessings of grace, wisdom and healing. I really don't think Gilda is fiction, for I fell in love with her, and as she and I both know, love is stunningly real.
Carol Lynn Pearson, poet, and author of *The Ghost of Eternal Polygamy: Haunting the Hearts and Heaven of Mormon Women and Men.*

This quixotic novel may well be one of the best stories ever to emerge from the Mormon imagination. Gilda Trillim is a complex, delightful character who calls forth the very best in human (and rodent) nature.
Jana Riess, author of *Flunking Sainthood* and *The Twible*

What a mad, marvelous, and compulsively fascinating heroine Steven Peck has created in this novel—a woman who can spend a year painting pictures of an apple seed and write a novel describing the contents of a single drawer. By carefully scrutinizing the microcosmos of everyday life, Gilda Trillim (but really Steven Peck) starts to answer some of the biggest questions of all, like "Where did God come from?", "How do complex patterns emerge from random chaos?", and "Why does anything even exist at all?"
Michael Austin, author of *Useful Fictions: Evolution, Anxiety, and the Origins of Literature* and *Rereading Job: Understanding the Ancient World's Greatest Poem*

Like *The Scholar of Moab, A Short Stay in Hell,* and *Wandering*

Realities, Steven L. Peck's *Gilda Trillim: Shepherdess of Rats* is a victory for the Mormon imagination in the twenty-first century. No one breathes life into the inner world of the Mormon misfit better than Peck. His writing is as complex and sophisticated as it is delightful and engaging. He shows why contemporary Mormon literature deserves a wider readership.
Scott Hales, author of *The Garden of Enid: Adventures of a Weird Mormon Girl*

Peck's novel-disguised-as-master's-thesis pushes not only the boundaries of genre but those of humanity and faith as well. Gilda Trillim's narrative is simultaneously absurd, grotesque, marvelous, and poignant—we need her messy spirituality, the euphoric animal vomit that is her manna from heaven, for through it she teaches us that madness and destruction can be vehicles for exploring the unreachable and communing with the invisible. Once again, Peck gives us a crucial contribution to Mormon letters which explores familiar paths like the atonement, as well as the more uncharted terrain of the feminine divine, with grace and insight.
Emily Gilliland Grover, Professor of English, Brigham Young University–Idaho

Gilda Trillim has sprung from Steven Peck's head as fully-formed and singular a woman as you'll ever meet. Hers is an engrossing, uncanny world, pulled into existence by an author at the peak of his creative power. Absolutely compulsive reading.
Emily H. Butler, author of *Freya and Zoos*

You are one of the lucky few to be living on this very planet at a time when a physical copy of Gilda Trillim's wit and wisdom can be placed into your waiting hands. I envy the roller coaster of colorful images and wrenching emotions your mind is about to enjoy as you uncover Gilda's spunk and spontaneity as a one-handed naturalist who writes creatively, paints particularly, and has a wicked badminton return. Come with her as she susses out the meaning of love through engaging with potheads and fishheads and attempt to understand her wide-reaching philosophical musings that stretch across the cosmos and then constrict into the core of an appleseed. Even though you are not a rat (unless you are and then congratulations for getting your paws upon this scripture!) you will find much to learn about the universe and finding one's place within it. By willing the one-handed, full-hearted, and perhaps-insane Gilda Trillim into existence, Steven Peck again captures the wonder and failings of being human and the mystical connections between the natural and religious world that make life so delightfully complicated.

Emily W, Jensen, writer, blogger, and editor of *A Book of Mormons*

Gilda Trillim:
Shepherdess of Rats

Gilda Trillim:
Shepherdess of Rats

Steven L. Peck

Winchester, UK
Washington, USA

First published by Roundfire Books, 2017
Roundfire Books is an imprint of John Hunt Publishing Ltd., Laurel House, Station Approach,
Alresford, Hants, SO24 9JH, UK
office1@jhpbooks.net
www.johnhuntpublishing.com
www.roundfire-books.com

For distributor details and how to order please visit the 'Ordering' section on our website.

Text copyright: Steven L. Peck 2016

ISBN: 978 1 78279 864 4
978 1 78279 881 1 (ebook)
Library of Congress Control Number: 2016954753

All rights reserved. Except for brief quotations in critical articles or reviews, no part of this
book may be reproduced in any manner without prior written permission from the publishers.

The rights of Steven L. Peck as author have been asserted in accordance with the Copyright,
Designs and Patents Act 1988.

A CIP catalogue record for this book is available from the British Library.

Design: Stuart Davies

Printed and bound by CPI Group (UK) Ltd, Croydon, CR0 4YY, UK

We operate a distinctive and ethical publishing philosophy in all
areas of our business, from our global network of authors to
production and worldwide distribution.

CONTENTS

Title Page of Katt's Thesis 1

Thesis Preface 2

Introduction 6

Vignette 1: Gilda Trillim's Maternal Great-Grandfather
Arnfinnur Skáldskapur 11

Vignette 2: Letter to Babs Lake—On Winning the Uber
Cup, May 1957 15

Vignette 3: A Letter to Babs Lake on Relationships among
Bottled Goods. Events Circa 1959 24

Vignette 4: Some Documents Compiled from Writings about
Her Stay in a Soviet Orthodox Convent. Events
Circa 1961 33

Vignette 5: Letter to Babs Lake about Her Studies in Junk
Drawer Ecology. Events Circa 1964 39

Vignette 6: Notes for Gilda's Novel Muskrat Trap. Letter
Written September 1965 about Events Circa 1949 with
a Note Added around 1986 46

Vignette 7: Gilda's Reflections on Her Melancholy.
Circa 1962 59

Vignette 8: Letter from Babs Lake to Her Mother Mathilda
Lake. June 1962 62

Vignette 9: Trillim Cooks Emily Dickinson's Black Cake.
Circa 1962 70

Vignette 10: An Account of Gilda's Vision under the South
American Hallucinatory Drug Ayahuasca. Circa 1966 75

Vignette 11: Gilda's Poem My Turn on Earth. Written
Circa 1951 99

Vignette 12: Trillim's POW Experience in Vietnam.
1968–1970 115

Vignette 13: Meditations at Apua Point, Big Island Hawaii.
Circa 1972   156

Vignette 14 Trillim in New York Notes. Circa Late 1972   185

Vignette 15: Article from *The Greenwich Peeper* by
Pseudonymous Author, 'Madam Alley Cat.'
October 15, 1972   187

Vignette 16: Interview with Reporter Dob Klingford,
Published in *The Paris Review.* July 3, 1981   194

Vignette 17: Gilda Writes an Event. Circa Summer 1983   209

Vignette 18: Letter from Trillim to Babs Lake from Nairobi,
Kenya where Gilda was Teaching a Short Course in
Writing. August 12, 1988   211

Vignette 19: Trillim's Reflections on Bodies. Journal Entry.
La Sals, September 6, 1988   222

Vignette 20: Fragment from Travel Magazine Article:
"Dreams of an Ancient Kingdom: Remembering Old
Siam" by Rose Butler. Published Jan 15, 1989   227

Vignette 21: Gilda's Write-Up for Her Mother's Funeral.
It Was Not Used there for Unknown Reasons.
July 13, 1989   229

Vignette 22. Babs Lake's November 3, 1996, Letter to
Her Mother   236

Vignette 23. A Small Fragment of a Text Supposedly from
Gilda, Found in a Romance Novel, Discovered 2002   252

Vignette 24: Gilda's Final Note Written Two Months after
Her Mother's Death. Given to Me by Babs Lake, 2013   254

My Thesis   260

For Jim Faulconer who made a difference.

Acknowledgements

I've been helped by many people and I would like to thank a number of people for help with this book including Christine Allred, Tana Arnoldsen, Michael Austin, Melanie Beus, Shelli Gustafson Birrell, Amri Brown, Sara Burlingame, Emily Holsinger Butler, John Crawford, Katie Snyder Evans, Steve Evans, Emily Grover, Karen Hall, George Handley, Erin Hill, Emily Jenson, Tracy McKay-Lamb, Dian Monson, David Morris, Kristine Nielson, Jana Riess, Ardis Parshell, Mark Quinn, Julie Smith, Aaron Taylor, Richard Tenney, and Jaren Watson. I'm also grateful to the permabloggers at ByCommonConsent.com who gave me space to explore the early stages of this project. Special thanks to Jenny Webb, an amazing editor, who edited the entire book prior to my submitting it for publication (all subsequent mistakes are mine). I'm also grateful for my wife Lori and my patient children who have given up so much of me to let me write.

An Academic Work Disguised as a Novel Disguised as an Academic Work

Note: Some references of this novel in the endnotes are authentic, some are fictional creations. Distinguishing between the two is left as an exercise for the reader.

Title Page of Katt's Thesis

Gilda Trillim: Shepherdess of Rats
Thesis
Kattrim G. Mender

A Thesis Submitted in Partial Fulfillment
of the Requirements for the Degree
Master of Arts and Sciences
in the School of Esoteric Literature
Mervin Peake Online University of the Arts and Science

Date
August 25, 2019

Thesis Preface

Call me Katt. My mother did.

I am Rusty and Chastity Mender's boy. This is my thesis. It will be bound in a light blue cover, with glow-in-the-dark star stickers gracing the cover added by my sister Wynona. For such I promised her she could do and I always keep my promises.

My thesis committee suggested that I give some personal details about my life to help the future reader get to know a bit about me. Not that I matter. It's just good to know the sources of things sometimes.

It is getting dark now and I've just lit the lantern. I'll start the generator in a bit. The sheep I'm tending are nearby up on the eastern flank of Waas, in the La Sal Mountains of southeastern Utah. I'm watching them for a month so the herders can take a short vacation back to Bolivia. My dad likes me to touch base with our family's roots and spend some time doing what Menders have always done for near 150 years—ranch sheep.

It is early fall. Elk are whistling their breeding status nearby. Just for fun I go out on the front steps of the round sheepherder's trailer and slip a plate call into my mouth and imitate their voice. I sound out long and loud like a lusty male. One ready to breed and fight. The two go hand in hand often enough and I get a lively response so press the matter on. Even though there is still a glow in the west, it's getting dark. I sit down on the top step and watch as the first stars of Cassiopeia appear above the hills to the northeast. The male is rubbing his horns through the branches. It is near. I walk down to the bottom of the steps and pick up a small aspen branch loaded with terminal twigs. One left over from a dead tree I chopped up for firewood earlier today. I rub it up and down the steps, feigning the action of a male elk making a challenge by worrying a low-branched tree with his antlers. The bugling male explodes into the meadow, nostrils flaring, looking fierce and undaunted. I let out a whistle long and loud.

Stanislaw has seen it too and rises up. He's a big white Maremma, fierce as a demon. With me he watches the rutting male. Even with my poor human olfactory equipment the musky scent is virile and overpowering. The dog's hair is rising, but he doesn't bark. We are both awed. The monster feigns a strike at an imaginary foe, his antlers dipping up and down in the air. He is powerful and wants to show he means business. What female would not be impressed? The elk bugles, its body tight, head tilted toward the mountaintops. I thrill to the sound. The reverent stillness that follows could not be captured by a thousand poems. The silence lasts for only a second before Stanislaw barks and rushes forward. There is the crash and rush of vegetation as the beast flees into the stand and then all is quiet again. The dog does not chase it long before he returns and plops down in his usual place near me. We sit together in silence.

Saturn is fully disclosed now sitting above the shadow of the La Sals and the Milky Way is starting to Cheshire Cat its way into the blackening sky. I go around to the other side of the trailer and start the generator. It kicks up with a single pull and the air fills with the smell of gas exhaust. I enter the trailer. Close the door and boot up my Mac. I pull up some videos on the elk rut and learn some things I didn't know. On YouTube I watch a bow hunter take a big one down near Medicine Bow National Forest in southern Wyoming. The man in the video is shaking as he approaches the beast. He says over and over, "Shit. Did you see that? Right through the heart! Right through the heart."

It's later now and I pull down my copy of *Red Dog Flying* by Gilda Trillim. It was written within about thirty miles from here in a cabin on the Utah side of Buckeye Reservoir. I am supposed to write a small article about Trillim for the Association of Mormon Letters by tomorrow. She is the subject of this master's thesis. I'm working on my degree in Literature. I'm doing it online from the Mervin Peake Online University of the Arts and

Sciences. It's not yet accredited, but they expect it to be such soon and are much cheaper than most schools. They were kind enough to accept me even though my bachelor's degree was not distinguished in any sense and I'd flunked out of another master's program.

I pull down a large milk crate heavy with file folders and place it on the floor. My thesis is a compilation of Gilda Trillim sources. I'm trying to ferret out whether Trillim was a mystic, a fraud, or a madwoman. I can let it slip now that I can't tell. But hopefully I'll shed a little light on the unanswered question that will ease someone else's path when they are trying to do the same at some future time.

My background for this? I decided to turn away from Philosophy at Brigham Young University when some of my favorite professors fled for greener pastures, those perhaps where philosophy was more appreciated. I finished my degree in English. I was never a good student because I struggle with tests as they make me anxious and jittery, and I can't spell worth a damn, so I squeaked by with many 'Cs' a few 'Ds' and graduated with only a 2.1 GPA. Be that as it may, toward the end of my program, I felt a call to study God. After graduating from BYU I went three years to Claremont's theology school, but was forced to leave after I flunked my prelims twice. I have terrible immediate recall and when people are staring at me expecting me to answer questions, I look as hollowed-eyed as a grazing ewe. If there is any pressure at all I slip completely away from coherence and appear even less insightful than a hunk of mutton on the hoof. It is hard to grow up among sheep and not to pick up some of their ways I fear. After my disgrace in California, I turned back to literature after being inspired by a friend of my Mom's cousin—we call him HT. He was strange, but they say you could sense something deep in his heart. Plus, he wanted to make something of himself. Like me.

My mother introduced me to the subject of this thesis when

she furnished me with several Trillim novels to read while up here on the mountain. They are odd, but of such a strangeness that suits well the long, lonely nights in the upper reaches of the La Sals. They left me pondering for days and I decided that I needed to bring these to the attention of others. Those who have time not only to read, but to stretch their minds to the distant stars set bright in cold mountain air. So for my thesis I decided to do a source biography on Gilda Trillim.

There are many I would like to thank for help on completing this thesis. First my advisors, Mary Locken whose passion for all things Gilda Trillim has been an inspiration to me. She first agreed to assist me studying Trillim's work when she found that, not only had I read a fair amount of the writer, but like the author, I was a Mormon, and that I had spent a significant amount of time in the La Sals—the same place that Trillim spent her final years before her death in Thailand in 1996. Dr. Locken was endlessly encouraging and assisted warmly in my efforts to bring this group of interesting documents to light. The other members of my committee, Lenoir Forb and Ravenstar 'Gerald' Nightingale, were also of great help in completing this work.

My father Roy Mender, or Rusty as he was known around the bunkhouse, paid for trips far and wide to follow the twists and turns of Gilda's life and allowed me to visit many of the Trillim Archives around the world including Russia, China, and Ethiopia. After reading *Dark Leaves in Winter*, he believes he was visited by Gilda's spirit in a dream. She commanded him to fund my studies of her life. He has never looked back from the require-ments imposed by that vision, including selling two hundred acres of good grazing land to see it through. I am grateful also for his love and encouragement in believing in me. My mother, Chastity Mender, has never doubted me. For that I'm most grateful of all.

Introduction[1]

In this thesis I explore one of Mormon literature's most important pioneers. You are unlikely to have heard of her, however, because sadly her reputation within the LDS community has largely fallen off likely because she was suspected of being a lesbian, a no no in Mormondom. Also unfortunate is that interest in her work among American literary critics has somewhat waned since its peak in the late '90s. Still, there continues to be a steady stream of dissertations, theses, and papers discussing her work. Despite her star setting somewhat in the West, she still has a large following in other parts of the world. For example, in China a major retranslation of some of her best work was just released this week in Beijing. She has an impressive following among a group of scholars in Ethiopia, where central aspects of her work seem to speak to the Ethiopian Orthodox mind with more affinity than in many other places around the world. Her largest academic following, however, is found in Russia, where Trillim spent a significant amount of time.

Trillim was born in 1936 in Burley Idaho, the daughter of Heber LeRoy Trillim, a potato farmer, and Margaret (Maggie) Kimball Trillim, a former librarian from Boston. In high school, her English teacher entered some of her work in a state writing contest. When she won first place, many realized that she had significant talent. Her experimental style quickly earned her accolades and a scholarship to Radcliffe College. After graduating she erupted onto the literary scene with her first book, the slim *Cattle Memories*. Her second book, *A Slouch in the Shoulders of Deity*, shook the literary world to its core, or at least those who were paying attention. It challenged previously held assumptions about what constituted literature and the ways it should be read. Her work's unusual style and challenging form have been often imitated but seldom equaled. Her final efforts in mastering the controversial style in which she wrote, i.e., constructing fictional works as strange lists, reached its peak after a yearlong study in what was then the Soviet Union.

It might be prudent at this point to give a lomtick of her writing, to ground you a bit in her style and in order to cast into relief some of the events that structured her later life. A chapter from her book, *Breathless Triangles,* is short enough to be included in its entirety.

Chapter 21. Wherein Pettiness is Laundered.

Objects: Cloud, figurine, lighter fluid, rat, helmet, paper cup, Post Office, translator, icterids, stories, fifteenth century, flat, municipality, lecture, blouse, angleworm, refugee, comet, quilt, holiday, porch, finger, saw, trout, penny, haystack, guitar, loom, shadow, rain, laundry bin, caterpillar, piston, soil, hen, nematode, steeple, mountain pass, Nancy, muskrat, ankle, Romanian, perfume, vessel, avenue, moat, pedestrian, brandy, suggestion, fairies, swamp, flax, soup, pocket watch, yam, baby powder, lentil, music box, plus sign, braid, wishing well, door knocker, toy soldier, dirt clod.

Action: flee, escape, canter, coalesce, inform, delete, bicker, saunter, deliberate, slouch, press, prostrate, hurdle, wander, peddle, fixate, blast, stare, destroy, argue, bless, forsake, delineate, hope, sit, flip, seek, slip, orchestrate, belittle, bounce, stomp, flicker.

Attribute: green, bright, overt, spritely, comely, glowing, dark, heavy, sanguine, overt, lazy, gray, gifted, mysterious, great, eager, obedient, quaint, clumsy, melodic, panicky, steep, obnoxious, high, witty, hollow, victorious, glamorous, purple.

In the manner of: swift, careful, vigorous, doubtful, loud, eager, calm, glee, fond, just, acidic, quirky, playful, shrill, late.

As you can see this is not easy literature. Early attempts to understand it revolved around creating standard English texts using the words provided. These efforts were especially popular in French circles[2] but it was vigorously argued by most scholars that this was not her intent and the text was to be taken as given—not reconstructed or folded into a more interpretable work. This reading was largely settled upon as a result of a debate between scholars at Edinburgh and Chicago. While both groups noticed that neither conjunctions nor articles were provided, each came to very different conclusions as to what that meant. The Edinburgh school prevailed with some stunning work by Susan Levant and Malinda Gregson, who showed that textual reconstructions were never Trillim's intent.[3]

Current trends have viewed her work as possibility generating literature—trends especially apparent in the copious writings of Ethiopian Orthodox theological seminaries and theology schools. The Reverend Hierodeacon Rellime Amada has been offering some especially compelling interpretations. He holds that Trillim should be taken as is, that the addition or withdrawal of a single word changes the possibility of the text and therefore its entire meaning. To reclaim the given possible, one must open oneself to how what can be constructed rests in the given; to the grace embedded in the text, and how that grace then operates in a person's life. Grace is said to thus release the virtual hidden into the actual. To wish for another word, or to redact what has been put forward, is to limit the possibility of the text. Only in the 'what is given' is the offered potential of the text opened and the meaning allowed to unfold. Amada believes she was writing a kind of redemption in which the 'saving' comes from embracing both the strange format and the words offered.

Trillim moved to Moab, Utah and the nearby La Sal Mountains in the late 1970s with her dear friend Babs Lake. It was there that she did some of her most important work. However, she felt slighted by her people, who never came to see her writing as worthy of being labeled 'Mormon literature.' In a letter to her sister she wrote:

"It makes me sad when I think about the way I was treated by some of the faculty. At my last reading they snorted and jeered. One even rudely remarked 'Poppycock' and walked out of the lecture hall. I don't think they want to remember me as Mormon or claim me as one of their own."

I believe this might have been at Brigham Young University. It is clear she was right. If you search for her work in the Mormon Literature Database she does not appear and her books, now largely out of print, cannot be found in any library in Utah. However, she remained true to the faith (as she understood it) her entire life and claimed to be a Mormon wherever she went. However, her take on Mormonism was unorthodox to say the least.

Toward the end of her life, her work took a strange turn. First the section 'In the manner of' disappeared, then the 'Attribute' section got shorter and shorter until it too vanished. Her work became stark—cold lists of nouns that took a darker cast. Words like 'chain,' 'pit,' and 'abyss' are representative. Most of the light playfulness she was known for disappeared, and a seriousness and intensity enveloped her work. Her books now came out more slowly, sometimes with years between volumes. Her last work can be repeated here in its entirety. It was called *Hammered Pliers* and it consisted of a single chapter:

Chapter 1: The framing dissolves in strong acid.

Objects: Moonlight.

She died shortly after its publication. I found a copy of this slim volume in a small English used bookshop on Jomo Kenyatta Avenue in Addis Ababa. Strangely the title page was inscribed: "To my friend David O./ The bravest man I know."

I would like to think that perhaps this was once owned by David O. McKay, ninth President of the Mormon Church (1951–1970), and I am tempted to imagine that he found her work as intriguing as I do. I hope that the Mormon scholars in the humanities will revive the reputation of this astonishing woman of Mormon letters whose name and work deserve to come out of obscurity.

Vignette 1: Gilda Trillim's Maternal Great-Grandfather Arnfinnur Skáldskapur.

As is traditional when one explores a life, it is not out of order to make a brief stop to examine Gilda's roots. I would like to look at one ancestor in particular to better situate and frame her unusual vivacity. Her maternal great-grandfather I believe captures Gilda's spirit more than any other of her progenitors. It is not that others are unimportant—certainly not—but rather this one stands out in a way that portends Trillim's adventures. The others are largely of that hardy pioneer stock that many of the Mormon faithful will recognize and appreciate: hard working; determined, undaunted by hardship and discouragement. Legends every one of them, but heroes and heroines of a recognizable type and manner and as such need little introduction or elaboration. Her maternal great-grandfather is different.[1]

Interestingly, her great-grandfather's name was first introduced to me in a page from my grandmother's journal long before the name Gilda Trillim meant anything to me at all. On the page, she makes a passing comment, "Oh that I were as lucky as Skáldskapur."

Arnfinnur Skáldskapur was an Icelandic sea captain who joined the Mormon Church while his ship was being refitted in Liverpool, England. He had a reputation for being something of an explorer-philosopher, yet he tended toward the fantastic. For example, he kept a journal of encounters with what he believed were mermaids. They were always sighted at some distance, so it is easy to disregard the accounts from our modern perspective, which has no place for such creatures. However, Arn (as he was called) would not be dissuaded. One of his grandsons wrote in a letter to his sister from *fin de siècle* Paris, "Gramps Arny showed us his journal of sea people sightings when I was just a little tyke. I tried to tell him there weren't any such beasts as sea people but

11

he would have non [sic.] of it. So I'm not surprised you cannot get him to take his medicine if he thinks it's been tampered with. Once something is in his head there is no talking him out of it."

After joining the Mormon Church in March 1866, he immediately resigned his captain's commission and left on the ship *Arkwright* with 450 other Saints under the direction of Justin Wixom. However, upon landing in the US in early July, he felt inspired to stay in New York and learn the art of daguerreotype photography and during the next five years became a well-known photographer of stage actors and actresses. In 1871, he took the Overland Route train to Salt Lake City, where he set up a photography business adjacent to a bank on the corner of Beech and Laurel streets. Soon after his arrival to Utah, he joined a gentlemen's club known as the Redbearded Horseshoers who met regularly to study the life and writings of Joseph Smith. He soon became the leader of the group. One of the few remaining pamphlets written by Arn contained the following paragraph:

"The Prophet Joseph Smith was a prophet and seer, but more than that he could wrestle the past into the future and vice-versa. I have it from John Taylor himself that when Brother Joseph found a treasure in the ground, the spirits that guarded it would try to pull it back deeper into the earth. But Joseph was more powerful than they all and he would lay hold upon it and with a yank heave it from the hands of those spirits. President Taylor said, "Now when he went to lay hold upon the gold plates those forces that make all things slippery tried to pull it down, but Joseph grabbed it by the rings and pulled, but he not only pulled up the plates he pulled the whole history of the Nephites into the world lock, stock and barrel. He made it real. Where once there was ordinary history he pulled into the universe sacred history.""

Arn began to teach that history was flexible and could be manipulated from the present moment just as much as it could influence the future. And through his photography Arn began to try to rewrite the past. He thought that through subtle manipulations he could do as he thought Joseph Smith had done to pull up new things into the past by a combination of faith and power.

He started his history manipulation experiments with small attempts at changing the past. He would photograph women in variously colored dresses. He would then hand-color the dress in the black and white photo a variant shade other than the one of which he had taken a picture. He would then save the hand-colored photo and approach the woman years later and show her the photo. When they disagreed on the original color, he would have her pull out the dress and examine it. His journal records years of failure, but as time passed, a series of successes began to appear. The blue dresses he was coloring red would be found in the possession of the woman, often after long storage in a cedar chest, actually turned to red. It seemed that the more recent past was harder to change (but not impossible). He reports that as his successes mounted he decided to try bolder manipulations of the past and would color the yellow dresses with, say, red and blue stripes. The discovery of the first red and blue striped dress stored by a widow named Rathbone sent shock waves through the Redbearded Horseshoers.[2] There was talk of deception. However, the final proof came when a pale blue dress he had colored with white and red gingham turned up for which he clearly had no access. The dress had been taken by a woman and her husband down to the Mexican territories right after being photographed. Several of the more skeptical Horseshoers wrote to the woman, named Tantamount Lee, and asked her the state of her dress. She replied with the following:

"'Tis a strange thing. I had not seen that dress but a couple of times in the five years we've lived here, for after bearing (due to the good Lord's grace) three children in the same, I had not worn it for many years as the children had done much to rearrange my figure. I remember as clear as day that it was light blue in color. It had been in my daughter's hope chest for those five hard years and upon receipt of your letter, I dug through the chest until I found it near the bottom. Now, you will think me soft minded, but my memory of a blue dress must be set aside in light of what I found, for it was a red and white gingham dress. So I dug out the picture taken those many years ago and to my surprise it has always been a gingham dress (though the colors are hidden in the colorless original) for the pattern is as clear as day."

It was shortly after that that Arnfinnur Skáldskapur sold his photography business and became the man you are no doubt familiar with if you know any Salt Lake History at all. He became quite adept at things like finding Spanish treasure, or in having bank accounts he had never mentioned suddenly becoming available and holding thousands of dollars. Even things like people in places as far away as Chicago and New York leaving him vast sums of money in their wills. The Salt Lake Tribune called him "The Luckiest Man Alive."

Of course, as you know, that luck was not to hold. After being named as one of the Apostles, he was gunned down just after the century turned new. The man arrested was 77 years old and claimed Skáldskapur had stolen his wife, 45 years ago. Arnfinnur's wife had been engaged to this man apparently, yet they had never actually been married, so the shooter was thought to be mad.

His ideas on the present influencing the past are interesting. Science demands that I dismiss them, of course, but as Jorge Luis Borges says, "Reality is not always probable, or likely."[3]

Vignette 2: Letter to Babs Lake—On Winning the Uber Cup, May 1957

I found the following fascinating letter in the Trillim Archives in Beijing during my last research trip. Her speculations are perhaps a little too bold, but do seem to portend certain trends in Mormon theology we see today. It was written to Babs Lake and dated May 19, 1957. It is intriguing to me because she draws on the work of Henri Bergson, the French/Polish philosopher whose work fascinated me during my time at the Claremont School of Theology. Bergson would have been much more well known in 1957 than he is today, but her tying his work to Mormon thought and theology reflects an extraordinarily deep understanding of contemporaneous evolutionary philosophy.

This work was highlighted in the 2010 Beijing Conference of the Gilda Trillim Society, and published in *The Gilda Trillim Quarterly*.[1] I cannot tell you how exciting I find these developments.

I've transcribed the whole letter, which was written in Trillim's rather bold, sloppy cursive. It took a bit of work to decipher. Some words I just could not make out (guesses are noted below in italics). She is also an abysmal speller, for which I have deep and abiding sympathies.

Dear Babs,

I must tell you about the mornings. At first light a strident rooster floods my dreams with his urgent boasts and slowly, very slowly, I slide into the realities of this new world. The air is heavy and thick and graced with a first-light temptation to pull the sheets back over my head to reprimand the dawn for its disturbance, but the bright glow shining through the jalousie carries with it the humid smells of breakfast fires, the river's stench of human wastes, and the essence of an odd foreignness, which drives my bare feet to the wood slats of the floor. I sit up panting in a slight panic because I have trouble remembering where I am and what I'm doing amid such strangeness. Then I fall back into the bed. I lie for a while running through the metaphors that I will use to describe this place to you. The rattle of a cart is like ... the rattle of a cart. The voice of the woman in the street berating her husband resembles ... the voice of a woman berating her husband. I think I am thwarted in my literary attempts because the otherness of this place is too new. Too striking. My mind finds it is all too novel to make the connections between these fresh sensual experiences and mere words. In short, everything is like nothing. I arise each morning on the edge of a horizon over which I've never peered. No wonder delight seems my constant companion.

Well, it's time to give you the tale in full. You've received postcard after postcard from me promising that I will give you the details in the elusive 'soon.' How weary you must be at my promises and lack of delivery! Well, settle back in your chair and prepare to have unleashed upon your beautiful head more details than you could possibly ever want. You poor dear. With friends like me, it's either feast or famine on the news front I'm afraid.

As you heard, we demolished the Danish in the final match of the Uber Cup. It was glorious. It was a first-class smashing. I'll have to say this without pussyfooting rococo hubris, because it is a fact that I was brilliant. I had a move that <flummoxed> and devastated my opponents. The press covering the tournament started calling it the 'Trillim Lift' (if you can imagine). You've played me enough that you'll recognize the move—the one in which I take a lob with my back turned to the assault, racquet arcing downward from my backcourt directed stance to catch the shuttle on the upswing of a backhand, on the upward side of the parabola framed by my swing (did that even make any sense?). It looks like the motion will lift the shuttle high and toward midcourt. I think what devastates my opponent is that it looks like a lucky return, badly played, and so they plan to do a return smash. What they don't expect is the fierce slice I've managed to perfect, which sends the shuttlecock driving just over the net fast and low. It's devastating, even if I do say so myself.

After the tournament, at a banquet honoring our American victory, a British fellow and an Indian filmmaker approached me about helping others learn my trick. How could I turn down a trip to Pune, India the birthplace of our sport? My novel is well-stuck and I was doubting my ability to pull it off by the publisher's deadline (soft, self-imposed, not a fixed point) so thought why not? I knew that you would yet be busy helping your family with the <lambing> and other spring activities so felt no rush to get back. So here I am in India!

Remember that semester we accidentally took that philosophy class? I still laugh when I think we signed up for a graduate course in Mereology thinking it was a class in mere-ology—an approach to art from the most minimal of expressions—like my own novels. I thought we would be listening to Moondog's music or looking at Mondrian's paintings. What's funny is we didn't know we were in the wrong class until midterm! Hilarious. But you'll remember Professor Boehme was always trying to carve the world into its parts and patch together wholes and, as you'll recall, pretty much wholes were just sums of parts. (Remember his thick Austrian accent trying to get us to learn mathematical Set Theory [Ze Un-i-yon ov de elements iz ze whol-le]! I still think he was in love with you, you got the impossible ninety-eight on your midterm while I got a twenty-three? Come now, we studied together the whole time! Oh, the romance that could have been, eh?)

Anyway, my sponsors, the American and the Indian (they are paranoid and secretive and likely delusional, but they have asked me not to write in a letter their names as 'communiqués' might be read in the post office here ['Hello' to whomsoever is reading this! Say hello to your paranoid handlers]) were determined to design a set of techniques that would make the 'Trillim Lift' just a matter of following steps A through Z. Like Prof. Boehme, they thought the 'technique' could just be carved from a set of individual movements that when added together could be summed into the successful execution of the move. What a disaster. First they tried to film me doing it, but I couldn't! I just couldn't do it on command. They would lob at me perfect setups for the move, but when I tried to do it, I just fell apart (and sometimes even fell down). I just could not manage it when I was trying to think about it. This won't surprise you. The real execution is nothing less than the instinctual level of play that occurs during a match, much like when I throw a tennis ball to our dog and she becomes one with the entire enterprise. Nothing surprising in the observation that it does not take thinking to play badminton well, and that once you've given your body the motions over and over it gets good at doing it without bothering to inform you what it is doing. To me it is not interesting or surprising that the brain learns to take short cuts away from conscious thought and its grinding slowness (especially in me).

But what does intrigue me, is what I am and where the me comes from when doing that lift! Boehme's little part/whole debacle fails! Set theory cannot touch it, because it's a folded up thing that no simple summation or partition can ever get its greedy little claws into.

Certainly, with Boehme, I would agree I'm a boatload of objects. Even the 'lift' is an object (and yes I'm convinced a situation can often be an object, since all objects are situations!). So what is the lift? It has its roots in hopscotch, I think. The long hours I spent throwing my brother's hockey puck just so—it would have to land flat or it would roll away. Hop, hop, jump, hop, pick up, hop, hop, jump, hop, jump. Those motions were essential. Then there was the invention of badminton, the rules, the culture, the tools, the implements, rising into existence like a poem or a novel. Then it had to come to Idaho and capture the

mind of Mrs. Beckwith who started a team. A thousand coinci-
dences bouncing around and through things until I find myself in
England, spinning around at just the right moment to capture the
cup and crown, and the imagination of filmmakers who want to
mass-produce the lift in an assembly line of motions. But the
motions are not just pieces of a puzzle. They are rooted and
grounded in the past in a way that cannot be separated from that
past. Can it? I did learn the basics of the game in a way similar to
what they are trying to do. Why should my lift be different from
that, such that I think it unteachable? But maybe you need more
than only the components of the lift, maybe you have to start by
teaching hopscotch?

(I can see you raising a finger preparing to dissect this, your
mouth twisting in that way that denotes flummoxed puzzlement,
your brow furrowing, then lifting to one side as you ask, "So if
the lift is an object, what sort is it? It certainly can be filmed. It has
certain boundaries, fluffy ones true, but certainly there is a
beginning and end. The beginning might be when the shuttle
crosses the net? Or when your brain first discerns the trajectory
of the shuttlecock's motion? Its end defined after the follow-
through of your strike?" Any and all of these things I suppose.)

The point is, my dear Miss Lake, the lift comes from nothing
necessary. It is a complex object (if you'll grant that), embedded
in a game called badminton that emerged in a given political
moment in the history of the world because a bunch of
colonialists were bored in a culture without a tennis court. There
is nothing necessary about this game. It <slouched> out of
nowhere, depending on gobs of little accidents. It could just as
easily exist in this world or not. And yet once there was
badminton, then the lift could follow. Badminton suddenly
creates space for all kinds of new objects: some tools, some the
decorations of badminton culture, some motions and interactions
within the game itself. It could have been that it never appeared,
or something quite different could have bubbled into existence,

like hitting small baskets with your elbows while standing on a balance beam (imagine the motions that that would have brought into the world! Motions as absurd as the lift out of context, but brilliant in the game of balance beam elbow basketing!) To do the lift outside of badminton would be nonsensical. Yet within the game it becomes the means of a powerful strike, which combines with many other objects, some of them unusually complex: me, the shuttle, the net, my opponent, the court, the rules of the game, the audience, the framework of a contest, the other team mates ... you get my drift? It is twisted up in a thousand knots.

Remember our class on the Nobel Prize winners and reading Bergson? Remember his book *Creative Evolution*? All of life is like this. Like badminton, things come into existence contingently, not necessarily. He argued that the beauty and wonder of life—its variety and amazing beauty—emerge from such events as created the 'lift.' One thing shows up in life's great drama and opens a space for another. He wrote how evolution creates spaces that create more spaces and thus creativity enters the world, and with creativity the possibility of freedom.

So I suspect you know me well enough to see where this is going. Religion! Ha ha it's never far from my thoughts. I drive you crazy with it. So just roll your eyes and sit back and endure what follows. You have always been such an indulgent friend.

You'll remember how crazy I used to get at my father's ridiculous view that God and the eternities were just an accumulation of more stuff. More family, more children, more and more acquisitions of worlds. An eternal game of monopoly with more and more squares on the board and more and more houses and hotels piling up on the spaces? Ack. How boring that seemed. An eternity of the same game? Forever? You'd have to have some sort of heavenly opium to keep you happy and sappy enough to make that appealing. And for women? Quadruple Ack. Such an eternity terrifies me. Eternity alone terrifies me, but this is horrific beyond imagination.

But when I look around at life. Its diversity. Its ongoing motions of creation and renewal. The magic and wonder of birds singing, frogs piping, trees flowering, pollinators pollinating, all emerging in Darwin's 'tangled bank' to more and more complexity, my heart thrills! Do not the eternities share some kinship with the magic and wonder of life itself? Creative evolution? Freedom? Are these not things we can expect the heavens to contain? Is not the fabric that makes up life and badminton some sort of eternal principle? Are not the 'Trillim lift' and the New Guinean mouse bandicoot both objects that have emerged from deep time as a result of a thousand contingent spaces being opened and closed and that form the basis and holiness of complexity?

This is what I love about Mormonism my root fabric. God is not a simple object without parts, without metrology (Boehme would be so proud I know what the word means at last), without history, without emotion, without meaning, but rather is complex, multiples. Mormonism looks at God and sees not just the 'From Alpha to Omega' but postulates an Alpha-prime that gave rise to Alpha. Well, my Mormonism anyway. I'm not sure my father would recognize it as his.

So here I go. Without you here to contain me, I go wild. I turn on my imagination and I see a God who has emerged from something. Perhaps we are on an ecological journey. Like life itself exemplifies here on Earth. Maybe the eternities hold wonder ahead! Maybe new structures will come into existence that never existed before! Maybe diversity and creation are eternal principles and God, us, and all of this, will become a part of something even grander, more wondrous, larger, more magnificent. An eternity of evolutionary unfolding into more wondrous and diverse things.

This is different from the static God of most religions who sits locked in a deterministic eternity of going through motions ordained by Himself or who-knows-what. Nor the view that God is sitting in some role that just sits out there waiting to be filled by some worthy applicant. No, this is a physical God. A God made of material who is participating in life. Life! The kind of life Earth so readily and amazingly displays. An eternal life where new 'lifts' emerge as the game changes and requires responses to that change.

So I wonder, dear Babs. What if the eternities are open? What if there is no set eternity to which we are heading? No teleology, as Bergson argued, to which life must aim. What if new emergences occur on the grandest scale of all and God Himself is participating in a dynamic and open existence? Like all life forms on Earth, we see our own bodies as a set of relationships, processes, and structures that have formed alliances of other entities, societies of chemicals, bacteria, and such that all work together creating something complex and beautiful. What if eternal life is the similar formation of relationships, alliances of objects many and varied? Changing. What sort of object would the relationships and federations of eternal beings make? Wondrous beyond the wonders of this earth life? Of course. Of course. Of course.

Maybe this is why we return again and again to the creation in our sacred places and in our scriptures? To be reminded of life in all of its manifestations! In all its wonderful surprises. And yes, if God cannot be surprised, then He cannot laugh, and if He cannot laugh, then he cannot weep, and if He cannot weep then we are nothing but reel after reel of a motion picture or television program and our lives are no more meaningful or subject to change than an "I Love Lucy" rerun (not that I don't LOVE that show).

This is why Satan's little scheme failed. He tried to make a machine, when nothing short of 'life' will do for the heavens. That's why Christ's atonement is so powerful and important: it became necessary because of the situation that arose. It's a response to the emergence of a new smashing strike to which one must respond or lose the game. I cannot imagine God is up there following some rulebook (or cookbook) that maps out all that must or should happen.

And so is this not grace? Is not the 'lift' embedded in a game I've been given, been handed, and with which I interact and grow in skill, in meaning, and in achieving something grander? Soon, if the 'lift' spreads (though the use of this film seems an unlikely route at this point, given how it is going), a response will be developed. It too will spread and the game will have changed. New opportunities will emerge, within the game, new 'lifts' new 'responses' will come and go. I'm sure if I were plopped down in a game in 1984 (have you read it yet? Get on it!) I would find myself lost. But that's how evolution works. That's how growth happens. Creativity. Meaning. These matter. An eternity without growth? I cannot imagine it.

Well, Babs, I'm diarizing again. These are conversations best reserved for a night under a bright Milky Way burning across a coal black sky on a cool desert night. When I get back, perhaps we can take the Greyhound down to Zion's or Arches National Park and spend some time in real speculation. Give my love to your mother and father. I hope they are well.

With love I am your,
Gilda

Vignette 3: A Letter to Babs Lake on Relationships among Bottled Goods. Events Circa 1959

This letter I give without introduction. It captures many of Gilda's future concerns. In this letter to Babs Lake, she returns to a world in which spirit flourished in an animated world.

Dear Babs,

I lost the second match and am out. I'm feeling a little blue and empty today. I can almost hear you telling me (in your musical lilting voice) to stop moping and turn to a good book. I will. I promise. Literature has always been my healing balm, the life preserver thrown onto the surface waters during my hurricanes and storms, and you are correct—or the you I imagine telling me to read is anyway. I need to find a book that will take me out of this world and plant me in another. Such worlds, I have no doubt, are as real as this one. Just because this world finds its existence principally in my head does not mean that *that* astral plane is less real than this one. For all I know I may be a fictitious character in the head of another being who exists in another sphere of existence. I picture him now, a biology professor perhaps, living in the mountains of the West, struggling to make sense of my life as a character in one of his fictions, wondering who I am and how I have come to capture his imagination, the two of us moving in a dance of meaning across the worlds—worlds different in ontology and subjectivity, each of us imprinting on the other new realities and new ways of understanding what it means to be. Surely there is room for such a multiple reality in which each of us plays with and constructs a world from the snippets of that reality we each claim. Am I mad? Or is he? Who can say?

I remember when I was young, ten or twelve perhaps, all things had a peculiar aspect—one that has since fled and no longer exists for me. I miss it terribly. It was a feeling of animation, a kind of visual hue, or perhaps better expressed, an existential flavor that could be discerned everywhere. I don't know why it went away, perhaps it has something to do with the demands and perceptions of adulthood, but back then everything had a living dimension, an active, almost fixed personality. I could recognize in objects a longing to belong. To fit in. Not that human preoccupations were theirs, no, but they had their concerns and these could be apprehended. I remember that were I to throw my shoe into the closet without his companion (and shoes were 'he's for all things then were gendered), he would languish in loneliness until restored to the company of the other shoe. He waited in the darkness among the other shoes longing for his bosom friend, like a lover standing on a coastal promontory waiting for the return of a sailor on a voyage long delayed. Each item in the world, or part of an item, was animated with spirit and presence, so that both the red wagon as a whole, and each of its parts, would disclose an individual demeanor. Its parts would form a society instantiated in its wheels, tongue, and bed, working together toward the emergence of a common disposition—a whole wagon. So although its many parts comprise a society of beings, the wagon was also a single entity, an animated spirit fashioned from its component parts but not decomposable to them. Spritely spirits all, individually or collectively construed, but each a conglomeration, a confederation and purveyor of a different mood or tone that manifest one complete eidolon.

Even those indisputable Platonic forms, the numbers, carried a psyche whose nature was as real and present as my grandmother's. For example, I recall that Twos were friendly and well-disposed to like those with whom they had the pleasure to associate. Nines more cantankerous and inclined to find fault and make demands of their brother and sister numbers. Fives jolly. Threes gregarious. Eight always seemed a little lost and unsure of herself, perhaps feeling resentful that she was not prime, even though she is found early in the sequence of integers where primes are abundant and easy to come by. Ones were never lonely as suggested, but rather joyful and encouraging—loved by all.

I remember one autumn day during this period. I was left alone. My family had gone to watch my brother receive the honor of receiving his Eagle Scout. It seemed unfair because only two weeks before he had been feted and cheered for receiving the priesthood. In a bitter mood, I milked our two cows. I was annoyed that they were forced to come into the barn for milking while the young steer was left to frolic in the pasture (although to be fair, he was earmarked for the dinner table and perhaps deserved what frolicking he could get).

At times when I was in such ornery foulness, I would give a hard slap to the cow's black and white hide. Normally the hand-on-leather strike would fetch such a vicious sound that it would soften my anger and allow a sprig of satisfaction to sprout through my beastly mood. But not today. I milked the poor beast roughly, and when I had finished mauling its teats and slapping its hide, I was still not mollified. I was yet banging things around in a rage. In my rampage I tipped over the pail. Now I was in a fury, flamed by my added fear and guilt that there would be hell to pay for having carelessly lost what was earmarked for Sister Hansen (one jug of each day's production went to one of a half-week's worth of widows who lined our country road like spices on a rack).

Now I *was* wicked. I knew it. It didn't matter much in the grand scheme of things for I was just a girl. No one was going to cheer me for getting twenty-one merit badges or for lumbering through an Eagle Project building a chicken coop for the 4H Club. And no one was going to take me to Flaming Gorge in the summer for backpacking and canoeing and I was never going to get to sit in front of the sacrament table giggling and hitting those around me nor would I be allowed to pass the sacrament to bowed heads reverently waiting to receive Christ. No, I was not important. I was not a boy earmarked by God to flourish in his Kingdom. So why not be fully wicked?

I remembered that Anne of Green Gables got drunk on currant wine, mistaking it for raspberry cordial. I was not sure what either was, but I remembered it was made of fruit and could be found in the back shelves of fruit cellars, so I descended into our earthy basement to find out if we had any. It was dirt-walled and cave-like. This storage room was fashioned to hold produce canned in the late summer and to harbor bags of harvested potatoes. The smell was dirt-rich—a kind of moldy scent that carried with it the fecund aroma of cool mystery.

It was a scary place. Behind the shelves could be descried cavernous earthy hollows that the dangling lamp could not penetrate. Anything could hide in these invaginations and, I was certain, did. I imagined dark things that could be felt, not seen—pale beasts, sensuously grotesque who stared from their secluded dens, hidden but present, disclosed but masked in invisibility. These were not monsters conjured from my brother's pulp magazines in which teeth and claw were the tools of destruction. The sharp protective accouterments his comics offered up, fashioned from some sort of atom and electron-laden thing, were weapons of physical matter that, in turn, might be fended off with other arms made of the same, like sword or spear, or be blown to bits by a bit of cold-steel southern Idaho weaponry.

The monsters of these holes were different. These malignant spirits were penetrative miscreations that did not devour flesh but menaced souls from the margins of reality. Such things could as easily follow you into a dream as into another room. I knew if I was quiet and reverential they would just watch—for now. Yet they were to be respected and avoided. One did not peer too closely behind the peaches or try to reach beyond the back row of green beans cavalierly. Caution was the order of the day. Even so they were manageable. By keeping your eyes away from the dark places behind the furnishings you could avoid contact and thus confrontation. Care was needed, but not so much that the whole place needed to be scrupulously avoided. You did what needed to be done, but did not linger or stay to play. While dark and dangerous, they just wanted to be left alone to mull over their world of gloom. These, however, were not the only beings present in that small grotto. There were many whose personality could be discovered.

When you entered the place from the rough-hewn wooden steps, you encountered a low-watt light bulb hung in the center of the ceiling by a long thin cord. Because you had to pull a beaded chain to turn it on, the bulb was left swinging, making the shadows dance with a steady cadence, as if a hypnotist had set the entire room into a rhythmic, purposeful swaying. As the period of motion decreased, the metrical incandescent pendulum slowed and the rocking shadows steadied and, in the dim yellow light, sturdy shelves were revealed.

The ancient wooden planks held an array of lost and lonely cans, along with forlorn and forgotten bottles and jars. Their disposition seemed to awake slowly, as if, unused to the light, they were trying to moor their emerging consciousness to something surer than the troubled sleep that the cellar imposed. They seemed to be blinking and rubbing their eyes, trying to grasp a world they did not understand and mostly feared. Of the myriad of bottled things, most longed to be opened. To be the one chosen, the one who would be carried out of the dank pantry and bathed in kitchen light. But others, those with faded labels, or rusted lids, dreaded your touch and withdrew to dark corners. Still, as with all things, I knew at that time every item of home production manifested a self, a personhood as present as anything that lived under the stars.

I found a small half-pint jar of what looked like syrupy blueberry jam. Feeling as dark as a witch, I declared by fiat that it was blueberry cordial-wine and drank it up. That amount of sugar filled me with such otherworldly power and energy that I knew I was as drunk as a homeless sot staggering through the streets of Boise. I wheeled about the house (such a fine acting job of inebriation I portrayed that I convinced even myself that it was no pretense), shouting words that my mother and father, had they heard me, would have washed my mouth out with their profanity neutralizing concoction of mayonnaise combined with Worcester and Tabasco sauce. Finally, I turned to the holy of holies in our small frame house—my parents' bedroom. A sacred place that we were forbidden to transgress.

As I entered still reeling from my sugar tear, I felt a secret presence—brooding and dangerous that watched over my parents' concerns. It sobered me. I approached the chest of drawers, its top arrayed with doilies, bric-a-brac, and small bowls holding coins and odd assortments of jewelry, cufflinks, buttons, and tie clips. I opened the drawers like a thief. The contents were disappointing, mostly loaded with clothes I had seen a hundred times on the lines in the backyard. My parents' underwear, Mormon sacred garments, held no interest to me and disgusted me in ways that their socks did not. That drawer was closed quickly. In another, I found piles of letters bound with twine tied in lovely bows. They were addressed from my father at an APO address and posted to my mother. I feared to pull the bow loose lest I not be able to configure it back to the way I found it, so I left them promising that I would one day read them. I fully expected to find the pageantry of their love story fully revealed on the pages of that correspondence. I also knew it would be as rich and magical as any found in a fairy tale.

I listened very carefully for the sound of their return, but hearing nothing I turned my attention to a small thin bookcase. It was of dark, almost black wood that gave the impression of solidity and seriousness. This I knew was my mother's. I could sense by the way it had been dusted and the way the books had been arranged with care, that this piece of furniture was attended, suggesting to my mind a sense of holiness and danger—an altar to a god that I thought might be watching with hand raised ready to strike if I offended the sacredness of the space.

There on the shelf I saw it. I can only describe it as a book that was calling to me, shouting for me to pick it up. It was as if this were a book I knew well, an old friend unrecognized until this moment, which demanded that I run to her and embrace her. The book was of polished brown leather and gold-gilded ends and on the cover was embossed a single word, *Proust.* I opened it carefully. I could tell the book had been opened many times as none of the gilded pages were still stuck together and separated as easily as a well-shuffled deck of cards. I thumbed through it eagerly. This jumped out like a surprised jackrabbit in the back pasture, (and I can even now find it easily in my own copy of the book):

I feel that there is much to be said for the Celtic belief that the souls of those whom we have lost are held captive in some inferior being, in an animal, in a plant, in some inanimate object, and so effectively lost to us until the day (which to many never comes) when we happen to pass by the tree or to obtain possession of the object which forms their prison. Then they start and tremble, they call us by our name, and as soon as we have recognized their voice the spell is broken. We have delivered them: they have overcome death and return to share our life.[1]

I don't know why, but this staggered me as much as the blueberry jam. I knew it was true. The world was alive with ghosts. In every object spirits lived, present in everything from objects as tangible as a stuffed teddy bear, or as airy as the number three—all had their viewpoint, their way, and their awareness. I knew this. The longer I stared at something, the more I knew its spirit.

Over the course of many years, I have returned to that passage again and again. For what was so true and present to me then has now utterly departed from me. The world has relinquished all animation. Things seem to be only things. And I wonder again and again what I've lost, for it seems to me that much *has* been lost. Where once everything could be counted on to feel something toward me, now I feel alone in a world of careless articles. The ghosts of my youth have all departed from me.

I think it was in the University that the roots of my animated world were wrenched from their rich, imaginative soil. And not just to the cold non-living objects of the world, but even life itself. As if it turned every singing bird or bouncing dog into just so many machines that tick tock to the beat of their own internal motions, movements established long ago when the universe came to be.

Yet I keep coming back again to this passage from Proust and these lines I found in the book you gifted to me at Christmas last year:

In those days we had never heard of passing up a chance to kill a wolf. In a second we were pumping lead into the pack, but with more excitement than accuracy: how to aim a steep downhill shot is always confusing. When our rifles were empty, the old wolf was down, and a pup was dragging a leg into impassable slide-rocks.

We reached the old wolf in time to watch a fierce green fire dying in her eyes. I realized then, and have known ever since, that there was something new to me in those eyes—something known only to her and to the mountain. I was young then, and full of trigger-itch; I thought that because fewer wolves meant more deer, that no wolves would mean hunters' paradise. But after seeing the green fire die, I sensed that neither the wolf nor the mountain agreed with such a view.[2]

And I am left wanting to shout at my professors, and to the empty self-thing that I have become, and who now seems so blind compared to that little girl who heard the silent voice of a book shout to her and who felt the weight of a shadow's dark watchfulness: What died in the wolf's eyes? What did Leopold watch leave that poor beast's being? And can we bring it back?

I am yours,

Gilda

Vignette 4: Some Documents Compiled from Writings about Her Stay in a Soviet Orthodox Convent. Events Circa 1961

A largely unknown piece of Gilda Trillim's life was uncovered due to some remarkable detective work by Peking University scholar Tang Whelan. He has been relentless in pursuing information on the 'lost year' as it is known in Trillim studies. The story of his discovery is worth a book or even a novel in and of itself as his research has taken him from rural Idaho to the heart of Central Russia.

Apparently, at the end of the badminton season in 1960 Gilda pulled a hamstring tendon during her final match against veteran player Sydney Fields. Most researchers believe that she fell into an episode of depression and returned to Idaho to work through her injury and its effect on her psyche. There were no known letters or even journal entries from this period. It appeared that she had cut herself off from all public appearances and made no contact with her friends. Interviews with her siblings seemed to confirm this retreat back to her parents' home, and her sister even suggested that she had a memory of Gilda returning home for a spell after her injury. Even so, the evidence was skimpy. And there were unsubstantiated rumors from various quarters that this was not true, however.

Due to the dogged determination of Dr. Tang, however, we now have the rich and incredible account (almost unbelievable, frankly) of the 'lost-year.' A book in Chinese was published this year on that missing time, but it is currently not available in English, although such an edition is planned for 2022.

Near the headwaters of the Lena River in Russia (near Lake Baikal) is the Convent St. Margarita of the Blessed Trees, an Orthodox Convent. It was a short-lived experiment in the marriage of faith to education, art, and science. Because of its remoteness and inaccessibility, and the willingness of nearby local leaders to allow its existence (with some evidence of bribery), it escaped the worst of the Stalinist religious persecution. The convent turned out to be a hidden patch of light in a dark era. How Gilda came to this place in the heart of the USSR is unknown, but it is here she spent a year coming to know an apple seed. Yes, you read that right. An apple seed.

Dr. Tang says that there is a great hall in the convent that contains literally scores of Trillim's chiaroscuro oil paintings of a lone apple seed, brown on orange, lit by a single candle. These were painted over the course of her year-long stay there. If this was not enough of a find, the convent archives yielded a daily journal that Gilda kept during her stay. While much of it describes largely mundane accounts of her quotidian activities — things like minor battles with the Abbess, or complaints about the unrelenting diet of bread, fish, and weak beet or turnip soup — there are profound thoughts on the relationship of observers to objects — like apple seeds.

As Dr. Tang documents, a few of her entries almost border on madness:

I sit down after my 45th painting and sigh and cry and then sigh again. I am no closer to understanding this seed than when I started. It sits there on the orange cloth, baiting me, calling me, daring me to find it out, to discover its way of being, to capture what it is under that brittle brown shell. I've painted it again and again, turned it nearly every angle, captured subtle nuances of its given aspect. I have been presented and handed all sides of this simple object, and yet nothing of what it is enters me. I've painted it in morning sun and gloaming cloud, in two seasons, and in afternoon and evening. I've placed the candle at numerous angles. I seem not to have come to know it at all. I thought by looking at it, its nature would slowly reveal itself. Give me what was hidden. I don't mean 'know' its soft inner fruit. Obviously, I could crush it, and smear its greenish pulp over a glass and peer at it until blurry-eyed, but isn't that just another angle? Wouldn't that mess just be painting 46 through, say, 67? Would I be any closer to getting to it than I am now?

It is silent. I've put it under a drinking glass and pressed my ear against its base for hours, not to hear the noise it makes—it makes none—but to sense its silence. To learn of the noises it does not make and in that quiet revelation find the seed as it is.

It haunts my dreams. It appears as mother, father, sister, lover. It comes to me as useless background and empty quest. And when I awake, I turn it ever so slightly and paint it once again. Come to me! Come to me sweet masked apple seed. Let me know one thing in this universe well enough to call it captured. Dear, dear apple seed, let me enter you. I welcome you! Enter me!

I have not bathed in days. If Babs saw me now, she would think me mad. Perhaps I am.

The Abbess kept a record too, which Dr. Tang has translated from the original Russian. He tells me that it documents how as Trillim continues this obsessive painting, some of the sisters seem to think that she is attaining a kind of holiness. A consecrated aspect begins to be ascribed to Gilda and a few of the sisters start to order and arrange her paintings in the great hall according to similarity of the perspective from which the seed is viewed. Candles are placed around this odd gallery, giving the great hall an aura of sacracy. The Abbess notes that the Prioress is uncertain this is proper, but goes along with it in silence. Hand painted icons of a woman resembling Gilda begin to appear and the Abbess thinks things have gone too far but does nothing to stop the apparent theosis of Gilda and her work with the apple seed.

One bitter winter night Gilda writes of a growing despair. It has been cold and gray for days and the light that seeps into the room where she paints seems constant and unchanging from dawn till dusk and her paintings have been identical for four days in a row. It seems to broker a stupefying sameness she cannot dispel. There is a pause in her work for about a week in which she also does not write. When finally the clouds break there seems to be a shift in her perspective.

My study of the seed has not failed. I just came from its cell, a cozy alcove situated about chest high outside my room that the sisters have given it—as if it were a new acolyte. Two of the sisters maintain a vigil there now and light candles throughout the night in the niche wherein it lies. When I carry it from that hollow to the chamber where I paint, they follow it, with lowly spoken prayers and chants. What happened I am not sure. My Russian is too poor to get them to explain in such a way that I can fathom the concepts. It has become a relic of sorts. I don't understand, but I do understand. Now when I look at the seed it calls to me. It is entering me in new ways that are hard to describe. The seed is slipping from the boundaries of otherness and even though I can see it no better than when I first began painting, now after 97 paintings I am slipping into it and it into me. The seed's being is becoming mine and when at night I am lying under the furs and wool blankets that ward off the Russian winter, I can enter into the seed. Not its inner seedy marrow nor inside the seed as a physical location, as if I were inside the biological substance that centers the hard brown shell, but inside the seed as seed. Inside the seed as if I were the seed. Inside the inside of the seed. It is hard to explain. I am becoming enseeded. I suspect it is becoming enhumaned. No one will understand this because words are failing me. But ...

It is at this point we begin to see the emergence of Trillim as confident novelist. She stops painting, yet she begins to assemble long lists of relationships to the seed. These lists are extensive. I'll just give you one for they tend toward the monotonous. She seems to be trying to enumerate every possible thing that might be interacting with the seed. The objects she lists are not just things but relationships.

List #31

{candlelight, the upward motion of air in candle flame, Sis. Aleve's movement, Sis. Aleve's breath, air from the east window, the clacking of trees tossing in the wind, air from the high window on the north wall,

the vibrations of a spider web as the spider moves delicately across the strands, the sound of the bells, {the presence of (gravitational pull of?): oak chair, icon of St. Peter, Icon of Christ child, Icon of Mary mother of Jesus, candle, iron candle holder, icon of Christ, floor stones, tapestry of boar, tapestry of peasants working fields, every stone of the convent, other sisters moving to and fro, the trees of the forest, the mass of water moving through the Lena}, the smell of the bread baking, the spider's breath through tiny spiracles, the aroma of the soup cooking, the stirring of the soup sending spirals of steam into the air diffusing spreading moisture throughout the castle, the temperature of the air, the stones, the whisper of the wind as it blows upon the abbey, the cloth upon which it sits, the light from the sun scattered by clouds entering from windows bouncing off of walls, stones, floor, ceiling, the call of the crows that nest outside the east window, the hush of snow falling on the high window of the north wall, the beating of my heart and of all the sisters', the whisper of prayers in the night}

These lists go on for hundreds of pages. It appears they were constructed over the period of about a week. The journal falls silent for almost a month (or a moon?) and no one knows what happens but when it opens, it opens with this.

Here is what the chemist in Moscow sent me: politic, linoleum and satiric and oleic acids, photogenic acid, quercetin-3-arabinoside, quercetin-3-galactoside, quercetin-3-xyloside, quercetin-3-rutinoside, quercetin-3-glucoside, 3-hydroxyphloridzin, phloretin-2-xyloglucoside, quercetin-3-rhamnoside, phloridzin.

I suppose my little friend must be the same.

So after scores of paintings, lists of relationships of the seeds and other objects, and a formal albeit isomorphic exploration (she did not use her own seed) of the chemical nature of the seed, one would think that Gilda would know that seed better than anyone has ever known an apple seed in the history of the world.

Yet the last entry of her journal is this:

The seed is in me in every way. It stretches my thoughts and stitches them together. It soars and descends through my being. My every waking and sleeping thought is of the seed. I have entered it and it has entered me. If a Zen master has achieved a greater oneness with existence than I have with this seed then she is surely Siddhartha and I will find her and study at her feet.

And yet, the seed remains masked. Although revealed it sequesters something of itself. It is hidden and unfindable in its revelation to me. It resists my final efforts to know it intimately, plenteously, fully. What it is to be a seed I know and I do not know. I have failed, yet shine in my failure like a burning sun. I am a seed. Yet it is as much a mystery to me as I am to myself.

I have recently toured the convent with Dr. Tang. It is no longer a working abbey (it was abandoned in 1968) but instead has been converted to a Trillim museum maintained by the Russian Federation of Trillim Studies. The paintings still hang in the hall. They are wondrous and could as easily be placed in the finest museums. The sheer number is staggering. We were also allowed to page through Trillim's Journal. It is charged with a power and electricity both palpable and sobering.

As I left, I put my name to the guest book. On every page, on the space left for comments, is penned in dozens of languages, (after words like 'amazing,' and 'stunning,') the same question, "What happened to the apple seed?" I added the question to my annotations and wandered from the magnificent cloister lost in thought.

Vignette 5: Letter to Babs Lake about Her Studies in Junk Drawer Ecology. Events Circa 1964.

This letter was donated to the Trillim Archives in Beijing. It was undated, but its authenticity is beyond reproach. Handwriting analysis, stable isotope analysis of paper and ink, and most compelling, a mention of the letter in another letter from Babs to her mother (referred to as "that crazy junk drawer letter") all confirm its authenticity. On a modest grant from the Trillim Studies Foundation, I traveled to Skjolden and can confirm that a small farmhouse, which was owned by a family named Vermeulen, once stood on the site high up the largest valley from the town. Much as Trillim describes it.

Dear Babs,

I don't know when I will be able to mail this. I am at the mercy of my neighbor's good graces and the unpredictable timing of his next whim to go into town. When Vager does, I will ride down with him and his sullen wife Disa and see if I can post this. No doubt you wonder what has become of me after our tussle. First let me get this out of the way: I am sorry. Really. I am truly sorry. I was unkind and insensitive. Take that as you are willing, but I mean it. Forgive me? Onward? Let's put this behind us. OK? Please? I really am sorry.[1]

I am living near Skjolden, Norway. I've taken residence up the valley from town in an old farmhouse, a cabin really. I'm dying of boredom. It seemed like a good place to get away. After all, the owners, the Vermeulens, would be overwintering in Portugal, so I'd have the place to myself. And who are they? I met them in England. They are both retired literature professors from Belgium and we hit it off splendidly. They said they would be delighted for me to spend the winter in their cabin and keep the old place warmed and lit. It's been a disaster. I forgot why no one vacations in Norway during the winter. Oh yeah. It's cold. Silly me.

I was in England to visit Edith Scovell. You'll remember I have always admired her poetry collection, *The River Steamer,*[2] and her translations of the poetry of Giovanni Pascoli. Her husband is an ecologist of some note, Charles Elton. He captured me. Not so much my heart (although a little of that as well I fear), but because his love for voles was infectious. Voles! The little tailless rodents that mouse around meadows growing plump and languid on soft grasses. He sees the world as a festival of inter-action, replete with connections that define and construct the world of nature.

Sitting in his Oxford home, hearing stories about snowshoe hare and lynx populations, entranced and captivated me. He told how these fervid mammal protagonists dance together in a sophisticated tangle of *fouette en tournant* around a pole of amicable balance. One that keeps either creature from dominating in the give and take of life's game. The feline and cony populations are linked together just out of phase as their numbers swing in contrapuntal motion growing and shrinking in response to the others' scarcity or abundance.

But these too are embedded in a wild Yoruba-like gambol of multiple dancers moving to individual scores enacted by hosts of other creatures: jays, birch trees, beavers, paramiscus mice, mosses, woodpeckers, muskrats, trout, bears, firs, marmots, pines, mushrooms, and stoat and on and on and on and on, all tousled in whatever motions they've been given by their instinct, course, accident, and inclination. Ever seeking individual survival.

His tales about the ways of life so captivated me that when I was offered this cabin, I could not turn it down—imagining myself an intrepid ecologist unmasking the mysteries of creature interaction. So up I came. I pictured myself enmeshed in natural webs thick and knotted, but I forgot that winter is not the most amicable time to make a study of the great outdoors. The snow is thick this year and smoothes out the landscape as if a nanny had thrown a downy white blanket over a child's play toys, thus dampening all contours and hiding everything beneath it. It also turned out that to move through this Cimmerian landscape is exhausting. Even with my yew and reindeer gut snowshoes, I find myself less bouncing through the woods, as much as slogging in a damp sweaty heat of a type that would not normally envelop me until after hours of badminton play. But even that warmth quickly turns to chill if I stop for but a second. Then when I start to move again it is back to sweaty heat with every exertion. So it's a bit like the lynx-hare cycle of an endless back and forth of heating up beyond comfort, followed by a freezing of blood and bone. The extreme back and forth between moods of personal climate end up sapping me of all energy and motivation. It is cold! Too cold for me to stop and consider my fellow creatures without quickly becoming impatient and discouraged.

I spent two days reading, but the library here is small and not well stocked and I found myself sunk in boredom so relentless that I was about to abandon the place and to make my way back to civilization.

But I was saved. I realized that there was an ecosystem I could study. Ecology is the study of the relationships among living things in an environment. The links extend not only among the plants and animals, but also among the rocks, soil, and sky. See? A large stone might provide the door to a badger hole, or furnish a launching point for an errant pine seed. A gap among the forest trees might provide a space that allows sunlight to stream to new and fragile seedlings stretching skyward to make the next generation of pines.

Well, there was little in the way of living things to study in my cabin, but I found a place of relationships, strange and varied. In every home, there is a drawer that serves as the catchall for things that have no formal place to call their own: the junk drawer. It is a place of mystery and peculiarity and it is to this that I applied my fascination with ecology. So here is my study dear Babs. You already know I am eccentric beyond reckoning, but let me add this bit to your arsenal of evidence that it is so! Here is my study:

A Study into the Vermeulens' Junk Drawer in a Cabin near Skjolden, Norway

The inhabitants: seventeen wooden pencils, two pins, six crayons, a small standard stapler, seventy-six paper clips, a spool of lead wire, twenty-four fishing hooks, a leather wallet, an expired ferry ticket, a tangle of reel to reel tape sans the reel estimated to be two feet in length balled up and held tight by a rubber band, a cigar cutter, four finishing nails, a box of tacks, a very small ball-peen hammer, a pair of needle nose pliers, a corkscrew, a red rabbit's foot, seven blue pipe cleaners, three red pipe cleaners, a tube of fly paper of the type to be stretched out and hung by a red loop, a postcard from Disneyland, eighteen bottle tops each from a different kind of beer, one hundred and six pale yellow rubber bands, seven large red ones; one nine volt battery, two mouse traps, one small leather dog collar, seven loose playing cards, two ten-ore coins, one fifty-ore piece, one Swedish krona, a carabiner, three skeleton keys on a ring, two loose standard keys, two spools of thread—one green, one black, a mini-bottle of Masquers English Vodka, a vinyl 45 rpm of Italian singer Timi Yuro singing Dolore stuck (maybe glued?) to the bottom of the drawer, three match books all from Norwegian Hotels, two empty film canisters, one compass, three German volksmarch medals, three corks, a small candle-wick burned, and a cabinet hinge.

Interactions: Fishhooks seem to act as a kind of parasite. Their topological configuration relies on barbs designed to frustrate the withdrawal of something penetrated; this allows them access to the inside of other objects. The wad of reel-to-reel tape has suffered the worst infestation. The point of three of the hooks have entered into the thin membrane and embedded themselves inseparably. One of the hooks has wrapped itself around the rubber band binding the soft ribbon and could be removed, but like all good ethnologists, I will not interfere with the system. Who is to say that the hooks have no more right than the tape to engage in their particular way of being in the world? I will not.

The wallet is huddled in the upper left corner, and its height has prohibited the pencils from mounting its leather covering and it sits alone, almost. A daring bottle top has secured a purchase on top of the billfold, anchored by its rough corrugated sides. The cap's hold on the wallet has also allowed two rubber bands and a pipe cleaner to negotiate an agreement to keep them topside and secures them from falling.

The dog collar has formed a ring enclosure within which are diked the vodka mini bottle, one of the volksmarch medals, three bottle tops, and the skeleton keys on a ring. The collar is of such quality that this trapped cozy collection seems quite stable, although one of the pencils seems to be worming its way through the gap along the side of the drawer—the proverbial nose of the camel into the tent.

The hammer has pinned two of the playing cards to the bottom and provides a barrier that has trapped the pliers, rabbit's foot, and corks. As if to show its worth, the corkscrew has joined the hammer in damming many of the objects into the upper right corner—ironically including one of the corks, the object of the corkscrew's desire. A pipe cleaner is breaching the barricade by mounting up the nine-volt battery trapped behind the hammer-formed palisade. A pen trying to vault the obstacle, but has only just begun. I have confidence that it will succeed, although perhaps not during my stay.

The many rubber bands form a substrate, which give a kind of soil and texture to the drawer. Many an object rests upon them and they seem to provide friction and resistance such that they add stability and structure to the bottom of the drawer, restricting movement and providing directional currents of item motion.

Only the film canisters and the candle seem to range freely, rolling hither and yon with every opening of the drawer. They jump the barriers from time to time by the skill imparted to round things, and by the dexterity conveyed by their momentum. Although, sadly, despite their potential they seem to cling to the front edge in a way that brokers a lack of imagination and a deficiency of pluck.

The compass points to magnetic north, as is its nature.

As I look at my object ecosystem. I cannot help but wonder what is it like to be these things, each jostling for position, each negotiating with their neighbor for what they will do next, which state of configuration they will enter. Each object is as much a part of the drawer-world as the next. All equalized in importance in the space in which they exist. And what do they make of me? In their non-perceptual perceptions what sort of cause am I? My disruptions—what legends come of them? What tales traverse the drawerosphere when I open the thing and my motions are translated into actions that reverberate down through the ages of drawerdom? Not human tales of course, but the tales the objects tell in object manifestations. What new world-configuration comes into being from the first seismic tremor that cascades out from my blundering efforts to unstick the stubborn resistance of the closed drawer? When my sudden tug on the knob propagates through the dovetail jointed wood? Am I a kind of fate? A destiny that is written upon all that follows ever after? How strange to think that I am a part of the strange ecosystem. Perhaps even a keystone species.

All of the drawer inhabitants were designed by humans for

purposes. But the drawer has nullified that. They are no longer available for human uses (thinking of the drawer as a kind of tomb). They are dead for the most part in that sense. Yet they go on interacting in that little drawer space. Powered by the vibrations that propagate due to the occasional drawer opening or when something new is tossed within. But once in motion they must settle their quarrels and make their alliances. They must adjudicate their place and position. They must open to or rebuff what offers they receive by other entities making demands. They network and parley. It is a dynamic place that drawer. All managed without sentience. Without perception. Without a modicum of apprehension. Yet full of drama. The junk drawer is a mad house.

Well Babs, I must go. This will seem quite ridiculous and silly I'm sure. Being bored in winter makes me crazy. But then you know me well enough.

Please forgive me. OK? For that. You know. OK?

As always I am your,

Gilda

P.S. Do the deists among the paper clips shake their knobbed ends at me, cursing my name for my disruptions, or do they bend their wire in petitions for grace? I wonder.

Vignette 6: Notes for Gilda's Novel Muskrat Trap. Letter Written September 1965 about Events Circa 1949 with a Note Added around 1986

Gilda's novel *Muskrat Trap* was an unfinished minimalist work found among her papers. These notes were paper-clipped to that work:

Even when I was a cricket-sized child, I wondered what it meant to be a free agent, for my mother would often advise as we left to play about the ditches and fields that supplied the spacious fairyland of our imaginative games, "Use your agency well." I'd also been taught so in Sunday School by my mother's friend, wide-hipped Sister Jackson. She said this world was where God would spy out our use of this precious gift of agency and weigh our individual application of freedom's grace in his almighty scales. She would stretch her fleshy and freckled arms wide and indicate the length and breadth of eternity and with a stern voice enjoin us to act well, for as free actors in the world our choices would be manifest in the flesh. And this would determine how our forevers would be spent. You are free, she would say, and in any given instant you can do what you will. Evil and good and all manner of in between confusions were laid out for our selection and it was up to us to reach down and take that which would disclose our character. Our acts were freely chosen. A gift from God.

However, even at that young age, when I examined my life backwards, there always seemed to be a kind of inevitability in every decision I made—a determination based on where I stood situated in life at the time. A given situation, combined with some fixed nature of my personality would determine the outcome. That suggested to my mind an impress of God's hand fixing who

I was and what it meant to be me. When I inspected my relation to past decisions, I could always construct a map of well-defined reasons, a set of explanations that could be proffered to ground my choices. A set of traces could be offered that gave a fixed account of where I'd been and where I'd ended up. It was as if I were a spectator explaining a game of badminton to a foreign visitor—the reason she falls to backcourt is in anticipation of her opponent's rush to the net, the reason she leaps up is to do an overhand smash—all actions in the game grounded in both what's happening on the court, and stitched to the player's individual style of play. Everything was explainable with well-determined reasons.

How was it that those things on which I staked my claim of freely owning always seemed conditioned on who I was and what was going on around me at the time? I could always point to *why* I acted thusly. Was it really free if what I was choosing was fully determined by the very stream of happenings? That whatever marched forward from the past to the moment just before my choice seemed to completely fix my next action? To decide otherwise than what I did, given who I was and where I was situated in life, would have been irrational. Or so it seemed. Perhaps the resultant choice would have been different had I been better informed, say, or had more ken about all the things that a particular choice would effect. Still, it always seemed that those things I did only made sense in light of who I was and where in the past I had come from. And by 'making sense,' I mean they were explainable, and if explainable, then they had causes, or certain given factors, that determined precisely what I did. Determined. That was the rub. It all felt inevitable. Extrapolating backwards it appeared that I was just the result of a thousand fixed choices based not in freedom, but in a long chain of priors that had anchored and defined me since my birth. The me that had been forged in the now was just based on all the antecedents that had clicked forward from the past like the hands of a clock. Where was the freedom? Where did it slip into this chain of tick-tocking causal determinism?

At about age fifteen, this line of thought propelled me into a crisis of sorts. I could no longer get my head around the idea of free agency or free will. I was told in no uncertain terms that I had it. And that it was up to me what I did with it. When my room was a mess, I knew that it was I who was responsible for the mess and its cleanup and if I was the one who left it in that horrid condition to which it was inevitably drawn, my mother would point out that it was my responsibility to make it otherwise. (To be honest, I wondered sometimes if it were really me or the room that had free agency, for supposedly it could be otherwise than messy yet it never seemed to venture in the direction of being clean and I seemed incapable of mounting a disturbance to its firm will on the matter of its state of uncleanliness.)

At about this time, I began an experiment to test the limits of my freedom in order to examine my actions to see if, at least in some sense, I could cause something to happen without it being attributable to another cause. To find if there was something I could really call 'freedom' in the things I did. I reasoned that I ought to be able to break the causal chain, or so I supposed. I wanted to impose my will purely and without reference to anything other than my will.

After sacrament meeting, if we were reverent and kept our fights, poking, fidgeting, and giggling, to a minimum, my father would take us out for an ice cream cone at the downtown drug store. We could have it dipped in a chocolate shell or plain. I thought to myself, can there be any easier test of free will than this? For surely it will be I that will choose the one or the other. So I made up my mind to decide the matter of which ice cream to get and then notice carefully through introspection what transpired in making that choice. So when we arrived I closed my eyes and with set jaw made my selection and then afterwards examined the case to see if I could determine why I chose what I did. But there were always reasons that seemed to determine my choice. Perhaps I had had two dipped cones in a row and to shake things up I would order a plain cone. Or perhaps, my sister or brother had both gotten a plain and wanting to buck the trend I would get a dipped. That decision, presented as free, always seemed to come from the situation at hand and was explainable completely by it. Does not an explanation imply a cause? And does not a cause imply another? Back and back until we are left with a long chain of events that rally the implication that I had nothing to do with it? I was simply stamping something as mine, which really had its roots in many, many priors and precedents (although these were not the words I would have used at age fifteen)?

Once during my experiments when I realized that a host of reasons suggested a dipped cone would be what I wanted, I broke from it at the last second, determined to do otherwise than the causes had led me to choose. So having made up my mind to get a dipped cone I suddenly demanded an undipped cone. I surprised those around me with the vehemence of my determination and the boisterous force of will that I shouted to avoid a dipped cone. As I was handed the naked ice cream, I felt a surge of pride and triumph that I had finally chosen differently than reason dictated. But just as I began a congratulatory lick of the prize obtained through my dogged agency, I realized that it was my very desire to push forward a free choice that had created a new set of causes and determinates. In my sudden change of mind, I had just followed another cause, this time the cause of my wanting to grab hold of a bit of freedom—a desire to do something pure as an agent in order to convince myself that agency made sense and was real. Sadly, even in this act, I had just followed a script, a strict outlining as closely anchored in inevitably as the motion of the wooden bird in my grandmother's cuckoo clock at the stroke of midnight. I was a victim of causes over which I had little say. I was seriously disturbed by the notion that even in as uncomplicated act of choosing the kind of ice cream style I wanted, I could not tell if I had done it acting as a free agent. How could I hope that in the wild gyrations of more complex actions in the world that I could recognize a hint of freedom in the jumble of my situation—a mess of happenings that masked those determinate causes, but that in reality bent me to their will instead of my own? I wallowed in self-pity. I was nothing but a puppet strung tight to forces that I could never understand. Nor ever fathom to any depth. For most of that summer, I walked like a wind-up soldier around the farm, firm in the conviction that I was nothing but a mechanical toy clacking to rhythms not my own.

My family had a cabin in Atlantic City, Wyoming. Punctuating the tip of the Wind River Range, this almost ghost town embraced about twelve families that trapped for mink, otter, beaver, and muskrat, or mined for gold and silver. These lonely lands made up the upper reaches of what further downstream becomes the Sweetwater River. We usually rolled into town during the late autumn because the school break was conveniently timed to coincide with the deer hunt, but for us it was a good time to relax. The potatoes and alfalfa had been harvested, sold or stored, and we could put our feet up a little. Often winter arrived with us.

I remember after a summer of taking on the burden of being an automaton we arrived to the cabin in what amounted to a full-blown Wyoming blizzard. Drifts were wafting across the road like the foam of a tumultuous ocean wave mounting a beach, and as the windshield wipers tried to push the snow from the front glass of our spacious Olds wood-bodied station wagon, our worry rose in proportion to the shrinking visibility. To make matters worse, the inside of the windows were fogging up from our breath and my dad had to roll down the window and stick his head into the storm to see where we were on the road. He tried to clear the moist film from the windows with his bare hand as he navigated through the storm. Worse for us was that frigid air was pouring into the car like water from a broken sluice gate. When we pulled up to our cabin, our neighbor Phil—an old trapper of about seventy years old or so—after hearing about our ride in, welcomed us kids into his home while my parents went next door to light and stoke the big cast iron stove, prepare the beds with warm blankets, and get something simmering for us to eat—all to drive away the cold frosting of our bones.

Phil set us on his couch, covered us in a sheepskin blanket, and brought us coffee mugs filled with Nestlé Quik hot chocolate. He was a grand storyteller. While we waited for our parents to ready the cabin, he filled our heads with tales about the early days of trapping when he was a boy. He told us about a raging wolverine he'd once fought after picking up a trap with the wily beast still attached by the leg and dangling from the steel jaws passed out cold. It revived just at that moment. Phil showed us a long white scar that stretched from his elbow to his wrist. He said the devil had gouged him a good one and then he pointed at me and said, "I weren't much older than you!"

The storm had passed by morning and there followed three straight days of bright late fall sunshine that melted the snow as fast as it had arrived. I told Phil I wanted to be a trapper when I grew up. Just like him. It seemed to warm him to me. Unlike my mother, he didn't seem to notice that I was a girl and say that maybe trapping was not the proper way for a young lady to occupy her time.

He took me to his shed and we picked out a set of traps to start my new career. He showed me how to set a spring foothold trap. He told me that if I really wanted to get a muskrat, however, I ought to use a wire snare. He took me out along the edge of a pond not far from the cabins and showed me the muskrat holes and how to set a snare over the top. We placed them partially buried under the loose loam ringing the holes found abundantly on the slight manmade ridge surrounding the pond. He taught me how to tell if a hole was actually in use or if it had been abandoned. He showed me how to set the foothold trap along the path from their holes to the pond and cover it with leaves and grasses so it was invisible. He showed me how to bait it with a few drops of anise oil to attract its attention and lure it to the trap.

I was of two minds when it came to trapping. Part of me really wanted to catch a muskrat, take its fur, and make something useful from it. Maybe a purse or a wrap. I imagined myself coming to the trap, finding a muskrat with the trap folded over it, and running to Phil to show him what a grand trapper I had become.

However, part of me liked watching the little bare-tailed rodents swimming in the shallows, diving, and frolicking on the banks. I had no desire to do one of these creatures harm, nor did I want to find one with its leg crushed bloody and mangled. I would imagine its body tangled in the cold metal of the spring-loaded trap or its neck strangled in the cruel wire and it would always bring a shudder.

My confusion manifested itself in setting the traps only in those holes that looked neither quite abandoned nor undeniably in use. I found myself not burying the trap entirely but nevertheless setting it. I would be as stealthy as a ghost in approaching the hole, but as noisy as a heifer when I snuck away. It was as if my efforts were alternating between undermining the successful capture of a muskrat and trying really hard to be a trapper like Phil. The two parts of me were at war.

One day Phil came up unexpectedly to check my sets. When he saw what I was doing, he looked at me and shook his head and said, "I reckon you can't teach an otter to build a dam." And he walked away. I was not sure if this comment was reference to my sex, my youth, or just a stubborn stupidity, but it cut me as wide open as if he used a skinning knife.

I went back and after lunch I knocked on Phil's door. He answered and motioned me in. He had been sitting at his kitchen table cleaning some of his guns and so he sat back down and commenced with the job at hand.

I watched him for a while and then said, "I really want to be a trapper."

He looked up and weighed me with his eyes and said, "Then do the things trappers do."

"But at the same time I really don't want to be a trapper."

He looked at me for a while longer this time and said, "Well, it's up to you."

That did it. Poor Phil. I unloaded all my worries about free agency on him like a pile of bricks emptied from a dump truck. He listened, all the while cleaning his guns, running stiff round brass and copper brushes down the barrels, swabbing them out with fragrant oil that when mingled with the spent gunpowder gave off a pleasant, earthy scent. After scouring them with the rod, he would slap all the parts that he had spread out on the table back together into a working rifle or pistol. It took me about all his guns to lay it all before him. The pre-existence. The war in heaven. The stuff from the Book of Mormon about acting and not being acted upon. He was as patient as a saint, because I realize now that there was no reason to think he was a Mormon but he listened nonetheless. He put on a kettle as I was telling him about my worries about not being able to tell if I was the one choosing to get my cone dipped, or if it was just a long chain of events eventually leading to me doing one thing or the other. While I jabbered on, the water boiled and he poured us a pair of hot chocolates, throwing a spoon of instant coffee into his. While we drank it slowly, I continued to list my reasons for thinking there was no real freedom of action in the world.

When I finished he shook his head and said, "That's a poser."

He took our cups back to the kitchen and came back with a tall glass of Kool-Aid and a plate of Swedish almond cake that apparently someone had brought over earlier, because I knew from experience and word of mouth that Phil was not much of a cook.

He leaned back in his chair and put his hands on the back of his head and closed his eyes as if thinking hard about something. Finally, he opened his eyes and said, "I think you're looking at it bass ackwards. Freedom to do sumpin' ain't just to do some nonsensical thing there ain't no reason to do. No, we always have reasons, if the reasons to do something are crystal clear and easy then there usually ain't no decision to be made. But it's when you got several things pulling at you and the reasons are mixed up and uncertain that decisions get hard and you have to be the one to make the choice. Being responsible means you make a choice always a little in the dark and that's what shows what kind of character you got. Freedom don't mean there ain't a pile of stuff going into it, you usually got reasons aplenty. Yeah, and after the fact you can pick out what they were. But it's more like being on a river in a canoe. Sure you are on a river, sure there are rocks and logs defining what you got to do, but there sure as hell ain't one way to shoot them rapids, but if you want to do it without sinking the damn thing, you got to make choices, sometimes bad ones and hopefully mostly good ones, that are going to decide if you make it to calm waters. It ain't about choosin' between two things that don't matter a lamb's ass like if you want your cone dipped—though as for myself I can't imagine choosing an undipped cone if'n you have a shot at a dipped one, but I suppose that bears to your point that I don't have a choice in the matter—but it's the ones that run you to the edge, that make you step into the darkness and hope you land that jump you into your freedom. It's when the causes are thick about you that you have to hitch on to one. Now that's agency. Not choosing betwixt things but figuring where to aim your craft through what rapids you find yourself in. And that's done caused you to choose what sort of person you want to be. Choose that and a pile of reasons sure do line up, thick and weighty. Seems to me you make a choice about who you are and what you are about, sure as we's sittin' here, but then that little stuff best be handled with a clear head and good reasons. You following me, Muskrat?"

I nodded. Pleased at my new nickname.

It was quite a speech. Longest I'd ever heard or ever would hear from his mouth for he was dead when we came back the next summer. I eventually came down on the side of letting the muskrats go. I chose that. Cause that's the kind of person I wanted to be.

I can tell.

Then apparently years later the following is written on the back of this in pencil:

I think often of Phil's words. That old Wyoming cowboy, a piece of driftwood, so smoothed by nature's roughness that he attained the kind of wisdom usually reserved for bespectacled philosophers whose jaundiced eyes have peered into the depths of being with such ferocity that they can snatch something of their own making from other worlds to plant in this one.

I've thought long on agency and freedom and how it exists in a world made of atoms with set spin and charge and which prance though the world marching to cadences well described and circumscribed. And I cannot find place for both my sense of freedom and my sense that I follow paths outlined by those lively atomic bundles.

I think often of my Sunday School teacher and her claim that we came into this world from a heavenly one, not much different from this, except perhaps more spirit-tinged and holy. That I was placed here to do and walk in a destiny outlined by a kind, wise father whose own will had set my fated circumstance to my soul's best advantage.

Yet I don't feel placed. Plato's vision of souls wandering too close to the mystical nets this physical world drags behind it and by such being captured in an accident of proximity seems to be closer to the mark. Not saved for the last days so much as being more cautious and careful about peering into the bemattered world that I did not go early. But finally bending too near this glorious place and being sucked into this thick material like the others. And no less randomly.

I was recently given a new book to review by New Yorker Cartoonist William Steig, called *Abel's Island*[2]. It's supposed to be a children's book. Far from it. It is an apt exploration of existence and meaning for any age.

The book opens with two Edwardian mice having a playful day picnicking and playing croquet. However, a storm arises and through a series of accidents Abel is lost in the ravages of a storm.

Heaven knows how far he was hustled in this manner, or how many rocks he caromed off on his way. He did no thinking. He only knew it was dark and windy and wet, and that he was being knocked about in a world that had lost its manners, in a direction, as far as he could tell, not north, south, east, or west, but whatever way the wind had a mind to go; and all he could do was wait and learn what its whims were. (p. 10)

Because I was meditating on pre-existence and life's relationship to freedom and determinism, this passage struck me hard. Indeed, is not that our common predicament? Facing the storm that happens along and tosses us in a world not of our choosing?

He is marooned on an island in the middle of a river with a current too swift to be negotiated by a mouse. Early in his adventure he notices a star he had formed a relationship to.

As a child, he would sometimes talk to this star, but only when he was his most serious, real self, and not being any sort of show-off or clown. As he grew up, the practice had somehow worn off.

He looked up at his old friend as if to say, "You see my predicament."

The star seemed to respond, "I see."

Abel next put the question: "What shall I do?"

The star seemed to answer, "You will do what you will do." For some reason this reply strengthened Abel's belief in himself. Sleep gently enfolded him. The constellations proceeded across the hushed havens as if tiptoeing past the dreaming mouse on his high branch. (p. 32)

Here juxtaposed are the elements of freedom and determinism. The star (God?) sees, but cannot help. Abel has stepped out of its influence. "You will do what you will do." Could be read as a claim about a determined course that might be said of a wind-up toy, but I read it by excising as unnecessary the final 'do' and see the sentence as an injunction toward freedom. That is why he finds his belief strengthened. He is out of the wind and into a world where he 'will do,' unlike the constellations, which proceed on their course.

Days pass and after several failed escape attempts, Abel realizes he may be here awhile, he wonders:

Was it just an accident that he was here on this uninhabited island? Abel began to wonder. Was he being singled out for some reason; was he being tested? If so, why? Didn't it prove his worth that such a one as Amanda loved him? (p. 34)

Why was he there? It was an accident. Nothing more. Tossed by a careless wind he arrived. He must do what he must do, like the canoeist in Phil's description of freedom; we are free to face the river, or life, with what resources we have, to accomplish what tasks have presented themselves in our confrontation with meaning and life.

In the end, Abel does escape the island by a bit of luck, a daring decision, and a continued resolve to find his way back to those he loves. But just as he escapes he is taken by a cat:

Abel realized that the cat had to do what she did. She was being a cat. It was up to him to be the mouse.

And he was playing his part very well. A little smugness crept into his attitude. He seemed to be saying, "It's your move." (p. 112)

Determinism. Playing a part. Making a move. Resolving on a stratagem to escape (which he does). All in a mess of choice and causality. None of it clearly free. To me this gets at the heart of what Phil was saying. It's not in the simple choices of this or that that makes freedom real, it's in navigating these perplexities on a scale above that. A scale with existential weight.

And where does this freedom reside? I think it is fundamental to the nature of the universe. One of its givens. I am reminded of the French Natural Philosophers trying to sort out gravity. They claimed that any explanation should be an explanation of why bodies attract. Why when you drop an apple does it fall? So resolved to understand the fundamental attraction of things they created a system of vortices that spun like whirlwinds creating the gravitational tug with which we all are familiar. Newton's genius was to shrug and say, who cares why, let's catalog and quantify its effects. And so today, why two things attract is just a thing matter does in the presence of other matter. Why? Who knows?

To me freedom is similar. We look for it bubbling out of the stuff of matter and in something akin to Descartes' vortices want it describable in terms of causes and explicanda. Yet perhaps, since it is so necessary to our understanding of everything that happens, like Newton we have to accept that there it is, sitting in us. It just is. Apples fall on our heads. We must make choices.

There is one more thing I notice. Freedom, if it emerges like magic from consciousness (like the conjuring of consciousness itself!) seems best recognized in the choices made for love. Those acts of love (or acts of choosing not to love) seem to create the most powerful evidence that freedom lives in the world; or at least to me that is where it is most clear. And those things I believe about God Mother and Father, that They are love, seem to be the best use of agency for the three of us. I could entertain that that is the most necessary place for freedom to hide, and maybe the only place it does. If so, it is enough.

Vignette 7: Gilda Reflects on Her Melancholy. Circa 1962

After her return from the Soviet Union, Gilda seems to have fallen into depression. Her friend Babs Lake took her on an Atlantic Cruise to break her from its chains. During that time, her spirits lifted significantly. She was reading *Moby Dick*, and this was found folded in her hardback copy of the book. It is a fascinating peep into the things she was thinking at the time and that later would inform her fiction. It is believed by most Trillim scholars that this was written about two days into the voyage.[1]

Here on a hollow deck. Of a hollow ship. On a hollow ocean. Gracing a hollow planet. Circling a hollow star. Secondary qualities without substance. Appearance without essence. Surface without depth. Is it real, or just me—falling into a slippage of self, a dysfunction of my brain, twisting reality into a caricature of a line drawing abstracted from something richer into which I cannot tap?

What if it's not me? What if this deep melancholy is natural? A response to a disease of sorts. Not something deviant or masking realities, but rather something embracing them? Attending to them with clarity? What if this depression of spirit is not a sickness of self, but of community? What if this deep detachment is a call to others, to draw the community's gaze to that one member who can no longer carry her self-imposed load? Like a fever. A signal to the village that something is not right within. A muster! A trumpet blast to rally the tribe. Quick. Run to her! Grab her. Hold her with your strong arms. Convince her by your swift attention that she belongs. That she belongs whether she can carry her load or not. Tell her: You are ours! The community calls, we will not let you go! What if in her struggles to get away she were told, you cannot go away, for you are ours.

You are ours. I am unworthy, she weeps and pulls away, runs away whispering, I cannot carry the load. It is too much. But the village comforts, we will carry both you and your load. See our arms? Are they not strong? Come one. Come all. There! Heave ho. Shoulder her burdens. You are ours! You are ours! See! We have your cargo. It is light for we are many and we can hoist it with ease. All your loads are secure. We will not drop them. Rest your mind, for we've got them, and we are holding all that you love tight. Do not worry; we will not let them fall. They are yours, and because they are yours, they are ours. Let me go, she cries. I no longer belong. Leave me alone. Leave me to be. Alone.

But we will not. We will not. We cannot. She is ours.

What if melancholia is natural? What if it is not broken brain chemistry, but broken networks of care? In a mythical time, call it the time of the cavewoman, call it tribal, call it the age of awareness, when we walked with others more closely, when we could read another's mood and contribution and tune ourselves to their comportment and disposition, could we then heed the call more keenly? Could we sense the community's ailments and disarrangements with more regard? Apply what medicine was needed with more fine-tuned dosage? Granting the magic necessary to attend to the broken community, in which a despondent member is but a fever of sort? A signal. A broken pulse beat in networks of care?

See my neighborhood now. Compartments of the lonely. We dwell alone, or in island families, staring through singleton houses lined up like rows of prison cells carved from the landscape, masking and dividing what community is still not ravaged by the sharp blades of modern life.

Or this metaphor. Our modern networks are like a spider web blasted with a stream from a garden hose: the shreds of the web remain, creating a mere semblance of the structure that once stood securely. Networked with solid moorings and tightly moored joints that could withstand what winds blew in the night.

Not now. Now under the pressure of the focused liquid beam from the water hose, it has been shred to the point that the lattice is a sparse and threadbare rag.

We boast about our individuality and hold up our independence like a plucked bird bragging that now without the weight of all those feathers it will be able to soar higher than its fellows. And the sickness grows. For what individual can carry the weight of existence? And in a thousand lonely isolation chambers we scream for help. We wander in a depressive fog and shout for aid, waiting for a community to rescue us. Yet like fledglings whose mother has fallen broken from the shot of a hunter's gun, we peep in the deserted branches waiting for a sustaining worm that will never appear.

And so in darkness we lie on the analyst's couch while he plies us with pills manufactured as blunt alternatives to the arms in which we long to be carried and think it natural to return to the individual cell, or our family's individual cell, to the hive of fragmented connections. We have become corporate. Industrial in our individuality—filled with efficiencies that care less, or sloppily Band-Aid severed relations, and ignore the organic roots that once nurtured and healed us.

Grab her? Hold her? For she is ours? We've forgotten how. And the we-will-not-let-her-go is lost in a palliative of duty, casseroles, and platitudes.

Vignette 8: Letter from Babs Lake to Her Mother Mathilda Lake. June 1962

I offer this without comment. I believe this letter found in the Archives gives us a deeper window into Trillim's soul than even her own writings.

Dear Mom,

How are you doing? Have your classes ended? How did your teaching go? I hope things are settling down for you a little, that your grading is over and you are relaxing. Although, I've never seen you relax, I think it might be possible in theory so I keep hoping one day you'll slow down. Ha ha ha. I like to picture you sitting by the fire with a volume of George Eliot in your hand, your granny reading glasses resting low on your nose and a smile on your face.

We have just arrived off the coast of Sardinia and in the morning we'll take a landlubbers' excursion. We spent two days in Montpellier and it was as lovely as you described. The winding streets, the wondrous cafes lining the Mediterranean docks (and yes we did have the octopus stew as you recommended). Since leaving New York the trip has been uneventful as far as the things you were worried about are concerned (hurricanes, icebergs, unscrupulous rakes trying to seduce me away to a life of passion and crime, etc.). As it always is with Gilda, however, it's been a wild and keen inward adventure. And yes she managed to get us into trouble. I think it has helped her spirits immensely and she seems to be more like her old self.

It started poorly though. The first few days she would come out to the deck with me to repose on the recliners, but seemed to take no notice of the surroundings. She would ask one of the deck waiters to bring her an apple and a paring knife. She would then slowly whittle away the pulp, eating not a bite, until she had extracted the seeds from the core. Then after a few minutes of staring at the pips she would begin to weep uncontrollably and nothing I would say could coax her from her dour mood. Whatever had happened in the USSR continued to linger and haunt her. And she refused to talk about it despite my many pleadings. However, the sea breeze and the ocean air seemed to steadily lessen these bouts of melancholy until finally one day I persuaded her to pick up a novel. You know Gilda, so what light and easy romance do you think she picked up? Of course, *Moby Dick*. It did seem to relax her, so I tried not to influence her away from it.

Shortly after this, two undergraduates began to scope us out. They would pretend to be circumnavigating the ship, but it was clear that we were the objects of some intense scrutiny. Finally, they stopped and dared ask us what we thought of the cruise and inquired as to whether we were enjoying ourselves. They wore white letterman sweaters and spoke in a most affected and nonchalant manner as they casually passed by. They were obviously silver-spoon-in-your-mouth frat boys, but get this (and you say there is no such thing as coincidence! Ha!), they were both on the badminton team at UC Berkeley! (I can see you saying in your Karl Jung voice, "Ah, synchronicity, perhaps.") At this Gilda's ears perked up, but she said nothing about her being the former women's world champion. At least she closed her book. We chatted awhile and finally one of them said, "I say, how would you two ladies like to play a round or two of badminton? We could give you a couple of pointers if you are interested in the game." I looked at Gilda, but she demurred and said maybe another time. We left on pleasant enough terms and it was delightful to see Gilda at least engaging in a measure of social intercourse. I know since her injury in the world championships, and her disappearance into the wilds of Soviet Russia, she has had a dark black cloud resting over her. This was the most positive sign I'd seen in weeks.

They were both humanities majors and the next day and the day after that too they stopped by to chat. They were both enchanted with some, as Gilda called him, Nazi philosopher[1] who had captured their loyalty despite the horrific connotations. Just to test them I told them I was Jewish to gauge their reaction. I was ready to heave them over the rails if they showed any distancing. They did not let a single shadow pass over their face, but seemed anxious to redeem their philosophical hero and rambled on about him for almost an hour. Gilda seemed intrigued (you'll remember she was a lit major), but my only comment was, "By their fruits ye shall know them."

The next day they loaned Gilda one of his books with some things marked to read. That night she laughed at it and handed it to me. I waded through some of the most dense and impenetrable text I've ever read. Finally, I gave it back to her and said, "Pure Nonsense."

She agreed but spent most of the night reading it anyway.

The next day the frats (as we started calling them), asked what she thought. She laughed and said, "He almost gets it."

"What do you mean, 'almost?'" they asked, genuinely concerned.

Gilda answered, "Ready-at-hand, he thinks the tool disappears when it's in use and only appears when it's broken or not working."

"You don't believe it? You don't think it disappears?"

Gilda laughed (and Mother you know how sweet her laugh is!), and said, "No. I disappear. The tool is the only thing that's left. He's got it backwards."

The frats began to protest, it being unthinkable that their Kraut could be wrong about something, and they started using all the words their Kraut had invented to explain his thought. Mostly this was done by hyphenating words. But Gilda would have none of it, but rather than argue she asked if they would like to play badminton.

They jumped at the chance. We walked to the upper deck where there was a court. While the crew set up the net, the boys asked if we would like to play doubles, with one of them on a team with each of us, but Gilda said we would face them together. They smiled knowingly at each other and said, "Sure, but if you change your mind after a couple of rounds we can do it the other way."

The racquets were of poor quality and almost toys, but in Gilda's hands I knew they would be lethal. They served first, an easy lob to me, which I returned. They were lazy and when I lobbed it back, they didn't even try and it went to the ground. Gilda served, it was a wicked drop and both guys rushed forward but missed it. They looked surprised. Really surprised. She served again, a killer, but they managed clumsily to return it short and Gilda rallied forward and did a hairpin that dropped like a sock right next to the net. Now they looked at each other with unabashed surprise. This was a game!

It was amazing. Every time Gilda would do some remarkable smash or stunning drive one of them would mutter, "I say!"

Pretty much I just watched while Gilda trounced them 15/7 and 15/5. They demanded another match. They were getting the hang of it and they managed a 15/9 in the first game, but a disappointing 15/3 in the second. I think Gilda was wearing them out.

In the end, they came up to her and shook her hand and said, "Who are you?" When they heard they had just played Gilda Trillim, they laughed and shook their heads and said, "Well done, my dear. Well played."

On the way back down, she tilted her head slightly and asked, "Did you notice?" And they asked, "Notice what?" And she said coyly, "It was not Gilda and a racquet being used reflexively to some purpose. It was not Gilda *using* a racquet. It was one thing, maybe you could call it a Gilda-racquet-court-net-game-situation-two-other-players-wind-sunshine object. But there was only one thing there. To separate us out would be to miss the reality."

They said that yes that is what their German says. That understanding is in the world. Not in the brain.

Gilda, laughed and said, "Understanding *is* in the brain. He's wrong again. When those things I see and hear and smell and feel combine with memory and construct the world, I understand. It's just that I'm a really big object. I'm composed larger than I am."

You should have seen the strange look they gave her, but in that strangeness was a kind of fear and admiration. We agreed to all spend the day on Sardinia together. I think the shorter guy named Gerald likes me. He is just a pup, but I'm flattered.

Later ...

We just got back from Sardinia. Gilda is taking a shower. I'm feeling strange. It was a weird trip. We landed in Olbia and had a pleasant lunch with our frat boys. We devoured a light meal of shrimp salad and some rather sweet Italian wine. We had not signed up for the group tour, thinking that we ought to be able to find ways to entertain ourselves. We decided to take the train up to Nuoro because there were some museums that looked promising and who can turn Gilda down?

We wandered through a delightful cobbled street. We decided to cut through a narrow alley that our map suggested would take us to a street that would lead us back to the train station. About halfway up the alley to the next street we found a man sitting against a recessed wall. He sat with a large wine bottle between his legs. He had no hat on and we could see an old and scabby wound with thin hair tangled in the scaly yellow crust, gray with pus. His trousers, grease stained and marred dark with odorous urine, were wrinkled around his legs like the baggy excess of a gray beetle grub. He wore only a sleeveless tank top undershirt stained with purple wine and vomit. His face was lined with hardship and his unshaved week-old beard was gray and coarse. We all passed by, looking down at him. The disgust on the frats' faces was clear and unmitigated. I'm sure I looked at him no differently. But on Gilda's countenance was puzzlement.

We had only gone a few steps further when suddenly Gilda ran back to him. She squatted beside him and grabbed him firmly by the shoulders and shook him hard. His eyes slit open and he mumbled something incomprehensible and slurred. But Gilda was undaunted. She roused him to a finer state of awareness and got him to his feet. He was talking to her, but none of us spoke anything but a smattering of tourist Italian, like "How much does this cost?" or "Where is the bathroom?"

She took him by the hand, and led him forward. He walked slowly, as if in a daze still talking to Gilda in a more and more animated way. We came out of the alley and Gilda steered him to the chairs of an outdoor cafe just outside the small street where we found him. The frats at first had suggested we abandon him and even demanded that Gilda leave him behind, but she would not listen. Once she got him seated at a table, she said to an obviously unhappy proprietor, "Caffè!" He did not move until she waved a few 10,000 Lire notes in his face. The frats and I sat at one table and Gilda and the man sat at another. A woman, perhaps the proprietor's wife, brought us all an espresso and menus. Gilda managed to order us all sandwiches and soup. When they were brought out the man ate slowly but without hesitation, interspersing his bites with repeated expressions of, "Grazie. Grazie."

The frats were tapping their watch and motioning toward the train station, but Gilda was not finished with the man. She walked him over to a clothier. She bought him some trousers, shirt, underwear, socks, and shoes. She also bought him a hat—a rather nice one. The frat boys were making snide comments about how in putting on new clothes on a filthy and wasted retch she was putting old wine into new bottles, but again Gilda just ignored them.

As they left the store, the man was weeping openly and mumbling things incomprehensible but unmistakably expressions of gratitude. The Frats were now silent and seemed humbled and subdued. Then she did the most surprising thing of all, we walked down the cobbled street a little further, she holding his arm as if he were her father, until we reached a shoeblack stand. She had him get up onto the raised stand and motioned the shoeblack away. Then she knelt before the man and polished his new shoes. There was no need of course. The shoes were brand new, but she did it anyway. Then she rose and paid the owner of the stand with a generous tip and helped the old man down from the chair—she was much taller than he. He was quite stunned. She took out a ten thousand lire note and placed it in his shirt pocket. She smiled at him and made drinking-from-a-bottle motions with her hands and negated it with a shake of her head. He remonstrated that he would do no such thing. Then she stood on tiptoe, lifted up his hat, and applied a generous and lingering kiss to his forehead. He became unglued and fell to his knees and holding onto the front of her skirt wept. She assisted him back onto his feet and holding onto his hands looked at him with such intensity it unnerved even me. Suddenly, she reached up and grabbed his face between her palms like she was holding it steady, forcing him to look into her eyes. She looked for a moment into his gaze, as if trying to memorize what was there.

Then she said forcefully, even harshly, "Who are you?"

He looked away, but then returned her unrelenting stare and started to answer, surprisingly in heavily accented English, "I am Anton ..."

She cut him off. "Not your name! Who are you?" She demanded.

The strange thing, and I can't really say why this came to me, but she did not seem to even be talking to him. It was as if she were asking these questions to herself. There is nothing that I can describe to you that would make it apparent that this was what was happening, but it just felt that way.

She held him like this for a few more minutes. Then suddenly laughed and said, "Yes! There it is. I see it." And she let his face go.

She shook his hand and said goodbye. We walked away at a fairly brisk pace, feeling the need to hurry so we did not miss the train. As we scurried away, the man stood and watched us for a long time with tears in his eyes.

We made it back just in the nick of time to catch the train back to Obila. No one said a word all the way back to the ship. When we got on deck and were saying goodnight to the boys, Gilda suddenly laughed and said something odd to them, "We are not thrown into worlds. We make them out of the stuff at hand." Then they excused themselves, claiming exhaustion, and said likely they would not come up for dinner and left us for the evening.

Isn't that strange, Mom? I've tried to bring it up to Gilda several times, but she just laughs off my attempts to get an explanation of the way she treated that man, and she says strange things like, "He was an apple seed with eyes. I wanted to look inside him to see what was there," or "Everything is being, and hides from us its fullness." It sounds crazy, sometimes, but the way she says it, it seems full of sense. At least for a little while.

I'll pop this in the morning mailbag. Next we are going to stop at Tripoli, then Cairo, Antalya, then Rome. I'll try to write when I can and tell you more of our adventures. We are fine and having a terrific trip. This was so worth doing. Give my love to Dad.

Love Your Affectionate Daughter,
Babs

Vignette 9: Trillim Cooks Emily Dickinson's Black Cake. Circa 1962

The following was written shortly after Trillim's cruise to Rome where she seems to have overcome her bout of major depression. This occurred prior to losing her right hand and her two-year imprisonment in Southeast Asia. As always her life's work has been to explore the connections between things: people, ecologies, and objects of all types large and small. This is one of my favorites because of the pictures that scholars found in an envelope tucked in her journal.

I went down, down, down to the heart of an apple seed. I searched its depths, scouring under every stairway to find its truth. I swept out the cobwebs of appearance and dug into its hard subterranean earthiness to strike some vein of richness yielding its essence. Beyond color. Beyond size. Beyond smell, touch, and sound, and at the middle of its being I found its unlimited capacity to hide, to withdraw into hidden passages, and to mask all its coordinates such that no map could be drawn. No logic yielded its ways and in the end what it disclosed of itself was naught but a meager caricature–a smudge, a line-drawing sketched from perceptions it was willing to share. I sigh at my failure.

Perhaps my approach was wrong. Perhaps to go in, to go down, I must go up. I must find all its fellows. Maybe, I'll expand and swell and enlarge myself and discover firsthand the root of connecting patterns and in such webs see what can be netted. Perhaps as always, the best approach is to start with baking a cake.

How about this one? Sent to a friend by verdant and bright Emily Dickinson with this note and recipe:

Dear Nellie,
Your sweet beneficence of bulbs I return as flowers, with a bit of the swarthy cake baked only in Domingo.
    Lovingly,
    Emily.

2 pounds Flour—
2 Sugar—
2 Butter—
19 Eggs—
5 pounds Raisins—
1 ½ Currants—
1 ½ Citron—
½ pint Brandy—
½ Molasses—
2 Nutmegs—
5 teaspoons—
Cloves-Mace-Cinnamon
2 teaspoons—Soda—

Beat Butter and Sugar together—
Add Eggs without beating—and beat the mixture again—
Bake 2 ½ hours, or three hours, in cake Pan Cake pans or 5 to 6 hours in Milk pan, if full—[1]

And what is a recipe? The blueprint of ecology. A harmony of relationships. The ideal form, which every kitchen demiurge must try to instantiate in matter (so imperfect a substance!)—An act of creation from the unorganized material floating among the carbon/nitrogen offerings budding from the earth: flours, sugars, eggs, spices, and flavors rich and varied. Endless mixtures and combinations creating worlds, nations, and countries undiscovered and lying curled snuggly in the capacious ether misting in cupboards and pantries well-stocked.

I start by taking raisins fashioned by grapes grown in the warmth of the San Joaquin Valley by a family who has grown grapes for many generations and who cherish their tended vines. These hand plucked offerings are laid out on newspapers (published in Fresno) by workers from Mexico who have come to bless their wives and children back home and make for themselves a finer life than they would have otherwise. Each fruit, graced by the sun, changes in substance as water is pulled through the fruit's hide initiating chemical changes that draw into being flavors delicate and distinctly raisiny, signaled by a delectable dark blackening. Raisins, a gift from: grapes, sun, growers, Mexico, and a universe's chemical underpinnings, and pulled from a box brought to me by a trucker and a grocer who have conspired under the rules of symbiosis to bring them dancing to my countertop.

I put these to soak in a brandy whose genesis was framed in a distant distillery in France from grapes of a different lineage, reared in soils whose ecology was conditioned by millions of years of separation from the raisin's sister-soil in California, each with communities of fungi and bacteria adding and enriching what flavors will emerge from the dark underpinnings of a thousand-trillion accidents. Then, aged in oak barrels fashioned from trees grown in the Tronçais forest, whose unique climate, soil, and woodland ecology create an oak with a density just so, from which a wooden plank will be made that will author forth a firm and sturdy barrel, produced by a craftsman with the ken of

five generations of barrel makers stored in his soul, a barrel that will slowly leach its own essence and nature into the brandy.

These are mixed and placed in a glass jar, made from sands carved out of sedimentary rock by ocean water, lifted and transported by wind to fall as rain down upon the pressed sandstone of Jurassic river deposits, themselves torn from ancient mountains long ago weathered to plains. Then beyond the material, scores upon scores of stories of how the glass factory was born through someone's dreams, pain, and determination could be told.

And so from around the world, gathered from ecologies many, from materials, objects, and substances with properties wrapped thick with the stuff of deep time and cantered across many spaces, and whose myriad stories of genesis and re-genesis call and peep to one another in tangled networks, sits my jar upon the shelf with raisins soaking, creating a new flavor in the world.

And so it goes for the batter, with nutmeg from exotic islands grown among the palms of distant shores,

And the sifted flour,

And the mixed and completed dough,

Until after baking, this object, this cake is born into the world.

The taste is subtle, a unique mix finished from staggering complexity, its creation an accident of unimaginable improbabilities and a network of earth processes and history. I picture in my mind the network of associations as if they were strung from wires connecting and fashioning the flavors. Wires running among the grapes of California, their growers, the newspapers which provided substrate for the ripening fruit, the oak of France, and on and on from the wheat farmer who grew the flour, to the sea captain who brought the cinnamon, to cows who provided milk for the butter from the grasses the bovines fed upon, to the slopes of Mauna Kea where the sugarcane was grown and harvested. The wires may vary in thickness like the strings of a guitar, with thick wires between say the citron and current where the flavor connections are strong and thin wires between the wheat made into flour and the man who delivered the gasoline for the tractor which harvested the crop. I imagine these wires stretching into the past, perhaps to the Pleistocene, which provided the material substrate for the soils of France, which add subtle shifts in the nuances of flavor gracing the cake. I wonder. Were I to pluck any string somewhere in this web of connection, how far would the vibrations propagate? Would there be any end to the music that would issue forth? The music expressed now as flavor drawn from my cake and combined with my olfactory apparatus.

Which all started with some tulip bulbs gifted by a friend and a favor returned.

Vignette 10: An Account of Gilda's Vision under the South American Hallucinatory Drug Ayahuasca. Circa 1966

Because of its length, I will pick up this vignette just as the vision described begins. Trillim provides extensive details about her decision to take ayahuasca. In the well-known *Look Magazine*[1] piece, she wrote extensively about traveling to Peru with her long time correspondent and friend, Russian anthropologist Valentina Czaplicka. There, she explains her interest and motivation for taking the hallucinatory South American shamanistic drug. There is much more that could be explored about the experience, but I want to focus primarily on the vision itself. Her complete journal entry of the event constitutes over two hundred pages, and although scholars (and true Trillim aficionados) will want to read the complete journal entries from the Archive, they are rather lengthy and full of technical details that are of limited relevance for this thesis. The primary question I want to take up in my recounting this event is whether it contributed to a propensity for hallucination later in life. This question has been considered in some detail by several researchers, but most thoroughly by Praskovya Blinova in her excellent treatment of the potential for ayahuasca to create long-term brain changes of a type that might explain Trillim's extraordinary claims.[2] She comes down on the side of such changes being extremely unlikely for Gilda's case.

However, I would like to draw on this hallucination to frame the discussion of Gilda's madness later in the thesis so for my purposes it is sufficient to recount from her journals the vision itself. Trillim argued that this incident was life changing, which in some ways could be taken as ironic, given the long-term disability that follows from this experience. After these events her writing takes on its more characteristic shape and themes.

We'll pick this up just before she takes the drug.

The unassuming indigenous hut was situated on the edge of a rainforest village that we had arrived to by river the day before. The dwelling was constructed of straight wooden supports, with round beams made of tree branches emanating from the three center poles. It was finished with wide pale-green plantain leaves covering the roof and sides in order to offer some shelter from the wind and rain. There were reed mats scattered about the hut for the participants to sit or lie upon. I chose one nearest the river and furthest from the front opening.

There was an old diesel heating stove near my mat. It appeared unnecessary given that the temperature in the hut seemed pleasant enough, if not even a bit too warm. It was just me and Valentina taking the drug. The old shaman gave me a collection of three old coffee cans. My friend explained these were to be used if I felt the need to vomit. Then she laughed and said, "And you will need to vomit." I had already had it explained to me that there was some inevitability in this unpleasant part of the experience.

The shaman, whose name is now lost to me, without ceremony brought the brown/tea colored concoction of medicinal plants in the black metal bucket in which it had been prepared. It looked like a mass of vine sticks and boiled green leaves. Valentina told me it had been simmering all night. It smelled weedy and earthy like the mud pies that I used to make as a child growing up in Idaho. He ladled some of the liquid into a blue porcelain glazed tin cup and motioned for me to drink. It did not taste as bad as I thought. It was bitter, but had a sweet edge; maybe they had added honey. Even so, I gagged, but he motioned with a toss of his hand and by tilting his head back that I should finish the cup.

Valentina was nodding vigorously and said in Russian, "Drink it all!"

I did and he gave me another cup. This was too much. I thought I was going to die if I had to drink more, but I held my nose and forced myself to swallow it quickly. This failed. It took six more attempts to get the whole thing down. My stomach started making noises and I had a sudden worry that I'd been poisoned and this whole contrivance was a trick to rob me.

The old man signaled with his hands that I should lie down on the mat and said repeatedly in bad Spanish, "Bueno. Bueno. Descansa un rato, Señora."

I lay down, but immediately, or so it seemed, I vomited violently into one of the cans, filling it nearly halfway. I tried to hold back, thinking he would make me drink more of the vile mixture, but he motioned for me to lie back down. I did, but was back up again in a few minutes vomiting. This happened at least twice more. I was filling my second can with a putrid smelling bile, when suddenly, almost instantly, I felt quite lighthearted and at peace. My stomach felt clean. Strangely clean. Not just in the sense of having gotten rid of some fetid poison, but my flesh and bones had been made virginal and innocent. Holy. As if I had been purged of all impurities and the taints collected over a lifetime of imbibing the dirt of existence had been washed away with clear water. My head felt weightless and the sounds of the others around me evaporated. And I mean evaporated. I saw the sounds bleeding into the air like the heat waves off a hot highway after a summer cloudburst.

I glanced at the shaman. His brown wrinkled face looked more beautiful than a Hawaiian sunset, each line signifying a grace of angelic perfection, his sparkling eyes like that of a god, shone brown with glory. He looked at me and said in formal German, "Wählen Sie Ihre spirituelle Lehrer sorgfältig!" I told him I did not speak German and he clapped his hands in delight and returned, "Jetzt tun Sie. Jetzt können Sie sprechen alle Sprachen." And I knew he was right, I could speak all languages now. I tried out Latin and Hebrew in my head and I could speak them each with ease. I realized that I no longer needed language and it seemed a blunt and bloated way of communicating—wholly inadequate to conveying even a modicum of what I wanted to say. I supposed, happily, that my thinking had reverted to Adamic, the language of primal Adam and God. I could speak with power such that in knowing a true name, I could create the thing just by naming it.

Then it was gone. The words fled me and I was back in the hut. Valentina was now vomiting, apparently having her turn at the concoction. All the smells and sounds of the place rushed back. I suddenly felt immensely sad for I could tell I had died, as I was now floating above my body, looking down upon the happenings of the enclosure. The shaman was busy handing Valentina a can. The air was thick with tobacco and other smokes. And the sounds! The music of the village was leaking with clarity into the room. There was the cry of monkeys, the sounds of crickets, frogs, and cicadas were clear and distinct. I could smell the smoke and the diesel and the strange assemblage of foreign scents. It never occurred to me that the soul free of the body would be able to smell. Then a lovely sorrow settled over me. I did not feel sad for myself, but for my mother who would hear of my death in South America and mourn bitterly. She warned me not to go on this trip. I had ignored her. Mothers are always right.

I floated outside and like a balloon began to drift higher. Very slowly, but unmistakably I was floating up, up, up until I was even with the canopy of the highest trees. There I placidly hovered. Looking down over the top of the rainforest as it rolled into the distance, verdant with living things, I could feel the life of the place like a ringing in my ear—a buzz that was felt, not heard.

Suddenly, I was approached by a gigantic dragonfly. It was large, electric blue, and it shimmered like a neon light blinking on and off. It said, "I am your guide." Its legs were strangely shaped, and I looked closely and they terminated in tiny badminton racquets. Three miniature birdies were being volleyed back and forth between each pair of dangling legs. I stared at the legs going through their motions and thought, "How mechanical it all looks! How forced. Like a machine." It said again, "I am your guide."

"I thought I would be met by my family when I died?" I said. Which was odd for I had not really practiced Mormonism for a long time and had ceased to even believe that it was possible to know what an afterlife would be like should there even be one. Yet I had kept up a hope that it was right in the broad outlines. There was, however, little room for dragonflies in what I had imagined for the hereafter.

"You are not dead," it said, "you are in the spirit realm. Learn what you can. I am your guide. What would you know?" It darted back and forth and up and down as it said these things, giving the sentences in cadence with its pitch and plunge. Yet all the while keeping the shuttlecocks in play.

There is one thing that has always perplexed me. Something that had puzzled me since the time I was a small child. I remember staying the night at my grandmother's house in Boise in the late summer. She lived on a tree-lined neighborhood street, not so busy as to be a major thoroughfare, but with enough traffic that one had to be watchful if chasing a ball into the road. I slept in a room near the street. I remember lying awake at night watching the shadows on the wall shifting and sliding as cars passed by, marking the room with small slats of light created by the passing vehicles' headlamps shining through the blinds. These patterned patches of illumination traced a bright path from one side of the room to the other as the cars moved past. Back then I liked to imagine it tracing my life on Earth. So the place where the patch began its sojourn across my room represented my birth, and when it was extinguished at the end of its trajectory, my death. As night progressed, the cars would become less frequent and I would mentally wander back to the pre-existence where souls lived with God until being born into an earthly life. Then, I pondered even further back, to the origin of everything. I wondered who made God, or when it all had started. There was a song we sang in Church sometimes, with the line, "D'ye think that ye could ever / Through all eternity / Find out the generation / Where Gods began to be?" The song dripped with mystery and filled my imagination with profound wonderings and unfathomable cogitations. Where did it all start? It was an enormous question. Big enough that as I looked at the bouncing dragonfly before me I was prompted to daring. I continued to watch the insect play about me like an opponent on a court for just a moment longer, then boldly begged, "Show me the beginning of everything."

"The beginning of the universe?" It inquired brightly.

"No. Before that. The very beginning. Surely, the 'Big Bang' as they are calling it now, must have come from somewhere. Yes? There must be conditions and capacities that obtained in something even bigger that made it possible for it to occur. Right? I want to know the beginning of everything. Of universes. Of whatever extra space graced existence such that a big bang *could* occur, and to see whatever conditions had to unfold to let that prior space evolve, and on and on. I want the foundational event. If it was God show me God. If it was something else show me that. And if it is a reoccurrence that repeats endlessly, then take me above it and let me look down upon it so I can understand what I am."

The dragonfly dropped the shuttlecocks it had been juggling. It stayed in one place now, hovering just above my eyes. It was silent a long time before it answered, "You will need greater guides than I."

And it disappeared.

The First Guide

I found myself on a red and white tiled checkerboard floor extending off into the distance until it disappeared over the horizon. Above me, a vault of a deep blue-black sky filled with numerous galaxies, stars, and planets that played above me in an as rich and varied dance as anything in our western night sky. There was music playing, the music of the spheres I guessed because it washed over me with such beauty and pathos that I felt I would be broken in half by the sound. It was like nothing I'd ever heard. As I looked at the orbs above me, it seemed that in some sense they were indeed dancing to the strains playing in concert around me.

A breeze was blowing and I noticed that from far far away in the distance, a moving point alone in the vast plain was heading my way. Finally, I could see that it was something like a dog running toward me. It was coming quickly and as it neared it resolved into a coyote—lean and hungry, its coat ragged and torn. It was wounded in several places along its flank as if it had been in a fight with another animal.

It approached me, addressed me in German (which I again understood), and identified itself as Herr Professor Schelling, a Natural Philosopher. He said he was the first of three guides who would show me what I wished—the beginning of all things. I asked him about the wounds he bore. He snarled viciously: "These I received from my enemies!"

He then growled savagely and nipped at the air as if trying to fend off an attack from above. He settled back down and scratched his neck with his back leg, then stood and said, "Follow me."

He took off at a run. I had a dream-like sense that I had to keep up with him and that if I did not, my journey would end there. Fatally. So I sprinted after him. We ran like the wind, and still I could not keep up, he was running too fast. Without under-standing why, I dove like a swim racer off a platform into the air. I found myself flying inches off the floor like Superman, my body occasionally bouncing lightly off the tiles. If I could just keep from landing I knew I would be able to keep up, so I concentrated harder and soon found myself flying capably through the air, like a bullet. I caught up to the coyote-Schelling creature and he led me across the tiles. Finally, after some time I yelled to him, "Where are we going?"

He glanced back and yelped, "To the beginning."

Soon the galaxies above disappeared, as if we had run beyond them, and now only a dark emptiness made up the dome of the sky. The eerie illumination that came from the tiled floor remained, although we seemed to be running through a vast and immense emptiness. We traveled like this for years, decades, centuries, eons, we ran the age of the earth, and of the universe and its birth in a fiery flash, but we did not stop and eons came and went, time unimaginable passed. Until at last we came to the end of the checkered floor which terminated in a precipice into nothing. At this edge we stopped. There was nothing but blackness above and before us, except far away beyond the rim and somewhat below us was a strange gray sphere.

"What is that?" I felt awestruck and frightened.

Afraid I should have known I squeaked. "Is it God? Plotinus's One?

The coyote looked at me for a long time and started coughing and threw up a pink mass, which it quickly ate. "It is the Ungrund! The ground from which all Being sprang! Even God and all the Gods! We are looking from the past, at a beginning so distant that you cannot fathom it. That is all there was once, if once is a word that can be used in this case."

"It was not sitting in space as you now see it from this place, it was absolutely alone, single, undifferentiated, and insentient, there was no qualia emanating from its substance, for substance it was, and substance it wasn't. You cannot comprehend. Do not try. It was not nothing, that is all that can be said. It lacked all motion, for there was nowhere to go. It could not be divided for there was no left nor right, no up nor down, no inner nor outer. No accidents. Just essence. No space nor time could touch it. For it filled all there was. There was nothing but it."

"Was it aware of itself?"

"Awareness takes difference. There must be something to be aware of? No? Aware of itself? Impossible. Certainly not as the self-contemplating itself thing Plotinus envisioned as first cause for it perceived no future, no past, no now. None of those existed. It was Not-nothing. Nothing else. It had only will. Not awareness. Not consciousness. Not perception. Only will."

"How then did we come to this?" I said, pointing back toward the place the galaxies had disappeared long ago.

"It annihilated itself."

"What?"

"It annihilated itself. The first great sacrifice. The one on which all others are patterned. The atonement that underlies all others and upon which all subsequent gods will pattern their own incarnations. It destroyed that oneness and became many. It created all lights, energy, matter, motion in one great act of destruction. It started deep time. It opened a universe in which newness and novelty are possible because differences exist and gradients parse out variance—difference upon which all things can work. It was will in motion. Yet without thought. Without awareness. Without sentience."

Long I stared at it. Trying like I did with the apple seeds to ascertain its nature. Finally, as if sensing my intent, the coyote continued, "You will get nothing from it. It has no parts, nor emanations to sense. It spans all dimensions—an infinity of such—because there are none. It is division by zero of zero. It exists and is all that exists. Therefore it is nothing. And everything. It is being and non-being. Everything, for it alone exists simply. And non-being because it stands in relation to no other thing."

"Surely the laws of mathematics hold, so there are transcendental realities even now when this thing sat alone. Are there not?"

"You speak from an age in which they exist. So this grounding is impossible to understand. Then (and I say 'then' only to give a hook for the mind to grasp, but 'then' and 'now' have no meaning 'when' this existed), there was no time, for what changed? There were no logical relations, for upon what would they be structured? When there is only one thing, what can be added or subtracted? If there are no circles, can pi find an ideal existence? What is logically possible when there is no contrary? When there is no 'either,' 'or,' nor even an 'and?' If there is no middle wherein can be found an excluded middle? If there is no possibility, where can we find an 'if' or a 'then'?"

I looked at my guide and said, "And yet here we are. Then at least the object had capacity? For if there were no capacity, surely it would be there still (whatever 'still' and 'there' might mean), would it not?"

Then the coyote howled long and loud. His cries piercing the silence with a yap that spoke of depth of longing. A yowl that vibrated around the universe. Then these words, "The mystery! Profound and without reasons! An event without a cause! The first true random act. Random in ontology! Who can understand? For the thing annihilated itself! And in that annihilation infinite dimensions open! As when matter is destroyed in your universe, utterly and irrevocably, energy in abundance is released, so when the original thing ceased, 'new' formed and dimensions were born. Universes many! Universes with differences! Variation! Change! And in that change, time! A sacrifice of sorts yet by what grace no one knows, yet in such however bringing into existence, through the first stochastic motion in a universe structured by randomness, the first moment in a random walk of unending change! And why not! Could there be cause and effect in an undifferentiated universe? No. But randomness! Sweet randomness! Therein lies the secret of all."

Suddenly, the Shelling-coyote looked around, frightened, "My time is nearly gone. The next guide comes. I must bid you goodbye. I am pursued and must flee."

He looked at me and sighed, "Opposition has entered the world. Just as I predicted was necessary!" He winked at me once and was gone.

I suddenly felt terribly alone. I sat on the edge of the checkered floor, my legs dangling over the profound empty nothingness. In the distance, the thing that would be all was expanding in an explosion of color such as I had never before imagined possible, colors I'd never seen; sounds beyond any musical note. Everything was born in this explosion? "Well at least beauty," I thought, as I watched existence unfold.

The Second Guide

As I watch the blackness that surrounded the odd sphere, something new appeared lightly above it and to the side. Shortly, I realized it was unmistakably heading my way. I could not imagine what it was as it moved through the profound emptiness, but as it got closer it was soon apparent that it was a sailing ship with sails unfurled and brimming with air and driving itself toward me. It steered toward my location and pulled up next to the tiled floor upon which I sat. A gangplank was lowered and off marched an aristocratic tortoise, its neck long and obscene. Upon its back rode a rock pigeon, and upon that plump bird's head sat a round and sturdy carabid beetle. This last creature provided voice for the odd trio. The ship was manned by a crew of rough and randy chimpanzees who moved through the ship's rigging like trapeze artists—executing fantastic leaps, daring flips, dives, and climbs amidst the cordage and sails.

The tortoise approached and the beetle hailed me from atop the pigeon, "Greetings! I, Charles Darwin, will be your guide for the next phase of your adventure."

The turtle made a kind of curtsy, while the pigeon bowed almost toppling the beetle.

"Which of you is Darwin?" I asked smiling, for despite the strangeness of our encounter, there was a sense of fun and carnival about the spectacle of these three guides and their introduction.

"Which indeed!" said the beetle. "You'll find as we introduce the tri-fold necessities that allow a maneuvering toward complexity my three-fold representation will serve you well. We are all together us, that is, Charles Darwin. At your service."

They bowed and curtsied again and bid me follow them onto the ship. I climbed up the plank and hopped onto the vessel. Once aboard, the gangplank was pulled in and we ambled toward the forecastle. The craft left behind the vast checkerboard plain and bore swiftly toward the exploding thing that was starting to fill the horizon with a wondrous display of brilliant hues and colors coalescing into a multitude of shapes and structures unimaginably gorgeous—beauty of such astonishing intricacy that I found words failed me, patterns with edges that folded and twisted into shapes that were indescribably stunning in complexity and rich in exquisite delicacy.

The imperial tortoise then for the first time spoke, its voice deep and compelling, and uttered with grave solemnity, "Behold the birth of all."

As we watched, bright lights flared and flashed among the swirling colors.

I whispered, "Are those stars caught in the act of creation?" And then it hit me—the flashes I was watching might be even more than mere stars, "Or are they the 'Big Bangs' that mark the genesis of entire universes?" I said in awe.

The turtle turned to me, locking its ageless eyes upon mine, "Come. Let us see." As if at his command, the ship steered toward one of the flashes. We gained its proximity with incredible speed and sailed boldly right into it. Out we popped into a new place, which I can only describe as an otherworldly province of blue and yellow. Words capturing the dancing structures within are beyond anything available in any language I have. They were not spheres, nor geometric shapes of any stability, and even in molten motion they seemed to have some regularity—following logic that was far beyond my ability to apprehend. Within, there were blazing flares bursting around us. "Are these explosions making universes?" I could not help but ask.

The worthy terrapin considered a moment then explained, "There are layers and layers of complexity we must sail through to get to the level of which you speak. Come. Hang on and we will find our way through the morass of rough oceans. But there is something in particular you must see." So, on we sailed, each time breaking for whatever flashes and flares we found in the places and structures through which we travelled. And as we entered a new flash or bubble, it opened into a new space of unfathomable depth and delight and through which we sailed until we entered a new flash of color and light. Again and again steering to a new level of existence, where complexity, rules, and laws varied in each, until we came to one in which the ship stopped. The apes furled the sails with startling speed, and we paused above what can only be loosely described as a planet—for it appeared to be a pulsating octahedron warmed by a similarly shaped orb casting off a rainbow of radiance as if it were this universe's equivalent to a sun.

The tortoise motioned with its head, "Behold the evolution of your gods!" And from the slime of that world arose creatures, instantiations of life. These changed, became societies, formed alliances, civilizations that grew in power and influence right before my eyes. Life grew in majesty and in power until they controlled the foundations of the light and matter in their universe in ways that made me gasp with breathless wonder. While it obviously all transpired on time scales unplumbed, it unfolded before my eyes and heart and understanding in a matter of minutes, as if my mind were enhanced to comprehend things unimaginable. But at the end were beings more glorious than I could grasp, encircled in an aura of exceptional light. They took that which they found about them in this place and created worlds and universes beyond imagining.

I sat on the deck in shock and buried my head in my hands and wept, "It is too much. I've seen the origin of the gods!"

"There are exalted and magnificent beings such as these shepherds in infinite spaces," said the tortoise, "These are those on your phylogenetic lines."

I wept, unprepared for a lesson on deep genealogy.

The rock pigeon flew to my shoulder and whispered in my ear, "Courage, my lady, courage. There is one thing more to learn. The three fold, the tri-fold structure that drives these changes and emergences."

The bird flew back to the great shelled beast, and that wise being looked at me and said, "Behold, we have traveled far, from the beginning to the now, but learn here the one thing that organizes and structures the all through which we have cut the waves with our prow. Complexity comes forth in only one way. Behold! Three things always exist. One! Wherein there is difference. Two! Wherein some structures are lost because they cannot abide, and some remain. Three! Wherein one sort of structure comes from something similar. Where there are two things and only one can remain, that which can take more of what is required to survive or do it better will go on. Behold! Variation. Behold! Differential survival. Behold! The inheritance of one thing that bestows its traits on another. Wherever the threefold is found, complexity will evolve. It will bubble up into a universe no matter how simple and humble its beginnings. You see the shepherds below? They were made this way. They wield this power to bring beings to themselves. It has happened on an infinity of universes and uncanny spaces. It happened on yours. It will happen on others. Learn it well. Complexity emerges in no other way."

"So your theory transcends all these places no matter what the law, what the structure of the world?"

The beetle chuckled at my question, "Yes. Yes. My little theory. My small abstract. It's the key to all being. For consciousness. For meaning."

Then I saw a hundred million worlds, with as many physics structuring odd and unique matter in each, and in those where complexity flowed, the three-fold held and structured that very complexity. Although often it was not sufficient, it was always necessary. And what forms! What remarkable life exists! In multiple instantiations of excellence! I'm weeping as I remember the things I saw.

I looked up, observing the ship resting in the quiet waters of an earthly lagoon. I could hear the sounds of surf beating upon the shore, and above me the blue sky was graced by white clouds floating comfortably through that expanse. I felt exhausted and small. I'd seen too much. My irrelevance to the greatness of the universe screamed from every pore.

"It is time to depart. For there is one more entrance into the universe that you must know." The pigeon was speaking now, "We will say goodbye and farewell."

Suddenly, as if in a dream I found myself on a sandy strand, watching the ship as it disappeared over the horizon.

The Third Guide

The beach upon which I was left, fronted a stand of tropical trees including a few palms. The sun had just set, and the first stars of evening were appearing low in the eastern sky. It was breezy and pleasant, although my hand felt oddly warm. I sat down and rubbed it and waved it in the air trying to cool it. The sky continued to reveal stars and I wondered when my guide would appear. The night unfolded. I looked at the heavens and pondered the wonders I had seen, the expanses of eternities that stretched out in dimensions of infinite intricacy and multiplicity, unfolding and condensing, in patterns of complexity unimag-inable. I thought about the rise of the shepherds, a higher order of evolved beings, who could manipulate entire universes. But why? What was their motivation? Power? Influence? What did they do?

"What did they do?" The voice startled me because of its mocking nature and when I turned there was a dark shadow standing between me and the ocean. It was not cast on the sand like a normal shadow, but stood like a paper cutout glued onto a photograph, like something added to reality that should not be there. It had a long pointed snout, strangely narrow and that bent upward unnaturally, its yellow eyes were crescent shaped slits, and ears sharp and erect, it was like a cartoon wolf, drawn sinister and distorted, and like a shadow two dimensional. It paced back and forth menacingly. A baleful creature that seem to emanate malice and ill-will. I suddenly became apprehensive, rattled that my hand hurt and burned so badly, and that this beast, unlike my other guides, seemed dark and treacherous. When it turned it was apparent that it was more like a sheet of paper than an organism of our world. A shade made flesh.

"Are you my guide?" I asked, feigning a bravado I did not feel.

"Am I in the presence of the Ghost of Christmas Yet To Come?" The creature sing-songedly mocked back to me, "Are you going to say, 'I fear you more than any specter I have seen. But as I know your purpose is to do me good, and as I hope to live to be another woman from what I was, I am prepared to bear your company, and do it with a thankful heart.' Fool, this is no fairytale, I can smell the fear thick about you. You are a worthless thing. Did you think you could drink a shaman's poison and live? Can you not feel the pain in your hand, getting worse, and worse, torturing you? Burning you up? Soon your body will burn similarly. You foolish girl, you wanted to see beginnings? I will show you endings."

It was true, my hand was burning so badly I could scarcely

think about anything else. The creature continued to pace back and forth, never taking one of its eyes off me, watching intently as I stood, my feet in the sand.

"Who are you?" I whispered, starting to shake.

"You know who I am."

"Name yourself."

"Name yourself." It mimicked me exactly.

"Please."

"Please."

I looked around me for a weapon of some sort but there was only sand.

It mocked again but with even more foreboding than it had yet mustered as it spat, "Throw a bucket of water on me and see if I melt."

Its pace became quicker. Inching nearer and nearer, I started to back away.

"Run!" it said. But I did not. I sensed that if I did, it would pursue and take me.

"Run!" it again commanded and threatened.

It needed something of me. It could not attack. It was coming to me that this thing needed me to run. To tear into the forest perhaps. I stood my ground.

I remembered when I was little, my father and I had once gone for a walk through the potato fields near our house. We were cutting through the tuberous crops when we surprised a cottontail that had been hiding under a pile of old railroad ties. But rather than running away, it looked at us for a second, and then bolted right at us! It was terrifying. Even my father jumped back in a panic and we both ran. We laughed and laughed because the bunny could have done us no real harm. I asked my father why she had done that when we were so much bigger. He told me, things fear confidence more than anything else. Most things don't attack unless they think they can win. When something comes at you like that, you had better get out of the way because if they are so sure they can take you, you'd better take it seriously. Wolverines can drive off a grizzly. Not because they are tougher than a bear, but because bravado works. Nineteen times out of twenty when a wolverine attacks a grizzly the bear runs off in a panic, just like we did.

I considered the horrid thing pacing before me. Then ran at it. When I reached the beast and lunged out to seize it, it was gone. Like that. It just disappeared. I looked around and the terror that had afflicted me by its presence had evaporated as well. A full moon was starting to rise from the east and as its light stretched out into the night, it disclosed a small figure walking toward me down the beach.

I could tell it was not tall, about three feet high, although distinctly human. It carried none of the menace of the previous specter. When it reached me it was clearly some sort of ape. It looked like a small human with long arms and a distinctly chimp-like face. It stopped before me and raised its right hand and said, "Greetings."

"Are you my guide? I've met Schelling and Darwin, so who are you?"

She gave a chortle and said, "You will not have heard of me. I am named Mbacoob!boo!a, giving strange clicks within the name. I will introduce her, or er ... me, to you later for your time is running out and you must hear her speak."

"The other guides were animals I knew, but what are you?" I asked because I found her a strange mix of human and ape that was disturbing the equilibrium of my mind. My hand was also still distracting me, but the pain had lessened somewhat, though it had moved more toward my wrist.

She chuckled, "I am represented as one of your grandmothers. But come. We have a bit of a walk and we must get moving if we are to get there in time."

We walked down the beach in silence, until I asked, "What was that other dire creature?"

My guide looked thoughtful, "It said you knew its name. What is it?"

"I don't know its name."

"I think you do."

"Satan? Beelzebub? Loki?"

"Are you so bad at this as that?" She was smiling now, almost at a laugh.

I thought of all the evil creatures from myth and fairy tales and listed a few, but she just shook her head like a disappointed parent, "Come now," she said, "You are better than this."

I thought some more and then a smile crept across my face. Of course. "Ahh," I said, "I see."

"Name it."

"Gilda Trillim."

We both laughed. An archetype so common as to be almost a cliché. You must defeat yourself.

"I never really defeated it. I just ran at it."

"Of course you can't defeat yourself. Can you? All you can do is cease to fear your darkness, then you are free to use it, overcome it, whatever. You did what needed to be done. You quit being afraid of it."

We chatted some more and finally I asked, "Can we just fly? My wrist feels like it is on fire."

"No, we need time to talk." She pointed out over the sand to the ocean, "Do you see where the waves break? There is a reef there. What do you know about coral reefs?"

"Not much, just that they are places where many kinds of fish and shelled creatures live."

"Why?"

"Lots of things to eat I suppose."

"Because coral makes a substrate that things can make holes in, holes that other things can cling to, holes that things can hide in. It makes space for lots of other entities, which in turn opens new worlds for the fish and other creatures. These in their way make places for other life forms, which once again change the world for even more new and varied plants and animals."

She waved her hands excitedly, "It's an upward spiral of making place, which makes more place for more life. Savvy? Life makes new, which makes more life. Life makes life richer. More things, more kinds of things, more relationships and connections and possible connections among the myriad things existing."

I thought about it, "Like a beaver dam makes place for cattails, brown trout, birds that feed on the dragonflies that arrive, and the birds that feed on them, and frogs, and more birds and snakes because of the frogs, and turtles that show up along with things like muskrats, which make room for the weasel and hawks and the many things that all have a place because the beaver made a home first by dragging a few aspens to make a dam."

"Yes, you understand exactly, the beaver dam changes everything, someday the pond is replaced by a meadow which will enrich the possibility of many small birds and mammals, provide forage for elk and deer that support wolves and on and on. Such is how the universe is made and unfolds in newness and novelty."

I nodded. I knew this and thought much about it. It is not surprising that my brain, steeped in a drug, brought out these themes that I had played with for years. The universe is open and surprising; truly new things spring out of nowhere. Some of these things that come about appear over and over. Like predators and parasites that appear in infinite variety and in countless manifestations and forms. Always where autonomous agents emerge they appear too—things that live by stealing what other riches individuals have acquired. Intelligence also appears in such variety that it would stagger your mind as things evolve to cope with the newness that the universe throws at it.

My guide looked up at me slyly, "But there is something that emerges that is so wondrous that it changes everything. It is this that I have come to teach you."

"What is it?" I asked, rubbing my hand. It was still burning fiercely and it was starting to distract me from the conversation.

"It is the currency that the shepherds value more than any other thing and expand their influence to encourage and promote it in the universe. But they are up against obstacles many. As your poet Tennyson says, life is red in tooth and claw and *that* is necessary for complexity to grow. The struggle to survive must always be present—individuals in battle with others to grab what rarities they need to provide for their own offspring. So the miracle the shepherds crave to share is balanced with the need for the universe to grow in complexity and opportunity and novelty. It is hard. For the shadows in the intelligences are always present, like your own, that you just met and face. This dark side comes from the needs of individual agents to survive. You would call it selfishness, craving, desire ..."

Her speaking suddenly drifted off as we rounded a small hill. Below us a campfire glowed in a small bowl where a group of humans were gathered, singing. The music was strange. Beautiful. Not like anything I'd ever heard. A small antelope was turning on a spit being cranked by older children taking turns at the effort. They were dressed below the waist in loose hide skirts, well-tanned, with vest-like coverings over their upper bodies. The women and men sported strange tattoos patterned in geometric shapes on their arms and legs. A male cut pieces from the haunch, and gave them to the children who speared them with sharpened sticks. The women's hair was adorned with flowers and the beards of the men were graced with beads and seashells. The meal was eaten with much chatter and laughter. Because of the distance I could only catch occasional words (again has it had been throughout this ordeal, the language was utterly transparent). I motioned to my guide to question if we could go closer. She nodded assent and we crept forward. The night was decorated with a night sky that would have normally left me breathless, but after a vision like I'd seen not long ago, such beauty, while recognized, did not fully overwhelm me.

The meal was over, and people sat down upon logs and rocks that had obviously been dragged there for this purpose. I was near enough now to hear their voices clearly and they were telling stories. The first I heard was about a beloved grandfather and his slaying of a leopard armed only with a rock fashioned as a device used to crush bones and extract marrow. The teller, whose age was hard to identify, maybe as young as 30 or as old as 40, showed the children with his hand turned into a claw where the grandfather had been wounded on his back and on his leg. The children sat rapt as the teller with clever exaggeration described how the grandfather had crushed the beast's skull. The children asked for details and the man telling the story produced from a bag tied about his neck a leopard's claw. There were ooohs and aaaahs as the children passed it around.

Next a woman told a story about why it was essential to share. She talked about a selfish goddess, who wanted all the power/mana/spiritual strength for herself, and so stole it from the other gods and goddesses who had spent time gathering it. One day she was caught in the act and the other deities gathered in council to decide what should be done with her. It was decided that she would spend her life as a thief. She was turned into a honey badger that would ever after have to stumble on honey and steal it from the bees with their dangerous stingers. But the goddess's husband, another of the great gods, thought the punishment too harsh, for he knew she would never be able to find enough honey to survive in the Serengeti. She would die. But the other gods would not be swayed to change their minds. So he transformed himself into the chirping and chattering honeyguide bird. As such he can lead his changeling wife to honey and who, after she opens the hive to extract the honey, shares the feast with her husband.

The next woman to rise was strikingly beautiful. Her black skin glowed in the light of the fire. I noticed that everyone, men and women, focused on her with devoted attention. I knew she was a shaman or priest with exceptional power. She radiated it. My ape guide leaned over and gave me an elbow and whispered to me with delight, "That's me in life! Mbacoob!boo!a. Listen to my words!" The woman began to speak.

With authority and power, she said, "Brothers and sisters and wives and husbands and children and small babies who only speak the language of the beasts. Lady Moon. Gift Fire. Antelope Friend who has sacrificed his life that we might continue to learn the ways of the shepherds who know many things. Who wield the power to make stars, like we do the stone tools of the earth we love. Those great ones who wield the power to make a sun, like we do fire with which to cook and watch. Who wield the power to make our land like we do the power to make our clothes to protect our children." Her voice was sing-songy and musically rich. As she spoke, she began a rhythmic cadence by slapping her hand against her thigh.

"Listen to me and you will hear words of power."

"Listen to me and receive the gift of the shepherds."

"Listen to me and you will find that in your heart you are a friend to all."

"Your hunts will be successful. And if they are not, you'll find that when you pass on to what follows that you will be made a guest at the shepherd's fire, whose hunts never fail." What followed was spoken with great force: almost yelled, and sternly commanded.

"Be generous with what you gather."

"Share your hunt or what you collect and do not look for it to return to you again through the same person."

"Be not afraid to take what others have shared. Have no expectation that what you share with others will be returned, nor try to return that which is shared with you—what has been given is given."

"A gift is a gift. The grace of the shepherds is generous and unfettered."

"For the shepherds, who made this starry sky from the dirt of the first offering, there is one thing they crave above all others. There is one attribute that they share and desire for you. It is this: that you evermore among yourselves and among the strangers that you meet upon the open grass and which have approached you with open hand and heart, offer the greatest gift which is—"

And with that I was suddenly awakened back into the hut. I had been thrashing about under the influence of the drug, but no one was watching me. In my delirium I had crawled off my mat and lain down next to the old potbellied diesel cooking stove. My right hand had fallen underneath and had been burned entirely away. I lifted up my hand to my face and saw only bones burned black which broke and which crumbled apart as I watched. I began to scream and scream and scream.

Gilda was taken by burro and jeep and canoe to Iquitos. She was in and out of consciousness. Several times her Russian companion despaired of her life. She stayed three weeks in the city hospital. Her mother flew down and stayed with her. Her arm was amputated just above the wrist, after which she was flown to Salt Lake City for further treatment. When she had regained some of her strength, she returned to Idaho for further convalescence.

One more thing is worth telling. When she was coming out of anesthesia in Salt Lake after repairing the bone around her amputation, and as her mother hovered over her in the recovery room, Gilda sat bolt upward and smiling at her mother as broadly as a court fool said, "She was going to say, 'Love,' Mom. I know it. The ancient shaman was going to say, 'Love.'"

Vignette 11: Gilda's Poem My Turn on Earth. Written Circa 1951.

The following theological poem was found in one of Trillim's high school notebooks. While the title appears to be tongue-in-cheek, playing off of the Lex De Azevedo and Carol Lynn Pearson LDS musical *My Turn on Earth: A Family Musical Play*[1] from the 1970s, and added years after she wrote this, the rest seems a kind of poetic theology. What is astonishing is that she seems to anticipate many current issues—like unscientific intelligent design creationism.

There is much informal discussion among Trillim scholars about what this work was supposed to be. It seems to be a play of sorts. Or perhaps a hymn of praise. It is clearly a poem and she draws on several poetic forms in its construction: sonnet, villanelle, sestina, pantoun, free verse, and even limerick. It is difficult to classify and lies outside the genre Trillim usually uses in her minimalist novels. There is the typical maudlin quality to such re-imaginings of the Mormon doctrine, as is found in Nephi Anderson's work, *Added Upon*, about the pre-existence. Nonetheless this one explores things like consciousness and free will in original ways. The poem is especially interesting in light of her just described drug-induced vision, which appears to draw elements from her subconscious portended in this work from an adolescent Gilda Trillim.

My Turn on Earth
I sing in praise of the High God!
Material Father.
Embodied Mother.
He that sorrows and weeps.
She that worries and cries.
Praise Him!

Praise Her!
For they stood and said, "These!"
"Praise them, we also are these!"
"And these will be made like us!"

And lo.
And lo.

There was a place.
There was a space.
Where matter was not yet matter.
Unorganized.
Wandering.
Here and there ascatter.

(The Spell)

Knot it.
Bind it.
Fasten it with glue.
Hold it.
Twist it.
Into a matter stew.

Shrink it.
Crush it.
Until it's just a tittle.
Pack it.
Stack it.
Until it cannot wiggle.

Until …?

Until Bang!

Until KaBoom!
Expanding space
Extending time

And then there was light.
And it all seemed quite right.

The children gathered round to watch
the great unfolding.

"Patience," said Father.
"Patience," said Mother.

And then a swirl soft lit appeared,[2]
Of stars thick spinning through the cloud,
Then another and another graced the expanding mere,
As light through night serenely plowed,
Then for joy the sons cried at a universe made,
And in ecstasy daughters clapped and sang,
For the foundation of delight was in matter laid,
And from that beginning all that would later emerge sprang,
"How long?" his children begged and pled,
"Before our warm bodies completed stand?
What wait before complexity will widely spread,
That we may in doughy matter gently land?"
"No one knows," said God, "What the future holds,
But we must watch and wait until it all unfolds."

Great is Their wisdom!
Mighty is Their watching!
Praise His mighty patience and Her forbearance!
For the universe spins as it must spin,
with matter in motion,
the laws are set,

and waiting and patience,
are also Godly acts.
For not until consciousness enters the worlds,
can They be heard and Their hand be raised.
For moving matter from those
courses to which it has been set
requires mind,
and mind matter.
And every act an agent.
And for every agent an act.

But lo, what horror did wetness unfold![3]
For substance found swift ways to replicate,
And thus began generations untold,
For suffering—pain undergird the second estate,
For through blood, semen and terrors thick rife
Complexity crawled mad in to the universe,
Growing, adding, emerging quickening life,
Bringing blessings though in curses immerse,
Then wept daughters and cried the sons at sere
Earth's monstrous demands in blood and tooth,
"Is there no other way?" wept mouths tight in fear
And Father answered, "Will you know the truth?
If freedom complexity and creativity will reign,
Matter must face its existential bane."

Then star bringer held up his hand.
And God nodded.
Mother bid him rise.

Stand still sweet parents swift and bright[4]
Holding back darkness, wielding light

For I have found the Apollonian way,

No need for messes, wet with clay

No blood, no semen, or menstrual mess
No offal, sickness, age, distress

Make it craftily designed and certain,
Forget this grassy, slimish, verdan

Here's how …

(And the children listened as he spake)

Tick tock tick tock[5]
Turn the steel precision gear
Now wind up the iron clock

Metal to metal, key to lock
Torsion, tension, forces shear
Tick tock tick tock

I will teach you how to walk
Set courses given, never veer
Now wind up the iron clock

All is determined, never ad-hoc
All to metronome adhere
Tick tock tick tock

Set with pulley, tackle, block
Let all in lockstep-click appear
Now wind up the iron clock

Toward exact prediction flock!
And every outcome engineer!

Tick tock tick tock!
Now wind up the iron clock!

A lone figure walks in the distance, His head bowed,
As the machinist unfolds blueprints
Exact and precise and shows his devisings.

The figure kneels and wonders,

Is a less cruel way possible?
Can this cup be replaced?
Can complexity emerge from other than freedom,
variation, inheritance, selection?
Is the machinist right?
Or is there another way?

The contriver can be seen
waving his hands and building a scale model
of a universe engineered to be set, certain,
no slop, all is measured and precise,
fixed, so that no surprises enter in.

The machinist shouts, "Where all is arranged from the
beginning.
And once in motion it starts to spin—
all ends are determined from
What beginning laid."

The other looks upward, is there hope in him?

While the Bringer with tinker toys played and stacked,[6]
Another looked at heaven's ecologies,
At life manifold, diverse within spheres,
Turning, emerging, knots in knots folding,

Living things striving upward creative,
Evolving, ascending, to new rife forms.

Who would enter this chaos? Pinning forms,
Spirit and matter joined, new made and stacked
Together, forged by bold acts creative,
To enable celestial ecologies,
To embrace topological folding,
So severe as to rupture holy spheres?

Alone to deftly hold those spinning spheres
Crashing, in sins of many confounding forms?
Who would stand to embrace such bleak folding?
Such a cross to bear! Against the world stacked!
On whom the fate of all ecologies,
Would rest? Who can dare be so creative?

As to fashion salvation creative
And reckless, to transcend all mortal spheres?
To save meek creaturely ecologies,
And those of keen humans whose godly form
Strains among its temptations sharply stacked,
And who against nature's lien is folding?

Who will stand to face staid fate's unfolding?
Against dark evil's relentless creative
Disillusionment, fierce against us stacked?
Search high and low among heavenly spheres,
Hunt among all conscious, sentient forms,
For one to hold tight the ecologies,

Willingly, lovingly, ecologies
Thick wrapped with matter and spirit folding,
Able to embrace hallow living forms,

And perform an act, holy, creative,
Beyond that which as yet emerged in spheres,
Endlessly spinning or in fell worlds stacked.

Who made the ecologies creative?
I. Send me therefore folding into spheres,
Where I will free willing forms, saved well-stacked.

"No don't send him send me! Send me. Send me," ticked the Tock,

I can engineer this with certainty,
such that none will be lost.
For every gear will turn as turned,
and every piece in place,
completing the whole
with exactness,
well designed,
ably constructed,
fit to all existence's need.
And all outcomes sure.

And then the tick-tock man of morning light sang:

Brood on blood spilled in thick fetid fluids that drain,[8]
in a broth of anguish lapped by tongues wet—
Slick behind bone teeth made to tear, crush, set
within flesh made to feel every rush of pain.
Watch razor claws that leave wounds spelling bane—
not quick, nor merciful—a constant threat
that mad suffering will never abet—
Leaving on existence naught but a stain.
That fate on creature, will thus fall to us,
and alone will our bleak children fall dashed,
smitten by nature's relentless cunning.

Think hard what cruel gains come of such a thrust,
where all we love can be cut and slashed—
Leaving us from mortal fears ever running?

Father/Mother in answer wept,

Since in complexity is freedom,
and machines made, even of
sweet biology are still machines.
We chose He that chooses life
over overt design.
We chose flourishing over
mandated determinism.

And they chose the life-giver.
And the intelligent designer was angry and kept not his first
estate.

*And Mother and Father gathered their children around them and
said:*

A Trilobite of order Redlichiida,[8]
Evolved into an Asaphida,
Though they all went extinct
Their time on Earth quite succinct
Permian seas still contained some Proetida.

Fish arrived in Devonian Oceans
With fins they could use for all their motions
For limbs, hands, and feet
Are for Godlings quite sweet
And allow them to apply crafty lotions.

Amphibians soon came upon lands

And in doing so formed little hands
They could hold onto walls
And make squeaky calls
Meeting all their terrestrial demands.

Reptiles next appeared on the scene
(Some shaded a glorious green)
The dinosaurs bold
Or so we are told
Also had quite a wonderful sheen.

A great calamity struck the lan',
And smashed into an alluvial fan,
The dinosaurs died,
'cross the world wide
Bringing joy to a small mammal clan.

There once was a Therapsid from Nantucket,
Who evolved into a thought bucket,
Finally stood on two feet,
And with spears hunted meat,
Using language all the better to thunk it.

Two alone stand and watch,
Hand in hand, waiting, wondering.

Could the machinist be right?
Could the way of the gear's precise turning,
engineered with care, laid out in set
exactitude without play—smooth running,
machines clicking and clacking forward
in righteousness, humming sweetly, into a
shiny and grinding future been
better in the end?

Many have followed him after all.

She turns to him,

"They will worship him when they get below."
"I know."
"The designer God."
"Yes."
"Omnipotent."
"Yes, working through consciousness has its limitations. Much better the myth of the God who can engineer any end."
"Omniscient."
"Yes. In a deterministic world if you know the initial conditions all else follows. There is great comfort in such a system."
"Omnipresent."
Looking down and spreading his arms he answers, "And here I am that I am. An object. Made of matter like them."
She laughs, "Yes. Like them. Our children."
"They will build machines great and complex."
"It's what they do with them that matters."
"Yes."
"I wonder, will they care for the world? Will they know the time that went into that cactus? That flower? That snake, that bird in bright plumage a half billion years in the making? Will they treasure the emergence?"
"We shall see."

He looks across the expanse,

"Existence is hard."
"Yes."
"We must prepare them for it."
"Yes."
"We are not machines."

"No. But emergence has its pleasures."
"Yes."

Sperm, egg, wet cells, sticky fluids spilling, sloppy, silly things[9]
slide across membranes inexact, error prone
accidents of selection slip, flesh swings,
through channels forming rough and brittle bone,
genes slip and slide through motions mostly right,
but cough and jerk from time to time, hiccup trip,
springs unwind, chemicals push through and fight,
splashing nonsense far and wide, loosing grip.
But from the grass the cheetah bolts, relentless.
Clear eyes focused on motion swift, fleeing.
Fleet legs stretching, back—a coiled spring, exactness.
Retractable claws in air stretch, seizing.
Chaos from below; quite a messy show,
But from above bides beauty's steadfast flow.

The children want the parents to hurry things along.
Evolution works at its own pace, selecting from
among the random variation, passing it on though
time, slowly. There are many false starts. Much waste.
The children become impatient.

Can you not by force move things forward?[10]
Just a little stir of the pot?
To hurry things along a bit?
Must consciousness be the only influence?

Just a little stir of the pot,
would make the stirrer culpable, so
must consciousness be the only influence,
as matter in motion does what it will,

Would make the stirrer culpable? So?
Bodies need to find joy,
as matter in motion does what it will,
with spirit to guide it to new ends.

Bodies need to find joy,
true, and claim those courses
with spirit to guide it to new ends.
But spirit needs a consciousness if it is to find expression

true, and claim those courses
shadowed by force and law.
For a spirit needs a consciousness to find its expression
in the courses through which matter flows

Shadowed by force and law,
constrain all, even I,
in the courses through which matter flows
from consciousness to consciousness.

Constrain all, even I,
so through soft influence I push,
from consciousness to consciousness,
my work to do,

So through soft influence I push
through you to put matter into motion,
my work to do,
only through you.

Through you to put matter into motion
all my glory, all my love is expressed.
Only through you
can the pot be stirred at all.

And so the children watched as things unfolded, emerged,
what wonders they beheld as things blossomed into being.

"Look, that Toodon goes upon two legs!
Its brain is large? Will it be our home?"

"Wait and see my children." Wait and see?
But no, a meteor strikes and all hope ends.

"But on that planet,
in that galaxy over there,
is that language?
On that one, hands?
On that far planet,
song like those in the heavens are sung?
There! There is an orb where intelligence reigns,
where behemoths use their trunks for tools,
then fashion more of rock and stone."

"Will that do? It's not like you in form, but it will do.
See they love and talk and sing like angels too?
Consciousness is there. Is it not? Can we go?"

"Patience my children, wait and see, perhaps for another,
but not for you."

"Then ... what's this? Little insectivores develop tiny hands,
Their eyes are focused straight ahead.
We watch as selection does its work,
on variations, random
threads, passing down generations of
these tree dwellers
chattering free."

"Cross your fingers. Hold your breath."

"A promising beginning sure.
Sociality makes their brains to grow,
their repertoire of sounds
and gestures grow and mount."

"Can it be so? They seem familiar."

Their tail grows smaller, the brain gets larger.

"Please, oh please. Let the tail go. Let it go!
Let it go away."

And it does. Down from the trees they come
and soon walking
develop a smooth and careful gait.
They hunt.
From rocks
they hammer tools.

One of the children cries:
"What a piece of work is protoman! How noble in reason!
how infinite in faculty! In form and moving how
express and admirable! In action how like an angel!
In apprehension how like a god!"

"Are they conscious
in just the right way?
Are the categories in place?
Can they reason, can they feel?
Can you touch their minds dear
God? Can you thus enter now
and influence the universe?"

113

And there, in Earth's glades,
A male and a female
Human squat across from each other.
A gourd of red ocher in the male's hand,
Each dip a finger,
into the bowl.
And each to each apply a stripe,
down the other's face.
A decoration.
And act of love,
making art.

*And consciousness entered
into the world.*

In just the right way.

Vignette 12: Trillim's POW Experience in Vietnam. 1968–1970

I have agonized over how to present this part of Trillim's life. It is crucial to my thesis and yet there is not a single account that does justice to the particular aspects I want to pick out. The following is constructed from scattered notes, an unclassified interview conducted by the US Army and another given by the American Embassy in Moscow. Both were obtained through a FOIA request. In addition, I have used letters from Gilda to her mother and to her friend Babs Lake. I've used recollections given in television and newspaper interviews. I also interviewed Podpolkovnk Vatutin, who was in charge of the Soviet attaché that brought Trillim to Moscow. The volume of available information is staggering, largely because so much attention has been paid to this aspect of Trillim's life.

In what follows, I've taken some creative license by imagining a narrative of what happened, i.e., this is a piece of creative writing, mixed with selections of her own voice to give a reality-based recreation of these series of nearly unbelievable events. However, it is based on a close reading of everything Trillim has said or written about the subject. In addition, I sent this to Lark Melk and Kaija Linnainmaa, leading Trillim scholars with particular expertise about her time in Vietnam. Their suggestions have been useful in getting an as accurate portrayal as possible. Still, many questions remain unanswered. For example, such basic information about where she was held prisoner remains uncertain. Scholars have suggested that it might even have been Laos, rather than Vietnam. The actual location has never been found, despite efforts by researchers such as Nguyen Binh, who spent considerable time looking for the camp.

I fear this attempt to construct an account of these events will be considered controversial, as any writing will always reflect the biases and inclinations of the individual investigator and I have not escaped this weakness. It seems this cross between creative-nonfiction and historical fiction may be the only way to capture these strange events. Whenever quotes are actually Trillim's I have marked them in italics. This includes several long sections from her journal.

Her most vivid memory of the events occurring early in her captivity was being transported in a small wooden wagon lurching slowly through thick tropical vegetation along a narrow two-track path. The cart was pulled by two small water buffalo. She found herself lying face down with her left hand frapped to her stump and both arms bound behind her back. Her legs were tied together. She tried to turn over, but she was also tied to the side of the vehicle. When she tried to move, a fierce pain shot through her side, especially whenever she twisted her torso. She remembered thinking that her ribs were surely broken. In her struggles to orient herself, she turned her head to the other side and saw a dead American soldier tied similarly next to her. He had an open head wound and his eyes were staring straight ahead, glassy and inanimate.

When the cart hit a pothole, it all flooded back. The USO tour. The helicopter ride back to Saigon. The bang. Tearing of metal. The crash. Major Oaklanding pulling her from the wreckage. Shots. The pilot slumping over after his head exploded in a spray of blood and brains. The look of pop singer Dick Flemming lying face-down in the mud. Artist Fran Treacle hanging from her seat restraints limply, her femur twisted at a right angle. The Major kneeling and putting his hands on top of his head in a posture of surrender. His signaling her to do the same. Being bound. Tight. Without mercy.

As she bounced along in the small wagon, she looked at the Major beside her and wondered how he had died.

Whenever the cart hit another bump, it felt like someone was pushing something thick and dull into her lungs. Where was she?

Back in the helicopter, the Major and the pilot had been arguing. The navigation system had glitched, then quit working completely. The pilot believed he knew where they were, but the Major asserted they ought to follow a river down below, which he had insisted was the River something she cannot remember, but the pilot was sure it was River something else. The Major ordered that they continue following the river. For what seemed like a long time they did. Gilda kept thinking, why does no one have a compass on this damn thing? She could see the Major's confidence wane every mile they traversed over the verdant landscape. Then the river just disappeared into the unending jungle below as if it had been nothing but a mirage. The pilot tried to circle back, but it started to rain. As the clouds descended, visibility shrank. She remembered that the Major and pilot were bickering again and insulting one another's competence. The pilot was sure they had crossed into Cambodia. Then a bang and a jolt. They went down. No one would have any idea where they were or where to begin to search for them.

As the cart made its way down what was now only a dirt path, it started to rain. Strange to see the Major with his eyes still wide open in the pouring rain—not blinking as the fierce raindrops struck and then beaded on the ocular surface. She could swivel her head around to the opposite side of the Major, where she could glimpse thick rainforest through the slats in the wagon's side. The vehicle, designed to hold hay, had been conscripted to carry prisoners. Despite the pain, she strained to get a look at who was driving the wagon. It was the farmer she saw first, but next to him were two Viet Cong soldiers huddled together and sharing an American Military poncho to keep off the rain. Soviet rifles poked out of the nylon gear.

Gilda began to weep. The horror. They had crashed. Good friends she had met on the USO tour were dead. And now she was a captive. She vomited weakly, and then looked up at her captors and said in English, "Please, I'm just a writer on a USO tour. Please, please help me." In answer, one of the men perched on the seat directly above her angrily barked something incomprehensible then cracked her on the head with the butt of his AK-47. She was knocked from consciousness.

She woke up confused and groggy in a small dirt-floor cottage with a bamboo mat on which she'd been laid. Straw was heaped along the edge of one wall. A small trench on the opposite wall served as a lavatory she guessed. She could hear voices outside, but understood nothing. Through a gap in the thatch she could see she was in a small village with huts of various sizes scattered about a small clearing in the forest. Within her field of vision she could see a peasant woman and some men, most in ragged Vietcong uniforms. Others were dressed in black shirts and trousers; these seemed to be in charge and drifting here and there among the huts of the village. Nothing, however, made sense and she feared to arouse anyone's ire. At night she was given a small bowl of rice, maybe the equivalent of half of a cup, and a piece of fruit by a woman who opened the door and laid the bowl on the ground and left.

No one but the woman bringing food visited her for several days. Nights were miserable, her ribs and head hurt from the blows. Almost worse, after sunset mosquitoes bit her relentlessly, leaving welts and itchy sores. She had constant diarrhea and her stomach felt as twisted and bruised as the rest of her body.

After about a fortnight of this, one morning she awoke to the sound of large trucks entering the encampment. There was much shouting of what seemed like commands. Hustle and bustle and laughter poured from the camp as well as other signs of excitement.

After about an hour, her door burst open and several men entered the hut. They were dressed in green uniforms, much cleaner than the ones she had seen around the camp. A short, bullish man spoke harshly to her, then said in broken, barely comprehensible English, "You Nurse?" Gilda shook her head, and said, "Please, I am a writer. Here with USO. I read my books to people."

He answered her roughly, "No, you Nurse spy."

She shook her head again against the accusation, pleading that she meant no harm to anyone. The man stepped forward and punched her in the gut. She curled up on the dirt floor of the hut protesting her innocence in small gasping whines. He kicked her twice and walked out.

She crawled scared and crying to her mat. He came back a few minutes later without his entourage and raped her. After, he punched her twice in the face, breaking her nose. He left shouting, "You spy. You American bitchdog."

That night the sound of the truck's engines signaled their departure from the camp.

For three days she did not stir, not even to eat. She did not slap away the mosquitoes. She peed freely on the mat and let the liquidly diarrhea pass through her like water from a leaking pipe. The old woman who brought her food tried to push rice into her mouth, but she would not take it. The ragged lady poured water into her mouth, which Gilda reluctantly lapped up. She willed herself to die. But death eluded her.

On the morning of the third day after her rape, she heard again the sound of the trucks entering the encampment. She crawled to a corner to hide. It was a different group of men, but on entering they quickly covered their noses and fled. After a few minutes the woman who had been feeding her returned with several other women. They threw buckets of water over her then motioned for her to remove her clothes. She did and they threw more water over her, cleansing the blood, fecal matter and urine from her body. Then they brought her some trousers and a shirt. These she put on slowly. She weakly tried to thank them. They did not smile, but rather hurried out of the hut.

She could hardly walk, but they pushed her forward to one of

119

the trucks. It was a troop transport vehicle with a canvas prairie schooner-like cover. She was thrown forcibly inside the back of the truck. It was dark at first, but as her eyes adjusted she saw she was not alone. There were two American soldiers sitting side by side on the left bench, both a bloody mess, their eyes nearly swollen shut. They were dressed in loose pants without shirts exposing badly bruised and bloody backs and chests. One's arm was clearly broken. They wore no shoes. They did not look at her. Perhaps they could not.

A guard climbed aboard, looked around as if inspecting something then climbed back out. In fear, she moved toward the front of the truck and sat on one of the two benches that rimmed the inside compartment. She sat on the opposite side of the two other male prisoners. An additional pair of Vietnamese soldiers climbed aboard carrying side arms and sat near the tailgate so they could look through the opening of the canvas stretched over the skeletal frame enclosing the back area. They paid no attention to the prisoners, but rather lit a single cigarette, which they passed back and forth to one another—saying nothing. One of the American prisoners seemed to perk up at the smell of tobacco, but then quickly fell back into his silence.

They traveled for four days. They stopped every few hours and allowed the prisoners to step out and pee in the forest. This at least allowed them to stretch their legs. At such times they were given a drink of water. Once a day they were given a little rice.

None of the American soldiers said anything to each other or to Gilda. Once only when they were on a break did she see any attempt at communication. One of the POWs limped up to a guard and looking at him miserably, tried to smile through his beaten and bruised face, and mimicked smoking by holding up two fingers and tapping his swollen and cracked lips in imitation of taking a drag. The guard laughed, slapped him, and walked away. The broken soldier never tried again.

They eventually reached something resembling a paved highway, or so Gilda believed because the speed of the vehicle increased and the ride became smoother. Ten years after these events Gilda wrote in a published interview:[1]

What was I thinking as I rode in the back of that transport? What thoughts crossed my mind in these horrible circumstances? These were a few: was it really only a couple of weeks ago I walked with my father and younger brother up to Delicate Arch near Moab, Utah? That we laughed at a joke about a shark and a lawyer? That the sun reddened and dehydrated us? How is it I find myself alone? Without allies? No connection to culture, meaning, language? I sobbed invisibly and soundlessly, not wanting to draw the gaze of my captors. I feared them. I feared them. I feared them beyond reason and beyond hope. I felt lost. I felt abandoned and forsaken. I smelled of my own shit and body reekings. My ribs and nose were broken. My face from the blows felt swollen. And more than these, my soul through violence had been poisoned and I could not shake the feeling that such damage had been inflicted that not even death would erase the taint—because it bored down to the core of who I was.

Despite the oppressive heat I sat shivering and trembling on that bench, knowing that I was helpless to whatever harms were presented to me. Whatsoever was handed to me I would take. I went numb for hours or maybe days, oblivious to sense. Not like a Buddhist monk whose thoughts have been quieted through mindfulness and attention, no, my mind was shocked to stillness like a piston frozen because no motor oil lubed the engine. I awoke during one of the nights on our journey, late. In the headlights of some car following us I could see that both the guards and my fellow prisoners were asleep—lightly, as people do in a moving vehicle, maintaining some modicum of posture to keep from sliding to the floor, but even so, their heads were bobbing on their shoulders loosely and unconsciously. Waves after waves of panic and fear bubbled over me; my breath became gasps for air that I could not obtain. It felt like I was being held underwater. I felt doomed. I felt damned.

I reached out. I called upon the God of my youth. I sent my mind heavenward pleading for him to take me back into his care. I knew I had abandoned him. I thought of the pictures I'd seen in Sunday School as a child in Idaho of Jesus with his soft chestnut brown hair, smiling down on a child and I begged, "Help me Jesus. Help me now. I'm lost." The truck rolled onward into the night. Why would he come to me? I had abandoned him long ago. And yet I hoped. I wanted to believe that someone somewhere was aware of what I was feeling and it mattered. Calmness drifted over me for a second, as if it were seeking a worthy vessel, but as I tried to reach out to it, it fled. I cried silently. Alone.

The trip is largely remembered as a progression of shifting olfactory sensations. The stream of smells seemed flighty and ambivalent, changing constantly, with particular smells never staying long before moving on. There were a few repeated patterns pushing through the slight whiff of wet canvas as the background aroma ping-ponged between the scent of verdant forest and the stench of sewage laced rivers. I remember suddenly catching a smell of burning wood or from time to time some strange pungent food. I remember vividly that the odors were ever present under that dark canopy, always growing more chaotic and foreign, but accompanied with a diesely infusion from the truck, an oppressive caustic background smell as the air wafted through the canvas shell.

I remember looking down at my stump and being reminded of what I had suffered to receive a vision of the beginning of creation. In the distant past, unimaginably distant, was a great thing that filled all of existence with undifferentiated substance. Where had I gone wrong? I cried silently. I had set out to discover one thing, the being of objects, even an apple seed. I'd spent a year coming to know one thing intimately, to discover one thing through and through. That pip. And yet it had eluded me. After a year, I still knew nothing. Then I had turned to the ecology of everything, objects, things, persons, living things, non-living things, noting connections wherever I could find them. But now I had lost them all. I had become empty. A void. A hole. A zero. I contained nothing that I wanted to own. I'd seen it all! The expanse of eternity! But now all my connections were severed. All my being sucked through the straw of human cruelty and emptiness—like an egg siphoned though a pin prick through which the yolk and marrow has been drained away leaving naught but a hollow shell, fragile and ready to break upon first touch of resistance. I was void. The empty set. Alone. Without value, I was cast aside. From the inside, all that I am had been stripped away, from the outside I had been forsaken. Nothing within nothing. I could make no sense of this. How had it happened? Once I was surrounded with people and things knitting together who I was, but they had all been unraveled, leaving me to drift alone in this faraway place. Why was not I dead? Like Fran.

Was Fran dead?

Before the accident she had been painting a picture of me. It had been sketched out on a drawing pad. Me sitting. Quiet. Demure. My real hand holding my fake molded prosthetic hand, a thing forever locked in a mannequin's unchanging position—fake palm up, my fake thumb angling toward the large joint of my fake index finger slightly extended, forming a circular hollow, my other fake fingers curling slightly toward a plane perpendicular to the angle of my wrist. The fixed gesture of someone about to make a point. Ironically, a point unlikely ever to be made. A point, like my hand, forever frozen in the simulacrum of point-making. Frozen and now lost—a meaningless gesture signifying nothing now lying abandoned in the dirt of the jungles of Southeast Asia.

I mourned for my lost fake hand, abandoned like me never to be seen again. I remember when I first got it. Its presence masked my stump from others. The plastic thing seemed at first unpleasant. It frightened me. It represented disfigurement and perhaps worst of all the mock-up lacked authenticity. Yet, as hideous as I found it personally, it masked the blunt blasphemous termination of my stump. A denial of beauty— unholy and scandalous that separated me from others in a way that made the artifice worth it. Where was it? Had it been picked up by a soldier? A villager? A token of triumph? A curiosity to pass around after a few beers? What had become of that abstraction of embodiment?

Now I had been wholly blunted, like my arm—my soul was now a ghost appendage dangling lifeless from my body—my future a ghost limb. I knew I would still feel emotional pain if I survived this. Just as I sometimes feel from my missing hand, so my ghost life could still try to grasp at something tangible, but it would only be a hollow plastic reproduction like my prosthesis, good for giving the appearance of a life such that I could still, no doubt, laugh at parties, plant a garden, or talk to a neighbor across a fence, but these would be artificial simulations, empty responses meant to represent the thing I used to be. The hand was gone. My future was gone. I wept at the loss. I was now a cipher signifying nothing. What sort of gadget could they make to attach to the rest of my life to give the appearance that there was something there?

Gilda apparently traveled north for several days. We know this because at one point in her narrative she tells how she looked to the back of the truck, the soldier on the right was bathed in sunlight all morning long. She was fed about a cup of rice a day, and given water three times in the same period. They finally arrived at a prisoner of war camp, a collection of cinder block buildings surrounded by cassava fields that the prisoners worked as slaves. No one has been able to identify this camp, despite diligent attempts to find it, and significant funding commitments to do so by The Society for Trillim Studies. Unfortunately, there is evidence that it may have been destroyed after the war.

When she first arrived, she was beaten and tortured to extract information. She was not able to explain the role of the USO and her part as an author sharing her work with the soldiers for entertainment. She suspected that they thought she was some kind of propagandist who read instructions to the troops. She was beat repeatedly with a switch across her back and legs, and they took a ping-pong-like paddle to her stump, which caused excruciating pain. This lasted three days. She was never raped again—she suspected because of the director of the camp was a Buddhist who held the guards to strict rules of military discipline—however, the entire duration of her captivity she expected it at any time creating a state of constant anxiety. Every time trucks arrived into the compound she would experience what we would now would call panic attacks or post-traumatic stress disorder, but which she described as "fracturing nervous tension."

She was placed in a small cinderblock room, one of many in a larger structure made of the same. The room was about three times the size of the bamboo mat that she slept on. A bucket served as a toilet. It was her only piece of furniture. A wooden door woven from thick branches blocked the exit until it was opened in the morning into a central hallway that resembled nothing so much as a horse stable. About every two days, she was allowed to empty her bucket into a trench that ran alongside the building. It was a constant source of a breath-stultifying stench.

There was one other woman in the camp, a nurse from the Netherlands named Silke Peeters with whom Gilda did not often have the chance to converse. Her presence at first gave Gilda a sense of comfort. As we will see, this was not to last.

The prison director, as mentioned, was a former Buddhist priest, who tried to run a compassionate camp, but many of the guards were cruel and unkind. The camp rules were strictly enforced. The prisoners spent all day in the cassava fields working, digging up roots for harvest, clearing out shrubbery, planting saplings, and such things.

The first week after her interrogation, they put her in the fields, but with her missing hand she could not handle the tools skillfully. She was slapped often during her attempts to work the crop because her hoeing with a single hand was unproductive and sloppy. She wrote that she never understood what people were saying to her. Although a few of the other POWs tried to help her and assist in her work, she was the source of constant attention and bullying by the taskmasters. Finally, early in the second week she was ordered back to her room where she would be forced to stay in the daytime while the others worked.

Because she was locked in her room during most of the day,

her first six months were ones of stupefying boredom and depression. During the long, unrelenting days imprisoned in her room, she tried to compose poems and stories, or spend long portions of the afternoon visualizing her life as a young girl growing up in Idaho. In the mornings, she would exercise, pretending that she was in a badminton match, bouncing back and forth along the length of her cell, swinging her arm as if battling for the world championship. Then she would run, jump, and skip in place for an hour or so until exhausted. After her exercises, she would lie down on her mat and take a short rest. Finally, she would do sit-ups and other exercises such as she thought she could manage within the enclosed space.

Then an event that changed everything for Gilda. I'll let her describe it.[2]

The rainy season was beginning and the air was humid, rich, and heavy. The steamy atmosphere made it ponderous to exercise and as I slowed down my activity, my mind would move in ugly directions toward things I needed to hammer down and relentlessly fight to keep submerged. However, I seemed ever more willing to follow my thoughts into the black. The sound of the rain was relentless and splashed through the small rebar grilled window onto my mat. Onto me. I developed a strange, indignant rash on my legs and torso. The pin-and-needle itching it produced made it worse than the maleficent mosquitoes. These had never ceased since I had arrived and their inglorious nightly feasts were unending. The welts they left marking the place of their meal were everywhere on my body. My only blessing was that my menstrual cycle had ground to a halt because of the constant stress and malnutrition.

We stopped queuing in the morning for our bowl of mushy rice because of the rain and I missed my chance to talk to one of the other prisoners. Since I did not get to work the fields, I seemed like an outcast even in my own bedraggled tribe so I relished the morning line up for rations, when I could steal a few moments of conversations and heal if only a little from my isolation. I always tried to get as close to the end of the line as time and circumstance would allow me, for I was more anxious for a few moments of human contact than I was for whatever meager pickings could be had for breakfast—a bowl of rice and a slice of fruit and a cup of thin broth, who knows of what kind. Sometimes Silke my only sister prisoner would stand by me and we would talk about the days before the War like a couple of old soldiers from the French trenches. My favorite conversationalist was Mike Norris, a funny and optimistic man who, with his cheer and smile, made the whole camp seem like a child's playtime adventure that would soon be over and we would by nightfall be tucked into our cozy beds back home with a mother's kiss planted on our cheeks.

With the rains, however, we were all confined to our rooms and our rations were handed out by the same old lady who usually ladled it into our bowls when we lined up outside. The guards did not stay in our building, which allowed us to shout out to the others and converse without being threatened for speaking like we often were. This almost seemed like a magical time because we could tell each other our life stories, share poems and memories, and do the kinds of things humans do to foster connection and community. It was not to last. Without explanation the contents of our wooden food bowls got smaller and smaller. The fruit disappeared and after three weeks of rain, it seemed we were getting only a few tablespoons of rice per meal. Then the evening meal disappeared. As our bodies begin to eat themselves, a silence fell over the prison. We were dying.

Nearly two weeks go by and the conditions become unbearable. A man dies and they know that they all must soon follow suit. Gilda begins to pray (her word) to her mother in long conversations. She became convinced that her mother could hear her in her dreams. She has recreated these prayers in poetry, but despite their enormous value, I'm going to skip them as they are readily available in her papers and are not necessary for this short introduction.

As Gilda was fading away, she writes:[3]

I decided to quit life. There was little point in delaying the inevitable. I looked at my skeletal knees, something akin to apples with pencils protruding from the ends. My skin was yellow and papery. I kept thinking how thankful I was that I did not have a mirror and did not have to look at the Jolly Roger face that no doubt would be staring back at me. I decided when they brought my daily trifle rather than take the offering I would give it to the rats. Since the rains had started, the rodents had become bolder and more aggressive. Several of the prisoners had captured and eaten some, but once rat blood stained their cells, the rats would avoid the place and these meals became one-time feasts.

On that fateful day my bowl was passed under the door. I picked it up and prepared to push it back. All my resolve melted. I greedily snatched a pinch and stowed it in my mouth before it could escape under the banner of my despair. I felt shame. Where was my resolve? A large black and gray rat was crouched in my windowsill sniffing the air. I took another pinch of rice and placed it on the other side of the sill. As I approached with the proffered rice, it made no sign of fear. I was no threat and it knew it. It waddled over to the rice, sniffed it cautiously, then without hurry picked it up in its delicate pink hands and nibbled it away.

"You are a fat rat," I said to it, scolding its insensitivity in parading around in such a well-stocked body. In answer it washed its face. I placed another pinch of the sticky grain on the floor, but before it could descend the wall, another rat came from under the door and snatched it up. The rat in the window, perhaps stinging from its mistake of not responding to my gift with alacrity, came down from the sill head first clinging to the cinder blocks like a spider. The two companions just looked at me sitting cross-legged on my mat with the bowl in my lap. I took two more lumps, stretched out my legs before me, and rested these offerings on each of my boney knees. Cautiously the two rats approached, watching not the rice, but my eyes as if trying to read there my intent and reliability. Slowly they came forward. The second one, a motley brown thing, strong looking and athletic, made a dash of such quickness that I almost flinched, but I held calm and it jumped on my knee and with its front paws, stole the rice and then bound under the *door. The larger rat seemed more circumspect, its caution more grounded in wisdom than fear. It approached with dignity and grace, as if it were a rat of rank who understood proper decorum in the matter of eating from a large monster's knees. It glided forward until it was even with my calves and then paused, assessing me. Finally, it conveyed a kind of rat-like shrug, climbed up to where it could reach the rice, and calmly ate it off of my knees. I did not move. I motioned to the bowl in my lap, tilting it forward so it could see the meager remnant remaining. It hauled itself up onto my thigh, balance-beamed its way to the bowl and calmly devoured its contents. It then climbed down to the floor, up the wall and out the window with a dignity that befit a queen. The next day I was anxious for the rats to return. I was growing weaker and the only exercise I could do was to walk slowly back and forth in my cell. When the bowl was passed under my door, I sat down on my mat with the bowl on my lap and waited, it wasn't long before my plump friend appeared at my window. She glided down the wall and came to my side but seemed reluctant to climb up on my legs. She stared into my eyes queerly as if waiting. The other rat came under the door and stood shoulder to shoulder with my friend. Much to my surprise we were joined by a third rat I'd never seen before, gray and musty colored, with only one eye, and a hollow cavity opposite the black bead on the other side. I liked her immediately. It wandered close to the other two, but stayed back a little as if testing the waters before committing to any action.*

I pulled out a clump of rice from the bowl, and offered it to my fat friend. She crept forward and then gingerly began nibbling it from between my fingers. She gave a soft squeak as if to say, "More please" so I reached in for another and repeated the gesture. This too she devoured. I took another pinch and passing my hand over the brave rat, offered the morsel to the fellow from under the door. He too demurely stepped forward and took the clump. He gave a squeak and received the second. By now the one-eyed girl saw which way the wind was blowing, and without much hesitancy demanded her fair share, and a second helping for a squeak. I offered them another, but they did not come forward. I even placed it under the nose of my fat friend but she would not eat it. They were close enough I could have easily grabbed them, but they just rested there observing me. There remained in the bowl a good half of the rice I'd been given, but even when I placed the bowl on the ground they would not take it.

I had the strangest thought. What if they wanted me to eat it? What if this is my share? Four of us. Three portions handed out. I picked up the bowl and began eating. The rats chirped in unison! What a sense of equality these small creatures had. When I put the empty bowl down, they came forward and I nuzzled them with my hand, each in turn— scratching them behind the ears, letting them run through my fingers. I found myself crying because it was the first physical social interaction I'd had since I arrived. We played for a bit, and when the old woman came for our bowls they ambled away.

This went on for another four days. Another rat joined our circus. I taught them all a trick of giving a little peep when I pointed at them. It was fun, but I was getting weaker and weaker and on the fifth day I did not try to exercise. I felt hollow inside. Emptied out. Like a gourd whose dried up seeds could be heard rattling around because everything else had faded into nothing. I was dying. When the fat one came that day, I said, "Well old girl, enjoy the rice while you can, I'll likely be going soon." She looked at me strangely, head tilted as if trying to make out my words. She turned around and left. The other rats remained and I gave them all the rice. I was disappointed that they did not leave me a share as before. I took it as a sign that they knew that for me existence was skittering to a halt.

I did not feel like practicing their 'singing' and so sat quietly while they milled around the cell. I liked that they never pooped or made a mess, as if they understood that this was my nest. They did not leave as I expected they would, but they stayed near and I stroked their head thinking about how short my life had been—how amazing, how horrible.

My fat friend appeared. I'd taken to calling her Lumpkin after Sam Gamgee's pony in Lord of the Rings. *I managed a smile to see her standing above me in the window. She started down the wall, when she slipped and fell to the floor. She was unhurt of course. Like cats, rats know how to take a tumble. It did wake me enough to notice that she seemed rather large, her belly extended in ways I'd not noticed before. I wondered if she was pregnant. She tottered over to me and climbed right onto my lap where the empty bowl was balancing. She peered in and I said, "Sorry girl. It's all ..." but I stopped because she vomited into the bowl. Had I had the strength I would have jumped to my feet to be free of this offense. But she didn't stop. She kept heaving and convulsing and acking and hacking with coughs and gags until nearly an entire cup of rat puke was sitting in my bowl. Throughout my life, even the smell of someone being sick would cause me to run for the bathroom gagging. Yet the smell of this vile concoction did not have that effect. I looked at the mess in my bowl. I was strangely drawn to it. It smelled sour, but it also had a sweet bouquet, rich and alluring. The funny thing was, I could tell it smelled vomity, but I didn't seem to mind the way I usually did. I could see that the mash contained fruit, the type I could not recognize, but there were large, pale fruit fly maggots still moving in it so I knew it had been not long in my friend's stomach. I stared at it for a few minutes. Lumpkin was cleaning herself on my lap, looking at me expectantly, or so I imagined. Finally, I dipped my finger into the soup and swirled it slowly watching the pink and orange striations blend into a livelier shade of fuchsia. I pulled a small sample up and breathed in its essence at close range. The aroma was redolent of a fine wine, with a spicy, vinegary trace. I found my mouth was watering as I placed the dab on my tongue. It felt like life. The taste was unexpectedly agreeable, almost alluring like a candied pudding. I could detect a bit of boiled cassava, bitter and starchy, and banana along with lilikoi. Before I knew what was happening I was two finger poiing it into my mouth with greedy relish. I finished by running my finger along the bottom of the bowl to mop up every drop and even squeegeed my tongue along the bottom to find every last remnant. It was a feast. Nothing to this day has equaled the exquisite delight of that sumptuous first meal of rat puke.*

My stomach felt stuffed to the point of bursting. Once again the bowl collector was coming down the center passageway and the rats wandered away. After I handed the woman my bowl, I curled up in a ball and listened to the rain. Why had the rats done this? They are creatures of instinct. Did they sense I was dying and their source of rice would dry up? Did some maternal instinct rise up out of deep biology and trigger passions for saving a nest mate or one of their offspring? I fell asleep with such ruminations, half in a state of wonder because of what had just happened. Later that night Lumpkin returned with another smaller load. She retched it into my cupped hands. I ate it without question, even licking clean some that spilled onto my mat. I felt stronger. That night I had to use my bucket twice, apparently due to either the sudden richness of my diet or some incompatibility between my own internal fauna and that of the rats', but it seemed a minor inconvenience for the nourishment that was coursing through my starving body.

That night the rains stopped for the first time in weeks. I took it as a sign that I would live. That I would get through this. In the morning I was still weak, but I felt strangely happy. Almost like songs were returning to my soul. When the rice was presented that day, it was like the world had changed. I gave it all to my friends—Lumpkin getting the lion's share. She brought me another load later that day, and then another that night. I was overwhelmed with gratitude and wept at the generosity and grace of the rats. I could not help even wondering if perhaps I was dreaming and in reality had passed out in a state of starvation and was witnessing the last throes of my famished brain constructing a fantasy rescue before it winked off permanently. But no, it continued. One-eye joined Lumpkin in feeding me and every day I grew stronger and more alive.

At last the rice rations were starting to increase, if only a small amount. The famine, or whatever had caused the lack of food during the rainy season, was abating and a small piece of fruit was being added. I surmised that over the course of the monsoons the rats had plenty to eat, but adored rice as a treat, because they continued to gather at meal times. Even so they continued to insist that I eat a little of it.

The rat vomit varied and included such diverse things as fish, which I was sure they were stealing from the camp officers' discarded meals, noodles, various forms of fruit and once or twice pork. I became accustomed to it and started to enjoy it more and more—looking forward to the arrival of Lumpkin and One-eye with their offering of heaved-up goodies.

About a month after the rains, the camp started to return to normal. I reckoned I had been a prisoner a year, although the passage of time was hard to mark. One day for the first time we were brought out for our breakfast, and the POWs were queued. The sight was one of horror. Skeletons, reduced in numbers by about half, stood in the line. I could not believe the skullish nature of the faces, I had not seen countenances like this before, save in magazine pictures of liberated Nazi concentration camps. I let everyone line up before me and joined the end of the line. Silke, who I was glad to see had survived, was near the front looked at me with a hollow empty gaze and came back to where I was. I thought she wanted to talk so I smiled at her. She looked at me and said, "So queen pig, you look no worse for wear." I was surprised and could not formulate an answer. It was true, thanks to the rats, while still thin, I was not like the thin hide-covering-bones aspect of those around me. I looked at her, my mouth quivering but with nothing coming out and she said, "But then who would not fuck their enemy for a bite at such times?" I started to protest when she answered her own question, "I wouldn't!" Then she spit in my face and walked back up to the beginning of the line. The man in front of me in line whispered back at me without turning around, "You fucking traitor. Bitch."

The group gathered under a small tree where they ravenously ate their breakfast. I walked up and tried to defend myself, but I was unused to talking and my tone sounded desperate and false even to me, "I did not 'fuck' anyone. The rats fed me." Colonel Pike, one of the older men who I had come to admire for his cheerfulness and calm, said, "You can't look that well-fed from eating rats. I know. And once you've offed a few they get as wary as coyotes." Many of the men nodded. Silke would not *look at me. I squawked, "I didn't eat them, they brought me food." Silke gave a sardonic laugh and spat, "Bullshit." A few of the men laughed. A young lieutenant whose name escaped me mocked, "Did they bring it on silver trays? Or did they use the regular dishes?" That brought a few more laughs. Someone muttered from the crowd, "I hope if it wasn't cooked to your satisfaction you sent it back." Then from somewhere else, "Oh, she was satisfied all right. Likely on well-stuffed sausages!" That brought as much laughter as those starving prisoners could muster and, except for Silke who laughed the longest, it quickly died down. Then Colonel Pike said quietly, but with considerable force and bitter unkindness, "Go away Gilda. You are not wanted here. What are you doing here anyway? Shouldn't you be dining with the rats? Go away. I can't look at you." As one, as if in a military formation, they all turned away from me, leaving me standing there alone holding my bowl of rice.*[4]

Over the next year, Gilda does not interact much with the Vietcong or with the other POWs who continue to shun her. Because she cannot work in the fields, she spends much of this time in a kind of solitary exclusion. She was now allowed out to exercise. She thinks the camp director thought she was a holy person. After all, she had survived the famine in an apparently almost magic manner. He let her wander the grounds with the understanding that she stay in the courtyard area in the center of the camp. When she was not walking in circles in this area she had to return to her cell, but the door was not locked until the other prisoners returned. She felt like this contributed to the rumors that she was exchanging sexual favors with the guards or the camp director.

However, now begins the strangest part of the story. Gilda continued to be fed by the rats. She grew strong under their care and her experiments, or as she called it, choir practices, became more elaborate and more organized. She trained them to squeak on command. To sing. After breakfast, a group of about fifty rats gathered in her cell and formed small clusters each made up of four to six rats. The rats would practice together singing in a strange and wonderful way. At first she would, after a fashion, play them as a kind of instrument. She would indicate by pointing which cluster of rats was to vocalize, and the height of her finger would indicate the note. However, as time went on this rat ensemble became more and more complex in its musical practice. Let me return to her words:[5]

The musical range of the rats was only about five notes, centered around eight octaves above middle C. Unlike a human choir, they randomized themselves in small scattered groups whose function I never quite made out, but seemed spatially consistent, meaning they arranged themselves in these same spatially defined groups every time they came to practice in my enclosure, even though the members of the group varied. This required some work. Some were arranged on the windowsill or on my mat or in the corner. Some gathered clinging to the walls some with heads aimed at the ceiling, others facing the floor, and still others horizontally, but the individual members of the groups that formed, all pointed their heads in the same direction. For example, the cluster that hung directly above my pillow always pointed their noses up. I have wondered if this spatial and directional arrangement conferred some tonal quality that the rats enjoyed or found meaningful.

At first I would try to 'play' them in ways that made sense to my human musical values, but as time progressed they began to extemporize and innovate. I was reluctant to let them do what they wanted, but in the end I just stepped back and let them sing while I listened. It was so different from human music that I feared it would be dismissed as irrelevant or nonsense by other musicians. If ever heard it would likely be ridiculed as a kind of random noise, yet as time went on I began to appreciate its complexity and nuance. The combination of voices the rats used in their compositions was not done in harmonies that humans would have found pleasing, but their consistency of use indicated to me that the rats preferred and even enjoyed a combination of notes that made no musical sense to me. I wondered if someday a rat Pythagorean mathematician would arise who would find mathematical principles behind these note combinations. Some brilliant rodent soul who would produce a ratty equivalent of harmonic intervals, ratios that formed natural combinations and chords different from ours but that the rats found pleasant. Though the music was not pleasing to the human ear, or at least my ear, I learned to appreciate their effort. It had certain minimalist tendencies, with long pauses between notes, blasphemous note combinations, or odd sections where the timing changed in strange ways. The rats had no way to lengthen their notes. So for a long extension of tones they achieved it by overlapping their barks and cries in ways that allowed a single note to be held as it was passed from rat to rat and from group to group; some of these continuing for as long as several minutes. The music reminded me a bit of Morton Feldman and John Cage, but the comparison is in some ways absurd because the rat music was too other to be characterized in human terms; its deployment and directions so unexpected and chaotic. Just when I thought I knew where it was going, it changed and surprised and perplexed me and left me wondering why they had done what they had done. Why make that move? Didn't it seem obvious that it should have gone elsewhere? Why did it go this way? Sometimes these compositions would last for several hours. I also noticed that there were repeated phrases that I came to recognize and commit to memory. For the first time since I arrived I wanted to live. I wanted to take this music to the world so that others of my species could enjoy the magic of these compositions.

We had two concerts a day, one in the morning and one in the afternoon while the other prisoners were working in the fields. The rats had an incredible sense of situational awareness. If a guard came toward the building, they would go silent. If he approached too closely, they would scatter with a swiftness that bordered on witchcraft. However, these occasions were rare and the concerts were usually uninterrupted.

The concerts began with the slow arrival of the rats. First Lumpkin and One-eye would arrive and feed me. As the food situation improved away from whatever had caused the famine (a disruption of supply lines, a bad harvest, or whatever) it was clear I was dining on the leftovers from the officers' kitchen, fruit and cassava. I even began to *put on a more normal weight, which offered further proof to my fellow POWs that I was sleeping with the enemy.*

The rats would arrive and mill about my cell. I would pet them and scratch their backs and bellies. Then, without a signal I could recognize, they would arrange themselves in their choir positions. The music always started the same way with the rats pointing down beginning the concert. From there it took off.

These gave me strange dreams if I fell asleep while the rats were singing. They were often about Idaho and my mother. In one, we are standing in the barn looking at rats running around in a strange formation like some kind of Rube Goldberg invention. It was not our real barn filled with a cement floor and modern farming machines, but an old-fashioned one with a hayloft and stalls for the cows. In the dream, my mother is standing on an alfalfa bail and trying to peer into one of the stalls, I can hear a cow moving around in it. My mother turns to me and looking at the strange formation of rats running through the rafters and struts says, "These rats are special. You are their God."

I laugh, "Don't be silly they don't worship me."

She looks at me and picking up an old-fashioned milking pail says, "It's not what they do that makes you a God, it's what you do!"

She then seeing I do not understand, quotes a famous Mormon passage attributed to its founder Joseph Smith. In the dream she seems to say it flawlessly, but I quote the real thing here:

"God himself, finding he was in the midst of spirits and glory, because he was more intelligent, saw proper to institute laws whereby the rest could have a privilege to advance like himself. The relationship we have with God places us in a situation to advance in knowledge. He has power to institute laws to instruct the weaker intelligences, that they may be exalted with Himself, so that they might have one glory upon another, and all that knowledge, power, glory, and intelligence, which is requisite in order to save them in the world of spirits.

This is good doctrine. It tastes good. I can taste the principles of eternal life, and so can you. They are given to me by the revelations of Jesus Christ; and I know that when I tell you these words of eternal life as they are given to me, you taste them, and I know that you believe them. You say honey is sweet, and so do I. I can also taste the spirit of eternal life. I know that it is good; and when I tell you of these things which were given me by inspiration of the Holy Spirit, you are bound to receive them as sweet, and rejoice more and more.[6]"

In the dream, my mother says, "Your rats are like these spirits God found floating about the uberverse. You are lifting them. Opening them to higher realms of glory. Like God did for us."

Suddenly the dream shifts and we find ourselves running along a high beam in the rafters in a long line of rats. As we join them in running, my Mom is shouting, "Keep up! Keep up! We could get passed very easily!"

The first time I had it, I awoke to find the rats still singing. It felt real. I thought about the dream, how they were moving to new unrat-like levels of consciousness. I thought about what my mother said in the dream, and perhaps in real life, for during my captivity I took these dreams to be a genuine connection with my mother. Not direct, like a telephone call, but indirect, mediated through a kind of spirit world like the shaman's visit. I thought about the shepherds that I had seen in my vision, lifting and helping other evolved creatures. Is that what I was doing? I wondered. Perhaps as my mother said, I was a God to these rats, not because they worshiped me, but because I was helping them. Lifting them to something new? I smiled at the thought. But I did not laugh.

From what we understand, these concerts go on for about a year, except rarely during the rainy season when the prisoners could not work in the fields and were kept in their billets.

One late afternoon the prisoners were pulled out of their barracks after their daily work was done. They were lined up and marched to the area where the officers stayed. Once there, they found a group of Westerners dressed in uniforms. Soviets.

The Soviet relationship with the North Vietnamese government was complex. They supplied weapons and advice but did not want to be drawn directly into the conflict with the

Americans. Therefore they did not wield a strong consistent influence. Its strength depended on the mood in Hanoi at a given time as to whether they were involved enough to satisfy the government. The group gathered at Gilda's camp was apparently on a tour to assess the state of the war to consider a request for aid.

The prisoners were lined up for inspection. They were not as skeletally thin as they were a year ago during the famine, but they were a ragged bunch—unwashed, unshaven, and filthy. Two of the Russian delegates walked the line of POWs in a bored pretense of caring. They stopped in front of Gilda.

"A Woman."

In Vietnamese one of them asked the camp director something. The camp director answered something back and the man nodded.

Looking at Gilda, but addressing his companions, he said in Russian, "These Americans are disgusting. Not even the most depraved Slav would allow themselves to become so degraded. Truly, capitalism is decadent."

Gilda then answered in flawless Russian, "Perhaps you should become a prisoner of war under the Vietcong to test that theory."

The man literally step backwards, tripped, and fell on his rear. With some dignity and help from the camp director he got back up and addressed Gilda, "Where did you learn Russian?"

"I lived a year in the USSR."

"What did you do there?"

"I studied religion with the Orthodox Sisters."

"What is your name?"

"Gilda Trillim."

The man looked closely at her face then said something in Vietnamese to the camp director, who gave a long and detailed answer to the Russian.

"He says you are a spy."

"He is wrong."

"How did you come then to be a prisoner?"

She explained she had been on a USO tour, that they had gotten lost, and their helicopter had been shot down.

He looked at her and then down at her arm and its missing hand.

"Did that happen in the crash?"

"No. I lost it before that."

"Then you no longer play badminton?"

It was her turn to be surprised. She tried to say something, but nothing came out except a weak, "No."

The man smiled strangely, "My wife's cousin's daughter played badminton. She took fourth place in 1961 in the first national championships. She lived near the Black Sea where she trained in anticipation of it becoming an Olympic sport, which of course never happened. On her wall was a picture of you. She talked of no one else. It is a strange world. I look at your face and am reminded suddenly of pleasant summers on the Black Sea."

Gilda looked away, "I'm afraid those days are over for me."

The man began talking to the camp director in a long and animated conversation.

At last he turned to Gilda, "We will talk again. I am sorry to find you in these circumstances. I will see what we can do."

The prisoners were then marched back to their cells. Shortly after, two guards came and escorted Gilda to one of the nice wooden buildings where the officers usually lived. She was put into one of these. It had a raised bed, a table, and a thick woven reed rug. Gilda sat on the bed and wept, scared that one of the Russians would walk through the door and do terrible things to her. It never occurred to her that her captivity was over. Nor that her strangest encounter with the rats was soon to unfold. I will let her tell it.

Endings churned like raging ghosts through the air, mixing and folding me, stirring time and memory into a froth of panic and despair.

Sitting on the bed felt like a betrayal. Decadent. A richness of extravagance that would demand payment. One I could not afford and would rather die than pay. I knew with certainty that through the door a monster would emerge and claim his due for this moment in luxury. I sobbed uncontrollably. Death awaited — no, I sought that. Death would have been easy. It was my powerlessness I feared. Death? I craved it, looked desperately to find it, but was too cowardly to move from my anguish on the bed.

The silent air boiled with panic. I was confused, as if I had entered another universe, like this one, but other and foreign. It looked the same, but its strangeness could be discerned because the very feel of existence had been reforged in ways there were no words to describe. My head spun and I sobbed, and even though I sobbed, one part of my brain, a cold and analytical corner, considered my sobbing and wondered at it from afar — as if examining my emotions from a coolly rational space. I held to that. A stoic glance emerging from the one corner of my brain that kept me from madness.

The door opened and in throat-closing terror I watched as a figure entered. It was a guard, but he did not meet my eyes. He was carrying a tray, which he placed on the table next to my bed and left. It was a white bowl of noodles with a large spoon laid beside. More food than I could possibly eat. Steam was rising from the dish and I could see pieces of duck, still covered in thick juicy skin, peeking through the surface of the ramen. I felt ashamed, but I could not stay away. I held the bowl to my nose and breathed in the thick moisture rising up to meet me. A part of me wanted to resist the meal, thinking I was being bought and paid for. Such grandeur and luxury would surely strike my initials on a contract of ruin. But the smell, the fragrant steam wafting off the bowl, and the combination of spices proved too much. I thought what happens will happen whether I eat this or not. I ate a piece of duck and some of the noodles. Hurriedly, like I did not want to get caught. I then pushed the bowl away.

The panic returned, I found myself half panting and half sobbing. I threw up into a basin placed at the foot of my bed. For some reason this calmed me. I sat on the bed, and tried eating the noodles again. I managed to hold down just a little.

I stopped sobbing and closed my eyes for a little while, but I did not lie down. When I opened them for a moment it seemed like the floor was moving, wriggling and writhing, undulating up and down as if it had become a small ocean. When things begin to resolve I saw that it was my beloved comrades. My rats. My friends. My peers. I instantly felt safe. Protected. Worshiped.

I moved to the floor to allow them to come to me. They pushed forward, gathering around me like kittens to their mother. They pressed against one another. Against me. Humbly I petted and caressed their dark bodies feeling their ribs, their heads, the scaly surface of their naked tails, their soft ears and whiskers tickling my skin, they were chirping loudly. Did they know something? I wondered. Did they know I was marked for death or worse? Did they in the multilayered fathoms of their souls and bodies sense that terrible things were coming and changes afoot that would end things forever. Is this why they were scurrying about me?

Suddenly, the door flew open. It was the guard who had brought me the soup. He was holding a bus tray, even so, it did not occur to me that he was there to clean up. I screamed. He rushed forward. In retrospect I can see he was trying to protect me from the beasts that he saw 'attacking' me. He yelled and stomped kicking and screaming into the mass of rodents. The sickening sound of bones crunching, and rats flying off of his boots sent volts of energy searing from every nerve in my body. I ran at him hitting him violently with my fists, he tried to back away, but I jumped on his back and wrapped my legs around his waist and pummeled him with my fists. He fled the room. I jumped free of him and ran back in.

The place was in chaos and the entire camp seemed filled with commotion. A siren was sounding and the sound of truck engines were revving throughout the compound, but I cared nothing of it and I ran back to my friends. A few dead, some wounded dragging broken legs, or staggering toward the holes and openings through which they'd crept *inside. And then I saw her. She was broken. Twisted. I picked her up. Her neck hanging loosely, separated from her vertebral column. Fatty Lumpkin. My beloved friend. Fatty. Oh Fatty. Not you. Not you little Lumpkin. I fell to my knees in agony and despair holding her little body, wailing. I held her warm body to my chest and spilled tears over her wetting her fur in patches of sorrow. Willing her to live. Please. O, please. If there are gods or goddesses. If there is a Heavenly Father or Mother. If you shepherds who can command the creation of universes can help me please bring her back to me. Please. Please. Please. Oh. Little Lumpkin. My little Lumpkin, don't leave me now. I pressed my lips against her mouth and breathed softly to fill her tiny lungs with small breaths. I pushed in the air so gently, so carefully, until I saw her sides rise with my breath. But when I released my kiss to let the air back out, with each exhale, blood seeped bubbling from her nose. I knew she was dead.*

I must pause in my narrative and tell a story before I go on because what follows draws too heavily on it not to be included.

My father had a favorite horse. It was a beautiful chestnut quarter horse with three white feet and a cream spot on its chest shaped like a butterfly—a generous and well-disposed mare. He called it Greta after the movie star. My brothers and sisters knew he loved us more, but just barely. He had likely spent more time with her than all of us kids put together. She pastured in the forty-acre field fenced out just behind our backyard, which she alone commanded like a retired thoroughbred. We didn't need as many horses as we drifted into more modern farming and by the time I was fifteen we owned only her. We didn't really need her either, but we knew she would stay until she died. She was part of us. My dad's only mistress.

One morning, early, about six, we were just sitting down to French toast when my mother stopped to look out the window as she washed up the egg bowl she had dipped the bread in. She froze, "Heber" she hoarsed out. Then she yelled fiercely, "Heber!" By that time we were all at the window or scouting out of the backdoor. My dad glanced out the window for a hurried second and then ran for the kitchen closet where he kept his loaded 30.06 Winchester rifle. *Through the window I could see three dogs chasing Greta: the Hansen's vicious German Shepherd, the Blinkman's mammoth Airedale that they used to hunt cougars, and a medium mutt that looked like a Dalmatian, border collie mix I'd never seen before. They had obviously been at it a while, because the poor mare looked like the fight was almost wrung out of her. The dogs were nipping at her legs, and although she was mustering a few last kicks, it looked bad. I glanced out the window and saw my dad lining up his shot against one of the rail posts of the back porch. He was as good a shot as anyone I knew and had won the state fair shoot off a time or two. Now he was shooting for love and it never occurred to me those dogs had a chance of surviving the next few minutes. The first shot took the shepherd right behind the front leg and it instantly curled up from a dead run to a furry tumbleweed. After scaring up a gnarled ball of dust in its tumblings, it lay still. My dad worked the bolt and chambered another round and sighted back up. The Airedale had stayed on the horse but not for much longer. I saw its head explode in a spray of red at the same time as my ears were muted from the report. The mutt had stayed back to examine at what had happened to the shepherd and was facing dead away from us. The next bullet ran up its butt and came out its chest.*

My dad handed the gun to my younger brother and sprinted to the horse who was now shaking and staggering on her trembling legs. Her mouth was massed with dripping white froth. I don't know how long the dogs had been worrying the poor beast but it must have been a while because I'd seen that horse run full out at a gallop for miles. My dad got to it and grabbed her mane trying to steady it when it tottered violently over onto its side nearly pulling my dad over with it, but he let go of the beast and jumped clear. A horse on its side was as bad as it could be. We were all running up to it by that time. My dad started trying to lift her himself, and waved us over to help. I had grabbed her halter off the peg on the porch and had her in it in what seemed like seconds. I tried to twist her head up hoping she would follow it to her feet, but she just lay there breathing like a bellows. She was soaking wet and hot as summer sand, steaming in the morning air like she was being cooked. Despite my Dad and Mom and brothers all pushing on her back and trying to lift and me trying to get her head going toward the sky, she was not budging.

My mother took my dad by the arm, and said, "There is only one thing that will help now." And out of her night coat pocket she pulled her bottle of precious consecrated olive oil. She must have grabbed it on her way out for this purpose because usually it sat in the cupboard among the medicines we kept at hand. My dad took the bottle and removed the cork and poured the entire contents onto the horse's forehead. Its breathing was still rapid and labored, its sides heaving like it was about to foal. He anointed it using the priesthood, then knelt down sealed the anointing and offered a blessing. He blessed it that its muscles would be knit together, and its heart be able to bear the burden of getting the proper amount of air to the parts of her body that needed it. Then he closed in Jesus' name. My mother whispered, "You've been blessed, get up." My father then stood up, straightened his coat, then looking at the horse knelt back down and shouted into its ear, "I command you to walk! Arise!" Suddenly that horse started beating its legs, and swinging its head to get some assistance from inertial motion. We all backed away. In her flailings she finally struck the earth with her hooves and climbed to standing in an explosion of movement. My dad was bawling—first time in my life I ever seen him shed a tear.

He spent the day brushing his mare's coat and making sure she was all right. That afternoon, when it was clear the harried equine was going to be OK, my dad came into the kitchen and pulled a cookie jar off the top shelf of the cupboard. My parents had been saving for an anniversary trip to San Francisco for about a year and it was kept in the antique ceramic. He pulled out about fifty bucks, which was an enormous amount back then, and handed it to me and told me to bike it down to the Bishop's and give it to him. I looked at my mom to see if she were going to countermand his order, but she just said, "Do as he says." There was a power that came from the heavens, but there was always a cost that had to be paid. Every farmer, rancher, and dairyman knew that.

I looked at Fatty. Her hair tinged with blood and this story flashed in my mind. There was no oil, but remembering a scene from the New Testament I spit in my hand and rubbed it into the forehead of my little friend. My companion who had saved me so many times before by feeding me the fluids fashioned from the juices of her own soft body. I laid my hands on her head, and blessed her, "Dear little Lumpkin, blessed and beloved sister, I bless you by the power of God to rise up and walk. Feel the joints of your neck knit with the bones of your back. Come back Fatty. Return from the dead. Be healed. I command you! Be made whole." Then I turned my face upward and plead, "Anything. I will do anything. Kill me if you want. But heal her. Dear God we have long been at odds. I've not believed in you for awhile, but please do what you can for my beloved friend." I paused and then screamed into the sky, "Do you even know what love is? Does it even matter to you?"

But the gesture was empty. Dry. I knew in my heart it would not work. Blessings are not for the far-gone. The injured beyond hope. No one ever tried to attach the decapitated head of a car accident victim. There were limits to how far faith could stretch even for those like my parents who believed in them as fully as the rising sun. Nevertheless, I stroked her fur for nearly ten minutes. Waiting. Watching. Looking for the twitch of her tail. The flick of an ear. The vibration of a whisker. But there was nothing. The camp seemed silent and the pandemonium of a few minutes ago had been replaced with a weighty quiet that seemed more threatening than the ruckus preceding it.

The rats were still there, but frozen. I looked down at the poor rat cradled in my hands, unbelieving she was gone. Animated no more. I leaned back on the floor and arranged her in a little ball nestled on my chest as if she were sleeping. I stretched out my arms like one crucified, for so I felt. Abandoned and forsaken.

Something strange began to occur. One by one the rats approached the stump of my arm and licked its rounded end vigorously—like a mother murid cleaning her pup. In the action I found the eidolon of my missing hand materializing, as if each stroke of their tongues were bringing into being a finger, or a knuckle, or the back of my hand. Or the spirit thereof. Then each would run along my arm to Fatty's body, still resting on my chest, and nip off a small piece, not an act of feeding, but of ritual it seemed to me, for they took naught but a single morsel. Then they ran down my arm to my good hand.

When the first celebrant descended my left extended arm to my hand, I curled my fingers around its soft body and blessed it. I found myself whispering queer augurs of the future. Strange prophecies poured out of me. I knew I was leaving never to return. And each of these souls I knew. Each was an individual unique and yet connected to each other and with the landscape in which they lived. Connected to the camp, to its refuse, to the forest that surrounded it, to the cassava fields, to the roads, and vehicles and I drew on those connections and proclaimed to each what its life would be like. How its descendants would fare, and gave what warnings I felt impressed to give. One by one the rats queued like patrons at a theater waiting to buy a ticket, until they reached my stump and followed their compatriots through this odd ritual. When it was over, Lumpkin was gone and on my chest was a stain of wet blood on my black clothes.

Last of all came One-eye. He licked my arm where my hand had been severed, but came and stood on my chest. He stood upon his back legs and squeaked and as he did the other rats took their positions on the floor and wall as they had in my small cell and they began to sing. I sobbed as they sang knowing I was going, knowing they had saved me. Unexpectedly, some change occurred in the lighting of the room. It became blue and holy and a strange light snow began to fall. Only it wasn't snow. It was tiny white moths drifting like dust motes in a sunbeam coming through a window after a thunderstorm on a summer day. How they sparkled and danced!

Still on my back looking straight upward I saw a figure descending from the sky as if from an immense height but oddly still within the room giving the impression that I was seeing into a new dimension, something like mirrors facing each other with reflections scattering light back and forth into a forever of ever smaller and more distant mirrors. *The woman, for woman it was, descended until she stood above me. She was dressed in a robe de style of a lovely blue silk, with several long strings of white pearls. A red sequin cloche hat just covered her short styled and straightened hair. Her shoes were gorgeous blue heels that shimmered like emeralds. Her black skin glowed like a shimmering pool on a moonless night and her eyes were bright and alive beyond life. Most amazing of all was her smell. It was of newborn babies, fresh autumn hay, rich moist soil, and lavender in the sunshine. It was of honey dripping from the comb, baked bread, and red sweet wine. It was of newness and pine. Just opened books and incense and beeswax. And oddly the fresh scent of manure and spring planting, and the milk of a mother's breast. It seemed so complex and full I wanted to melt into her.*

"You are a shepherdess," I spoke in a hushed tone.

She laughed and helped me sit up. Her hands were warm and she sat on the ground next to me, her arms enveloped me. I laid my head on her shoulder and she stroked my hair. The rats continued singing, but each of their dark eyes was on her.

Finally she said, guiding my head up so she could look in my eyes, "I have many names: Goddess, Heavenly Mother, and, yes, Shepherdess will do."

"Have you come to save Fatty Lumpkin?" I was breathless with hope as I asked.

"No. She is gone." She had tears in her eyes.

"The shepherds can form a universe with such wonder and they cannot heal a rat?" I whispered in frustration and despair.

She looked at me seriously, but radiating such love it was difficult to hold onto my anger.

"You would have me end your suffering, dear Gilda. Not hers. I cannot stop suffering, it's always there. Things go as they go. That's the way of it. Things go as they go, weaving in and out in a dance with other things. Even I am subject to the movement, the bargaining, the exchanges with the things that appear and disappear in the world. Suffering is the price of being."

"You are not in control?"

"Control?" She laughed sweetly, sadly, "No. Like you I make deals with the things and events that surround and envelope me. I have my whims, but so do they, and we must strike an arrangement if I'm to make what moves I wish to make."

"Please. Make your whim to bring Fatty back to me ..."

"No. Would you force the rats to sing your song rather than theirs? Daughter, is there not something crucial to the song being for and from them that makes the essence of the music vital to what it is?"

"Yes. but ..." I trailed off.

"Ask daughter. Only in questions does grace unfold."

"I thought you could do anything."

She laughed, not a twitter, but booming as if I'd said something hilarious.

"You don't understand. Life will unfold as it will. There is nothing I can do to save her. She is dead. Do you remember what brought everything into existence, the infinite universes, substance and objects?"

"The coyote said it was randomness."

"Randomness rules all spaces! Dear child, not even shepherdesses can see but a short way into the future—and, oh my, only those trends so large that we can't miss them because they are stable and linear. Determinate futures—we can see to their end—but not many. No. No. No, Dear Child. That is why all things must be accountable, both things sentient and not. Those not, must follow such wisdom as is found among all the players struggling to find place in the tick tock of machines and the movement of agents. Those thus endowed with sentience must choose those paths through which they are led. We guide where we can. Offer advice. This is the grace we bring into the world. We offer wisdom. Nothing more."

"Then you cannot heal a rat wounded unto death? Can you not heal the sick at all?"

"What the mind can do, we can often do. It is a powerful thing. Limits should not be easily assumed."

Her love was overpowering. She was smiling at me. Her eyes shone like emeralds in firelight.

"Can I come with you?"

She took my hands and I was surprised to find I had two.

"No. But I have counsel. You may take it if you wish. You would be wise to do so. You will doubt this one day. You will question your memory. You will remember how hollowed out and empty you were and you will imagine this but a product of your shocked and ravished mind. But try not to doubt this one thing. You are filled with grace. A grace that comes of being who you are. Objects and events do not change the wonder and complexity of what you have evolved to be. Remember your friends the rats. You have followed our own desires and work in this lifting. We shepherd you and yours, you have done so to them. Remember the songs you have learned. Shepherdess of Rats."

She turned as if looking at a clock or something in the distance.

"It is time for me to leave you."

"Must you go?"

"Yes. Father and I are going dancing. I won't miss that."

Then she reached down and took my face into her hands and kissed me on the lips, then on the forehead.

"I love you daughter. And love, my dear, is everything."

My head was racing in strange circles. I held onto her, breathing in her luscious scent and ambience. I did not want her to go. She stood up and smoothed her dress. The rush of emotion bursting through me like an electric current brought forth a sudden silliness because I did not know what else to say, "Your shoes are beautiful."

She looked down at them and smiled, "Yes they are." Then she bent down and whispered in my ear, "They ought to be. I am a shepherdess after all."

She turned as if to go, but paused, her head tilted as if listening. It was the rats. During all this time they had continued to sing, providing a background to Heavenly Mother's visit that I had not noticed until this minute. She then gracefully walked among them touching them on the head and stroking their backs as their voices continued to squeak out their strange and fantastical music. Then she raised her head and from her pursed lips issued the most lovely chirping I'd ever heard. She joined the rats, taking her turn in holding the notes, pausing when necessary, adding, amending, joining in their aharmonic chords, it was rapturous. I could swear that in the chorus I could hear the distinct voice of Fatty joining in.

The music ended and the woman turned to me and clapped her hands in delight. "Gilda! Look what you've done! You've brought a new thing into the universe! You've created a new niche! Novelty! Newness! Shepherdess of the Rats, indeed!"

She laughed and ran over to me and kissed me one more time, "Now I really must go. But one thing. I know you think you are tainted. That you are poisoned. I tell you in no uncertain terms, you are not. You are not. You are a creature of love and nothing can touch that. Nothing."

"But, I'm so broken."

"Oh, my dear child, can't you see? We are all broken. It comes with existence." Then she smiled, "Broken yes, but not unhealed. Believe that."

I nodded, "I do. I do believe it."

She turned to go, smiling once more at the rats, and as she did I said, "Mother. Please take me with you."

She turned to me and smiled, her eyes moist and shining, "Not yet. What would Babs think if you left her behind?"

Babs! I'd not missed a day, or more likely, not missed an hour without thinking about her. How could I have forgotten her in this moment of such significance?

"But perhaps I can leave you with a blessing?"

I nodded, unable to speak. She came over and stood behind me and laid her warm soft hands on my head as my father had when he had blessed me as a child. Then she pronounced a blessing. The words she said are gone or maybe my mind never articulated them, as if she spoke in a language that only my heart could understand. But the power, the wonder, and the magic of that moment will ever be with me. I am weeping now just remembering the joy and feelings that poured from her mouth. I remember that snatches of my life appeared. Random events moving backwards in time—I was a young woman playing in a tournament; I was helping my mother saddle a horse; I was a child holding my father's hand as we walked through a hardware store. Until at last I was nursing, suckling at my mother's breast. Warm milk poured into my rooting mouth. No, it was not coming from my mother's breast, it was coming from the shepherdess's hands, pouring into me, through my head and down my throat like a spirit-filled colostrum abundant with body heat and healing powers. The taste! The joy of it was as if a thousand spring days of sunshine and green sunny mornings were condensing into a thousand summer nights, with stars bright and clear shining through every blackness life offered, scattering shadows rooted deep within the hidden crevasses of my soul, chasing them away like tumbleweeds in an April storm or like ghosts on an October wind sailing off to distances from which they could never return. I saw autumn leaves gracing aspens, dancing and playing in the wind with the sun low and billowy clouds like ships sailing across a deep blue heaven, and too, I felt the glow of a winter moon cold on virgin snow alive with a sparkling dance. It was the milk of passing days. Of laughter. It was singing carols with frosty breath in the dancing lights of a window framed in blinking colored lights, a tree adorned with popcorn and silver in tribute to the child king. I saw me as a toddler capturing bees in a jar and bringing them to my mother laughing and holding me tight as we pressed our ears to the lid as the bees hummed their summer work. It was my old Labrador retriever curled by a fire. My grandmother rocking softly, the soft click of needles knitting. I cried and cried, but no tears of sorrow. The milk was healing me. Bringing me the life that mother's milk always brought. I was being brought back to life with every swallow. I felt light infusing every cell until I knew they would burst into a thousand new universes. I could bear such joy no more. I turned around and we wrapped our arms around each other and she held me tight and sung a lullaby stroking my hair. I cannot describe it. It was existence itself. When it was over I was shaking. Sobbing for joy. I was changed. Forever.

We both trembled and cried together until finally she pushed me gently away. Then with her thumbs wiped the tears from my eyes, she pulled me close for one more quick hug, then turned and stepped away.

Back into the sky she ascended. As she did however I saw she was joined by others, until there was a small group of people swirling around her as she and they ascended together—each as magnificent as she.

As soon as she disappeared, the crash and commotion of the camp returned. I sat there numb, and strangely, all I could think of, and all that seemed important, was what she said about being broken. And being healed.

Footsteps approached and the door opened. The rats did not hesitate this time and scattered, leaving the few dead who had been killed in the previous visit lying strewn on the wooden floor.

In walked the camp director, some of his men and the Russian visitors. They found me sitting on the floor, Lumpkin's blood covering my chest, and the bodies of dead rats lying here and there. They were shocked silent for a moment and then one of the Russians said to the camp director, "Please clean her and this room up." It was translated and the director gave a reluctant bow and ordered something to one of his men.

Then one of the Soviet officers, a Podpolkovnk Vatutin, the same whose niece had played badminton, squatted down in front of me, speaking as if to a child, "Miss Trillim we have made arrangements for your release. Tomorrow we will return to Hanoi and you will fly with us to Moscow. There you will be turned over to the American Embassy. Do you understand?"

I nodded. I asked if the rats could come. He said he was afraid they must stay. I nodded and the men left. A few minutes later the old woman who collected our bowls came in. She led me to a nearby small river that I did not even know was there. She took off my bloodied clothes. And gave me a bar of lye and lard soap and motioned me into the calm still waters. The bank was sandy and shallow and I had to wade about ten feet to get enough depth to submerge myself. The water was magical and cleansing. I scrubbed away years of neglect. I washed my sheared crop of hair with the harsh soap, and scrubbed every part of my body twice, three times, and finally a fourth time. I did not care that we were not alone and there were other women nearby washing clothes. My body seemed hollow. I was reluctant to scrub Lumpkin's blood from my chest and breasts, but at last I did. Weeping. The old woman did not seem to be in a hurry and I stayed in the water until the skin of my fingers was wrinkly and swollen. Finally I walked back up the sandy bank and she handed me a paper-thin towel. With it I dried myself as thoroughly as I could. She then handed me not the shabby dirty clothes of a prisoner, but the black shirt and wool pants of the Vietcong soldiers, including a black and white checkered scarf. She gave me a conical straw hat and looked me over approvingly.

As we came into the compound, the other prisoners were returning and upon seeing me dressed in the uniform of the enemy they said nothing, except for the Dutch women who shouted vehemently at me, "Whore!" Their faces however were of such disgust and anguish that their judgment still haunts me.

I was led back to my new room. The murdered rats were gone. The carnage cleaned up. The old woman entered and showed me some propaganda pamphlets written in English that had been laid on my bed. As she turned to go, I wrapped my arms around the old woman and kissed her on the cheek. She seemed surprised and smiled awkwardly, bowed and left.

That night the rats sang for me for the last time. It seemed stilted and forced, as if we both knew this was goodbye, and we wanted to make this last time meaningful and significant, but were trying too hard to make it so, and in the effort recognized things were as they were. I sat on the floor and listened. When it was over, I held a few of my favorites and let them scamper over me, licking me, and squeaking what I took to be their goodbyes. At dawn, I heard the diesel engines starting and intuited that I was leaving. I looked at my friends and started to cry.

"Remember me. OK? Remember Fatty Lumpkin and her grace. Keep singing. Please keep singing."

Suddenly there was the sound of footsteps and the rats bolted for their exits. One-eye turned just as he departed through a crack in the

154

wall and looked at me and squeaked and was gone.

As you know, Trillim was indeed taken to Hanoi and flown to Moscow. There, after the American counter intelligence officers at the Moscow embassy had extracted everything she could remember about the camp, her fellow prisoners, the trip from the camp, and the Soviet relationship to the Hanoi government, she was flown to Washington where she was met by her family and friends.

I will leave it here. Much has been written about her stay in Vietnam. But I think Gilda's recently discovered final account that I just reported will suffice better than anything I could add.

Vignette 13: Meditations at Apua Point, Big Island Hawaii. Circa 1972

This represents a well-known fragment from Gilda's Journal. It is one of my favorite pieces in all of the Archive. Anything I could add would be superfluous and take away from the depth of this work. I therefore provide it without commentary.

No one will find me here. To the southeast hangs the friendly gibbous orb I've known all my life occasioning a path of serene white moonlight reflecting across the top of the ocean, fulgent in the breakers. To the north a sulfurous fog steaming off of Kilauea obscures the low stars. They say in a few weeks the lava might reach here and cover this spot. I hope not. Perhaps the ghosts of the ancient Hawaiians will hold it at bay. This is a sacred spot I am told. I gently breathe in good sea air. I am sitting on a spit of land jutting out from an unpretentious lagoon that makes this place susceptible for basking in nature's sorceries. I am alone. Inhaling the moist oceanic ether drives away the fear, or some of it anyway.

I look back over to my bivouac and see the reflection of my fire against the black lava rock wall that guards my camp. What was that rectangular ruin of piled stones once constructed to be? A temple? A home? A hut for a fisherman who whiled away his time mending net and line to catch his family's dinner? I want to think temple. This seems the kind of place I would raise one had I the inclination to give into certain temptations. I just cooked a pan of Japanese noodles and opihi that I picked from the wave-caressed rocks this afternoon.

A kind old Filipino man who ran the little mom and pop store in the town of Volcano introduced this delicious shellfish to me. When he saw I had a transradial prosthesis, he asked if I had been in Nam. I answered yes, managing to lie while telling the truth since I was implying that's where I lost my hand. He told me his son had died there. His eyes watered and we were soon talking, I told him I had been a POW for two years. I don't tell *anyone* that, but it all spilled out of me like a confession. Soon we were both in tears telling each other stories that burst from us like some sort of emotional flatulence. Ironic given the purpose of the trip was to leave that event behind.

He then told me about Apua Point, the loneliest spot on the island—a six-mile backpack from the most southern point of the Chain of Craters Road. He told me about the opihi, something he would normally never tell a tourist. He also warned me about the rats that would try to steal my food. He didn't know that the promised presence of rats would guarantee my visit to the spot. Isolation and rats. What could be better?

The taste of opihi may have been worth spilling the beans about how I spent the last few years. Wow. A delicacy worthy of royalty. A gastropod that clings to the rocks like a barnacle, they are found throughout the islands. I climbed out on the rocks to gather them, watching the untamed waves beating the island back into the sea with such violence it left me holding my breath. With each smash of the waves against the rocky shore, I felt a surge of wrath from the ocean both frightening and exhilarating. One slip and I would be feeding the crabs and fish below.

You have to sneak up on these little hors d'oeuvres. Like the clams beguiled by the walrus and the carpenter in *Alice in Wonderland*. If you make your intentions known you lose them. You have to climb among them without touching them, then squatting down, work swiftly, by sliding a knife between their shell and the rock, all before the next murderous wave strikes. You can pry them off of the hardened lava with a flick of your wrist, but if they catch what you are about, they clamp down on the basalt and you've missed your chance. I don't even think you could chisel them off the rock face.

Shaped like a conical rice paddy hat, they are open on one side and therein lies their precious meat, a gelatinous mass that I scooped into the Chinese rice noodles boiling in my tin mess pan. When the shahe fen was cooked, I was delighted to find that the fleshy mass had shaped itself into a little rubber miniature of a snail-like creature complete with a slug-like nose, upraised neck, and little antennae. And the taste? Indescribable. It tasted like all that I fancy in seafood, fashioned and condensed into a single untamed flavor.

My first night I placed the remains of my dinner on a flat rock and waited hoping to lure in some rats. They never showed. I sat near the pebble-sand shore and watched the waves and composed a poem. This one:

The Moon
The woman on the newly hardened rocks
of ancient lineage—was seeing the stars for
the first time in ages. The moon—old friend,
distant comrade—grinned at the cooled lava
as the sea ebbed and rolled at the pahoho's
black and jagged edge, old friends reuniting.

She stood singleton, alone, a stranger amid the
supposed rats and mongooses that wound their way
among the succulent xerophytes along the shore
(the clever beasts survive by snatching whatever the tides
toss out in its heaving or whatever they can
take from trekkers to this lonely spot,
though none came to her).

She was wild and unafraid of what ghosts
might abound. And of which she'd been warned.
She too, like the kindred moon
and the natal rock, was brewed from the violence
of an exploding sun. She felt the kinship of

158

an essential and elemental reunion—reunited sisters.

She reminisced. She and the waves and the rock and the
moon told their singular tales and even as poorly
as they understood each other, some implied
gesture came through and all were content
to sit and ponder their separation and their reuniting.

At this moment. On this night. Each alone and each
together, bound by bonds of old magic and power
that not one of them understood nor even wanted to,
as they bathed in the darkness and the light
remembering and forgetting.

It is the second night. To get to the end of this rocky promontory,
I passed a line of squat and stunted palms, ragged and unkempt.
Not like the tall and stately palms that line Southern Californian
boulevards. The fronds are stringy and torn, displaying a
wildness like some ancient forest hermit, bearded with tangled
rattan stripped from the fibrous bark.Woven in the nest-like mess
found at the base of the leaves, debris from the wind gathers,
adding to a bedding structure that guard the gargantuan floating
seeds provisioned with their own milky supply of fresh water.
Around the trees, sun-bleached coconuts are scattered haphazardly about—a few have leaked a phallic root probing the sand
for anchorage.

I walk carefully over the rocks to the end of the jetty and find
a flat rock to act as a seat. My lap is my desk. Tonight I want to
ponder objects again. To explore the old questions that interested
me before the disruption that stole so much from me and
replaced my ruminations with jagged scars and unhealing
wounds.

That past must be set aside for a time. Stoically, perhaps, but I
must seize again old puzzles. What is it to be an object? How do

things connect? I fear everything must be repackaged in light of things my mind or my heart now wants to orbit. Twice now in vision, love has pushed itself forward as the first principle of concern. First in my vision of the cosmos, and second with my vision of Heavenly Mother. I don't know if I've gained insight into the outer world or inner, or if there is a difference, but I seem to be being led, either by my brain or the universe—it's hard to say which, for it is hard to escape the old quandary of whether the world wheels in freedom or by fixed determination—if these experiences are immanent or transcendent.

I open my gambit with the moon. I look up and see its face. I know light waves are bouncing off its surface from the sun, disclosing the presence of this object that lies 238,900 miles from the earth.[1] I learn more by seeing the variation in color and texture. I see craters and I have explanations as to why they form, giving me a hint that whatever the moon is, it is craterizable. Recently, a few men have visited there and brought back rocks that reveal more about its rocky surface.

I also look out over the ocean and consider the rise and fall of tides swaying according to the moon's pleasure. Yet much of this immense sea remains masked. Like the apple seed I so long labored over that I tried to trick into revealing its nature, yet as always some part remains hidden. As Heraclitus says, "Nature tends to hide itself."[2] I wonder if the only way to understand the moon (or an apple seed) fully is to be that thing. Yet even that can't be right. I cannot even fully uncover myself to myself, so what could the moon reveal to itself? I often surprise myself and discover myself in new ways. I understand myself no better for being conscious. Therefore as a meaty object I am a mystery to my conscious self: I cannot feel my liver livering, or my kidney kidneying. Does that mean that this thing that makes me, that binds me to cells, to organelles, to the structure of bone and flesh, runs deeper than I can feel? I don't know what it means to be the moon or a seed. I should back up for I do not mean consciously.

But I notice that things 'feel' other things. They interact. They touch. They react to each other, like the items in my study of junk drawer ecology.

So it seems like a thing-in-itself is not revealed even to itself, but only in relation to other things. Alone an object or a thing is nothing. A moon in a universe that held only a moon would not be there. It would have no properties until it related to other things, things that, relating, give it size, structure, and all the rest. The moon is revealed by the light of the sun, by the pull of the earth, by the foot that walks and leaves footprints in the dust. And I similarly find myself manifest by the moon and its shine. By the relations in which I stand—by rocks and ancient lava, by the photonic absorption of the light of thousands of stars, by the sound of the ocean splashing against the shore, by opihi and its shell, by the sedges and sparse plants pushing through grains of sands, by the relationship of those plants and the sand as individual grains and individual plants and their shells, by the birds which pipe on the shore and their feathers which fall on the ground and are washed to shore from the sea and that gather with other detritus forming bands of debris of which that feather is but a piece of the structure that traps the foam of the sea, upon which small fleas dance and play and capture meager nutrients created by bacteria decomposing that debris with patience and relentless acts of decay, and by the palms which create shade and places where certain molds can form that create spaces for newer sanctuaries from which to launch new plants and plant systems into the world. Here I stand in relation to an infinity of other objects and an infinity of relationships of objects to one another, which create new objects like the waves created by moon and ocean which structure and mold other objects and on and on and on. Is there so much of me that like Whitman I can claim I am multitudes? How can such a small person stretch out and reach myriads of infinities upon infinities? How is their room for all those relationships? How can I hold so much? To be me must take infinite work as relationships compound into more connections than I can fathom. It cannot be conscious, of course, because even my neurons are part of a deeper structure—pieces of chemicals, the relation of brain states formed by some flicker dispatched from, say, a fly that happens to skip past my eye, which in turn launches a cascade of neuronal triggers that cause my eye to blink. An event that signifies nothing but a random event, most of which must be ignored or perish in trying to actively attend to everything. There is too much for that. My brain must be selective.

And so I let go. I cannot hold it all so I let go. I let the moon bathe me in its light and let the sound of the waves wash over me and feel the fresh breeze play upon the palms and rocks and cry and career through objects. I integrate these into a feeling of peace and enjoy the flavor of the objects around me and suddenly I am no more multitudes but am one thing, a unit, a moment. I take in a breath and sense that the tangle and bundle that I am melts away into a puddle of one. I am suddenly a gift to myself. I am not bracketing *out* questions of what defines me but bracketing *in* a wholeness, a stitching. I do not want to say I'm 'one' like some Siddhartha for I'm not. I am still many, but I've come to be a togetherness. A unity, not a oneness. Like wine aged into one flavor. Its parts can be separated, but its flavor is unified and coherent despite the multitudes it contains. Or, more crassly, the corkscrew that pulled the cork, a device that comes together to form a simple machine, created by combining machines like the wedge and lever to create a new thing that in its unity relates to the wine in specific ways. A community. An ecology. An inhabitant of a universe of objects, uses, relationships, creating novelty and hope. And there it is! A new object. Perhaps every object is just a confederation among other objects. Objects are just connections coming together in a community of interrelationship. Relations all the way down. Can you think of a single counter example?

Where of love then? Tomorrow. My sleeping bag is calling me to its folds.

Later

They showed up about noon. I had just taken a pleasant swim in my miniature private lagoon. I was sunbathing naked on the beach when, thankfully, I heard them approaching from a long way off because they were arguing about something. I hurriedly dressed. When they walked into camp, I greeted them cordially enough. They were as friendly as a couple of Labrador retrievers. She had sandy blonde hair curled in the humidity and was wearing a yellow flowered bikini top, cut off Levis, a straw cowboy hat, and some expensive hiking boots. The woman was also tall, tanned, and athletic. He was rather more nondescript, rotund, wearing gym shorts and sneakers. His hair was long, dark brown down to his shoulders. He had a short beard.

They plopped their packs down by a rock near the shore and he introduced them both with, "Hi I'm Mikey and this is my old lady, Judy."

She was bending down to fish out their canteens, but popped up long enough to wave. I intentionally waved back with my stub, startling them for a second, but they seemed not to be bothered otherwise. He told me that they had come down through the Kau Desert. I said nothing about my route. They were hiking all the way to Hilo through Puna. I tried not to let my disappointment show.

"We heard there was water here and thought we would stop for a few days."

This was supposed to be a time of solitude. This was a time to reflect and sort things out that had been confused for a long time. In our short conversation I had learned enough about them to know I had no desire to spend time with them and I was feeling desperate so I flat out lied, "Yeah, I heard the same, but it's all dried up ... supposed to be over there by the trees, but I can't find it."

I was pointing in the opposite direction from the water. The water was hidden in a small cave a few hundred meters westward and even with the detailed directions I'd been given it had been genuinely hard to find. The entrance was masked by some fairly thick shrubby and if I hadn't noticed birds coming out of it I might never have found it. The water was brackish, but serviceable.

"Damn! These islanders are always filling us with shit. They say one thing and it turns out that it just ain't so. Especially when going to somewhere they want left alone. They want to keep it for themselves. About fifty-million times we've been told something and it's crap. They were probably hoping we would die out here."

"Oh, I doubt that." I said, although thinking, who could blame them? This was quite a pair. Given their equipment they were rich and given their accents they were from New England. A perfect combination to get snowed. The irony being that this time they had not been led astray by Islanders but by the *haole* they automatically assumed was on their side.

"Well we started with three canteens apiece and still have got a full one each, so we've got enough to make it to the Chain of Craters Road tomorrow. We'll have to hitch a ride to the Park and fill up there. How are you fixed for water?"

I smiled and said I had enough to get by.

I showed them another camp about fifty yards from mine, identifiable by a ring of stones, but not protected from the wind by the remnant wall of a Heiau like mine.

I went for a walk. Looking for shells and just wanting to be alone. I felt guilty for lying to them about the water, but not contrite enough to want to spend two or three days with them. When I got back they were boiling dehydrated backpacking meals in seawater. Eggs and stroganoff. I was not going to tell them about the opihi. It seemed like the knowledge had been given to me as a trust. I was not going to betray it.

Looking back I feel miserable. They were not bad people. Generous. Talkative. But to me they were intruders. Corsairs of solitude. It made me combative and ornery.

The rest of the day I mostly avoided them. I went for a walk toward the Pali, an escarpment that rose from the coastal areas up toward Mauna Loa. I got back in time to watch the sun set, nothing spectacular, but nice. In Hawaii, I suppose because of its tropical latitudes, it gets dark quickly and when I returned to my camp, the backpackers had a roaring fire going. He was playing a ukulele he pulled from who-knows-where and they were singing some songs. For a moment I was annoyed, because I enjoy the silences of the wilderness, but I soon noticed that they were not that bad. Actually, they were pretty good and were pulling off some lovely Richard and Karen Carpenter-like harmonies. I listened while I got my own fire started and found myself softly singing along. Just as my fire was starting to reach a respectable burn, Judy came over.

"Hey," she said. "We've got plenty of lasagna, we actually made three of the packets, just in case you wanted to join us. No worries if you want to be alone, we just wanted to offer ... you know, in case ..."

I resigned myself to their company, "Sure. Why not?"

Mikey gave me a royal welcome and made a place on a driftwood log they had pulled out of the surf just past the lagoon where it had been wedged among some boulders channeling the waves into a nook that held a small debris trap. I sat across from them with the fire between us, but they had kept the blaze small so that it was not inconvenient to interact with them across the flame. I remember our camps in Wyoming were usually graced with a fire half a person high and you would have to stand if you wanted to engage the person across the flames from you.

He kept playing while Judy made us paper plates piled with freeze-dried pasta — it had to be more than three packets — along with some freeze-dried corn. We all sat on the extempore benches and ate in silence. It took me a bit of balance and maneuvering to situate the plate on my lap in a way it was secure, and then use my left hand to eat with a small plastic fork. I'd left my mechanical hook in the car, not realizing I'd have to dine with company out here, so I felt like quite the spectacle. They were polite and said nothing as they watched my dinner-dance, my posture maneuvering and making endless adjustments with my stump designed to keep my plate from being upended. I managed. When it was over, we tossed our ware into the fire and watched the remains blacken, then burst into flames.

We sat for a while in a comfortable silence, then he reached into his pack and pulled out a pipe. The bowl was ceramic and the shaft, a cork-covered steel. He held it up and said, "OK if we smoke this?" I gave him an assenting shrug with a wave of my hand and said, "It's cool."

He loaded the pipe from a baggie and lit it with the flame from a twig. After puffing it to life he took a long hit and handed it to Judy and she did the same. She held it out to me and holding her breath hoarsed out, "It's local. Puna Fire. Want to try it?" Then she exhaled a thick bluish tinted fog.

I'd not smoked pot since high school and since my last experience with a hallucinogenic had cost me my hand, getting high in the presence of a burning flame was not something my nervous system would let me get away with. Still, there was a slight temptation, but something inside me beat it down fairly quickly. I said, "I gave it up ... I'm fine ... so you two enjoy."

The pipe was back in Mikey's hand and he raised it to me in salute, as if both acknowledging and honoring my choice. They smoked it quietly, like me, watching the fire. Finally, he took a long draw, and then curled his fingers around the bowl making a funnel, and blew hard into his hand-fashioned trumpet, forcing abundant smoke out of the stem. Judy put her face over the smoke and breathed it in deeply trying to catch it all through her nose and mouth. She tried to supercharge him but he came up coughing, "It's all resin, babe."

They stared at the fire a while. Judy then said, "Wow. That was some gooood Shizzz."

He answered, "Wow. It's like ... Wow."

"Puna Fire."

"Yeah, Puna Fire."

"Good Shiizz."

"Fine, Puna Fire. Better than that Maui Wowie."

This went on for a while until it turned into a similar commentary on the stars, on the waves, and on the island.

"Fine Island."

"Wow, really fine Island."

"Yeah, fine Big Island."

They started giggling and things until I figured I'd best go. I stood up to leave, when Mikey said, "So, sorry, we didn't mean to leave you out. What snacks have you got out here? We packed light and forgot munchies, just the meals. It's all that freeze dried crap."

I explained my provisions were not much better. Mikey looked disappointed, but just shrugged, "OK, sit down and listen to this wild story we heard from the guy who like sold us this shizz."

Judy giggled. "Mikey, tell her that story. It will freak you out to the max."

Mikey was watching the waves from the surf roll in with a strange look on his face, like he had to keep an eye out for things, "You tell her, babe, but tell her it is creepy so watch out."

"It's creepy."

I have to admit I was curious. For they no longer seemed to think everything was funny. My two stoners seemed unnerved and watchful, even as high as they obviously were.

"Go ahead, I'll listen."

"OK but remember, man, you are going to be creeped out."

"Creeped out to the max."

7

"So creepy."

"Yeah, uber creepy."

"OK, what happened?"

"Well, like the dude who sold us the weed, said that this was like true. It happened to his mother when she was like a little girl."

"Yeah, like a little kid girl."

So you get the idea. This story went on with constant interruptions between the two of them. Many distractions and asides. Several attempts to find something to eat in their packs and finally eating some nuts and raisins that I finally gave in and provided. There was a growing spookiness that had them almost cringing and whining in fear at one time, but in the end I had the story. It *was* creepy. I'll tell it straight not as I heard it from the scattered and tossed fragments they offered.

It goes something like this:

The grower who cultivated my friends' pot was from an old Hawaiian family. One of the Ali'i, the rulers, and had married pretty much along those lines so that he had claims to the line of chiefs. His mother told him how when she was a little girl, her very pregnant mother one day started screaming and ordered her to go get her father. She never forgot the puddle of strange smelling fluid between her mother's legs. She ran like a reef dart down to the cane fields where her father was a foreman for one of the sugar bosses. He had a horse and they climbed aboard and galloped for their home. When they got there, the mother was passed out limp on the floor. Her belly was sunken. A bloody mess was splashed all around her legs and waist. And most eerie and strange, a slime trail leading out of the house shone in the morning sun sparkling. They awakened the woman. She screamed and bawled and they could get nothing sensible from her. She was weak and shaking and finally whispered, "My son has gone down to find his ohana." At that moment, her auntie showed up so the pot grower's mother and her father started to track the queer slime trail through the shrubs and grasses. It led through the 'akoko to the strand and there on the black sand beach was a small shark flopping and flipping toward the shoreline. They ran toward it, still following the silvery trail that they had followed from their house. When they got to the baby shark it was exhausted, its dry gills working slowly in immediate distress. Her father picked up the shark and rushed it into the surf. He cradled it in his hands moving it through the water, spinning it in small circles until it regained its strength and skittered away. The pot grower's grandfather watched a long time, waist deep in the gentle surf. He turned to come back when the little girl saw the terrifying dorsal fin of a great white roaring toward him from behind. The little girl screamed and pointed and the man turned around and saw what was coming and rather than run, turned to face it. She saw the treacherous beast open its mouth but stop before her father. After a moment the beast turned around and fled the reef toward the open ocean. Her father slogged forward and fell on his knees and offered a prayer to Heavenly Father for his wife's deliverance, for the Melchizedek Priesthood, and that he was in the tribe of Manasseh, and of the sharks. Then he turned to the little girl, "You need never fear the sharks, your little brother will protect you. He is a shark and you are ohana."

After the story, a strange feeling settled over the group. The waves near us crashing and sparkling white in the moonlight seemed pregnant with mythic power as if a shark could appear as we watched. The night on the other side seemed menacing and watchful. Crouching, ready to pounce.

Finally I whispered, "They were Mormon?"

He seemed surprised by my question and said, "Yeah, how did you like know that? Whoa. This is like creeping me out."

"There was some Mormon stuff in the story you told."

"Wicked strange. Are you a Mormon? Is that why you don't do the doobie?"

"Yeah. More or less."

"Yeah dude was a Mormon, but says he was like exorcized when he did time in Kulani prison for stealing cattle up on Parker Ranch lands. Slapped him harsh they did, but fact is he learned how to grow emjay when he was clearing land for the Hawaii DSS to make that arboretum north of Hilo Town."

"Excommunicated."

"Yeah, whatever, he was Xed out of existence."

Judy weighed in, "Tell her about the nightwalkers."

"Man ... You don't want to go there. That's some wild ass shizz that was, like man I'm all creeped out even worse about that."

"Creepy is as creepy does."

"So like tell her anyway. I ain't heard nothing like that. Tell her."

"You tell her!"

"OK. I will. So he says this is true. He says he's like seen it five or six times and he knows his brother died from them. He says his brother was no way old enough or drunk enough to like have a heart attack and they got him sure."

"What happened?"

Mikey interrupts, "Nightwalkers got him!"

"Nightwalkers?"

Judy again, "Yeah, at night these armies of old time Hawaiians come marching through the streets all ghost and see-through like. You can hear them singing old Hawaiian songs and they come with their war clubs and all and if they find you awake they kill you with a blow from the clubs. It don't leave no mark but you are dead nonetheless. Doctors will tell you it was a heart attack or a brain stroke or some such nonsense. At night you can hear them marching. He says the only thing you can do is drop down and pretend you are asleep."

I could not suppress my smile, "Can't you just hide under your blanket? Aren't there rules about ghosts getting at you under a blanket?"

"This is real. Lots of people have seen them! Not just a few and in every case if they hadn't pretended they were sawing logs it would have been the end. Believe or don't but man you are a fool if you don't. And if you don't take this serious you'll likely end up losing your other hand."

"Mikey!"

Realizing what he just said, he slapped a hand over his mouth. Then said soberly (especially given how high he was), repentantly, "I am so sorry. I am. Really, really sorry. I didn't mean no offense. It's like the weed talking. I didn't mean nothing. It's just you can't ignore the mysterious things of the world. There are stranger things than we know. But you know ... crap ... I'm really sorry."

I wasn't offended. I was tired of this conversation with a couple of flower children dosed up on wacky weed, however, and so decided to exit the scene.

"Look, no worries. But I'm tired and think I'll go to bed. Thanks for dinner. That was very generous of you. Goodnight."

I stood up. I felt sort of bad. They were both obviously in pain thinking they had offended me. And who knows maybe at some level I was. He was right. There are dangers in the world and taking ayahuasca and letting your hand fall in a fire is pretty foolish. But that's not why I was leaving. I was tired of their youth and their sense that life was nothing more than chasing a more exquisite high. Worst of all, I was missing my solitary contemplations because of them.

As I was walking away I could hear Judy scolding Mickey, "You shithead! Why did you say that? We were having such a nice conversation. Man, you are really an asshole you know that?"

I couldn't make out what he mumbled back.

In the morning, I went on a small sunrise hike to see if I could catch sight of some monk seals that I'd been told visited a little cove occasionally. When I got back I planned to make breakfast for my friends and apologize for my abrupt departure and let them know I had no hard feelings. They were gone. On my sleeping bag they had laid some wild flowers and a package of freeze dried chili. On a note they had written:

Namaste, We got up early to make a run for the road to get some supplies up mauka side then head north past Hilo and up the windward coast. It was groovy to get to know you a bit. I hope we did not offend or leave you with a downer about our stop in this quiet paradise. Should you ever find yourself in Boston please look us up and say hi. We leave these gifts that you might remember us more fondly than we deserve. Love is all you need, but we are still working on it.

Peace and Love,

Judy Hauptman and Mikey Singer

OK. That was sweet. Now I felt guilty. They were just exploring the world like I was and I had been anything but gracious. I'd done everything I could to drive them away—not helping them find water, leaving coolly after I'd been given a generous meal, ignoring them when they wanted to talk. The irony was running thick in the air around me. What did their arrival interrupt? My contemplation on love. What did I do? I drove them off. What did they leave me? Their love. Ouch.

So here I sit. The day has progressed and I feel glum. Disappointed in myself for treating the others so shabbily. I cannot bring myself to wish them back. I feel torn and disappointed that I drove them away and that they left. As if to reflect my mood clouds have gathered. Rain is rare here on the edge of the Kau Desert so I'm not over worried about a downpour, but the overcast sky and increasing wind seems to remind me of the guilt that I can't seem to suppress.

I try to shake it off with a swim, but that backfires because the wind is whipping up the waves making it choppier than makes for good snorkeling. I start to climb out and cut my leg on a piece of coral and although the wound is not deep it stings in the salty water. I get back to camp and realize I'm out of water. Mostly because I didn't pull some out of the little cave in the presence of the others. I didn't want to give its location to the hippies, and so my misfortune starts to feel like a just punishment for bad behavior—*So you want to reflect on love do you, why didn't you start with the nice couple from Boston?*

I pick up my apple cider jug and make an easy climb down the fifteen-foot drop into the cave and standing on a little ledge fill the bottle. I decide not to clean up my wound so near to the source of the spring, so I climb back out and scramble back to camp. I trip on a driftwood log the flower children left on the trail, apparently while dragging their benches over last night. I lose about half the water and find I'm limping slightly because in the fall, I may have twisted my ankle. I call them several names, then remember how I treated them. I'm frustrated with myself. I'm frustrated with them. I'm frustrated that I have been made to feel so lousy. I'm frustrated with the wind and the coral that cut my leg open. I'm angry the sun has disappeared.

I clean the wound and test my ankle for real damage. It's already feeling better and I can walk on it, but worst-case scenarios start to run through my head: What if I get injured and can't walk back to the car? No one knows where I am on the Big Island. What if ... what if ... what if.

I sit on my sleeping bag and fall on my back then turn over onto my side and start to cry. Why not? I'm feeling sorry for myself. I don't even have a hand. I've lost badminton. I've lost two years of my life. I've lost everything I've ever valued. Has anyone been through this much? I can't even go camping without it being ruined.

I fall into a heavy sleep and when I awake it is late afternoon. I'm groggy and thick headed. It was not a good nap. I stand up and walk away from my camp to use the bathroom. The Filipino man who gave away so many secrets about this place, warned me that the ghosts of the ancestors here are erratic and unpredictable, given to whims, and dangerous when not respected. He said that when I use the bathroom, that I should explain my need to the spirits of the place and apologize for despoiling the land and then to cover it all with soil. I think the notion that I should make such a fuss about taking a pee quaint, but I had followed his advice so far on this camp—making a game of thanking the ghosts for the use of their land. It did make me feel good—like I was tapping into something deep; recognizing the sacracy of the land. But this time I ignore the advice. I pee on the ground. I feel disappointed in myself and in response raise my middle finger to the landscape. How dare it make me feel like I owed it an apology for peeing! But the act feels like a transgression. I've breached something and the place doesn't feel the same.

As I leave and start to walk back to camp, I catch something out of the corner of my eye, but when I turn toward it, nothing. It is strangely unnerving. The impression of motion was strong, but I don't see so much as a bird. I think to myself, I know there is nothing to this, however if I ignore my fear, it will just keep pestering me. Better safe than sorry as they say. So I return and say, "Look ghosts, I had to pee. So sorry and all that." The foreboding does not go away. I slept longer than I intended and I find that when I pulled out the water bottle and bandaged my leg I didn't zip my knapsack back up and mongooses have pulled out some trail snacks and scattered them about.

I need more water, so I return to the cave for more. I have trouble carrying more than one canteen at a time with only the one hand, so I make two trips. I start the fire and go back to the large boulders and crags where the opihi are found. I climb up on the black volcanic rock and start to pry some of the little gastropods up. I've loaded up only a small number into my camp pan. I bend down, working on one when I glance back just in the nick of time and see a rogue wave bearing down on me. I scream and leap up the rock in a half jump, half spring, getting out of the way just in time for it to crash at my heels. If it had pulled me in, I would be lost. I'm shaking. I've lost my knife and pan both which I left behind when I fled the wave. I stare at the water crashing below me and I feel an anger and a presence from the ocean. It feels like it is reaching out for me, trying to find a way to pull me back to it. I force my rational mind to take control. I go over the facts at hand, spell out clearly the laws of the universe, and dismiss any intent on the part of inanimate objects. I start to settle down when I see a figure dart past a slit formed by two large rocks obscuring all but a small section of sandy shore. I'm filled with fear that pimples my skin and sends chills down my back. I climb a little higher and move off to the left about 100 meters, not the way I came in. I don't know who is waiting for me. I get back on the shore and carefully approach the lagoon and my camp. I see no one. My fire is burning nicely. I look for footprints and don't see anything obvious or new. It's all as it should be. I scan the shoreline looking for who I might have seen back on the rocks. There is no one. I shout, "Hey. I see you! Come out of there." Trying to trick whoever it is out of the shadows, but no one appears.

I return to my fire. I feel like I'm being watched and I keep turning round and looking up and down the beach, at the rocks, up to the Pali. But there is no one here. With my pan gone I cannot cook my noodles so I munch on them raw. It's not as grim as it sounds, but I miss the warmth that the cooked food brings. And I miss the opihi.

"Gilda!" A low voice. Almost a bark.

I spin around again something moves out of the corner of my eye, but no one is there and there is nowhere they could have gone. I shout:

"Who's there? Show yourself!"

But no one is there.

The sun is starting to set and I'm scared. Terrified. Malice surrounds me. My knife is gone so I look around for a weapon. I find a piece of driftwood with just the right shape for a club. I stoke the fire high and wait.

The sun has set and I'm watching the fire. I get up and walk around facing away from the flames and stare into the darkness waiting, watching. The fire pops and I jump. The sound of the waves and the wind masks any other sound. In the complexity of those reverberations of the wind through the rocks and palms and grasses and over the top of the waves one can hear multiple voices. And in the break of the surf channeled through the flutes and horns of a thousand crevasses and cracks, the symphony is complex and varied. I hear within it voices. I hear song. I hear the thromb of ancient drums and the chants of long dead warriors. I feel the curses of Kahuna and shamans. I hear the howl of ghosts. They all are proclaiming one thing: I do not belong here.

And then I see them coming from the Pali. Nightwalkers, moving white and insubstantial toward me from a great distance. I don't know what to do and like a child I dive into my sleeping bag. My mockery of my friend's story seems to be condemning me. I can hear the tattoo of their tramp and the refrain of their cadence call as they bellow their war chant and send it riding on the wind. Demonic ethers spill from their voices corrupting the landscape and poisoning the air. These baleful apparitions will offer no quarter to the embodied. I know that with certainty. I am breathing like a captured animal—my chest heaving, sweat soaking my shirt, I am trembling like a hypothermic ice bather. They will find my body mongoose-gnawed and cold. A prayer starts to form as I wonder how I will die. And I know I will die. There is a certainty that I am about to leave this world that is crystal clear and undeniable. It is not a belief, but a kind of knowledge. I am doomed.

I pause in my fear as a little thought surfaces. How will I die? How exactly will they kill me? How effective are their spectral weapons? Other than terror, what power have they? To my mind suddenly comes the message a biologist friend of mine wrote from a bed and breakfast he and his wife were staying in near Bar Harbor, Maine shortly before I left for Vietnam:

It appears this bed and breakfast is haunted. Last night as the crescent moon's light breached our western window, a ghost materialized, passing in through the dressing table mirror. A great sea captain he appeared to be and when he saw my eyes fixed upon his visage he let out a terrible and otherworldly moan. But I smiled, and he, flummoxed at his impotence, let out another Jacob Marley-like wail. It seemed too textbook to me. Unoriginal and hackneyed. "Come," I said reproachfully, "let's have no more of these carnival ride shenanigans. I am a man of science. Tell me by what metaphysics you appear. Demonstrate by what chemistry, however strangely mercurial, you are structured." So we spoke long into the night, but not of natural philosophy as I intended, for the conversation turned to the gray of the sea and the song of whales and the deeds of courage that pressed forward will one day tame the stars. We showed one another our scars won by honor and accident. And as the rosy-fingered dawn began to blank the eastern stars (laughing together at his reference to Homer, for there is ken shared between the living and the dead), and as the smell of bacon and coffee from the kitchens below wafted into the room, he bowed and doffed his hat and departed.

A creative work obviously but as I recall it, courage gathers and I stick my head out of my bag and challenge the nightwalkers: "Tell me by what metaphysics you appear! Demonstrate by what physics you are bound! I will have no more of your shenanigans. Name your power or fade away!"

And suddenly I start to laugh. The absurdity of my curled up in a shivering ball of jelly to avoid warrior ghosts hits me full force. I laugh and laugh. Now I am shaking in mirth. In sidesplitting laughter I fight my way out of the bedroll and face my demons. But they are gone. The sound of their march has become the knock of a piece of driftwood lodged in a narrow rock spillway of pulsing waves beating forward and rolling back dragging the log back and forth in this slotted trap. Their chant?

The play of the wind among the palms and rocks. The wraiths revealed against the Pali? The moonlight drifting in and out of the thinning clouds.

A bit of beef. A blot of mustard. An underdone potato.

I am again surrounded by the soft light of the moon, which is now fully disclosed. The waves speak again of ancient things, processes at work for eons. I am bidden again to wonder and mystery, not of the type suggested by superstition, but that demanded by the deep occult of things existent.

It is time to look at love. I am no longer afraid. I pull the book I want to explore from my pack. It will serve as the basis of my investigation and the moon will light it. The book deserves a book-length treatment of its origins in full but I'll sketch it only briefly.

In the summer of '58, I was at the University of North Carolina, Chapel Hill teaching badminton to young girls in several sports camps being run by the PE department. It was to last over the course of the summer. During my time there I decided to sign up for a graduate course in writing poetry. The class itself was a waste of time (the teacher was a model of affectation and theatrics and the students were more inclined to snicker at his poetic recitations than be moved by them). The students, however, formed a cadre of fellows that made the summer delightful. There were students from multiple disciplines like the biologist who gave me the 'haunted inn' piece above, historians, students in English, and some from religion. I will not name them (there was one whose name you would recognize if you've followed American poetry). Quite the band of merry bards were we.

Often, we would gather at a pub on Franklin Street to read to each other our best work—not like in class. There we would read our throwaway poems because the teacher, no matter what a poem's worth, would listen to a student's poem with his eyes closed, his fingers folded together and his index fingers buried into the bridge of his nose. He graced his face with a look of rapture. It became a game among the students to read in class their most devilishly awful and hackneyed doggerel and listen with an undisclosed smirk as he praised it to the moon. The real game was to suppress your giggles as he extolled the virtues of every poem. But in the pub we were a master's class at the height of our craft. Our best work was put forth and received honest and often brutal critiques.

One of the students from the religion department was a strange and ethereal girl. Her skin was translucent, almost an Alice blue. She had a sharp, delicate face with round (more than generous) ears that could not be kept contained within her thin straight hair. I'm not sure I ever knew her real name. We called her *MT (em tee)*, from the initials, *Mus timidus*, a nickname that she seemed to enjoy as a mark of acceptance. She was pathologically shy. She rarely shared her poetry and she never offered critique or advice to anyone. When she did share an offering, it was always stunningly complex. She used technically challenging forms with such beauty and grace and insight that offering advice seemed silly (although we tried and which she took with appreciation). She read, and even spoke, multiple medieval languages. She was unique, weird, wonderful, and quiet.

She was always there. She seemed to follow us around like a puppy. When we would slide from pub to pub to put down a few beers, she would order one but take only a sip or two from each, leaving a string of unfinished drinks. When we ordered a pizza or fish and chips she would nibble on a little but not touch much. If you wrote down everything she said over the course of the summer it would have amounted to only a page or two of text. We all liked her and encouraged her to interact, but she would just hide her smile behind her hand and mumble something we rarely caught. Her teeth were strangely misaligned and we speculated how this might have affected her self-confidence.

At the end of the summer we were devastated to find out after she missed several of our outings that she was in the hospital. She was diagnosed with a rare form of cancer on the right side of her heart. Given its location, the doctors said there was nothing they could do and she would likely not last more than a few weeks. The truth was from the time she was admitted until the time she died was only ten days. When we finally heard about her being in the hospital we came immediately, but it was on the seventh day since her admittance. She was optimistic and seemed not to be as sick as the doctors were saying. She was clear-headed and animated.

We visited together as a group and joked with her for about an hour after which her mother, who had come from Vermont, said maybe we should let her get some rest. As we were leaving, *MT* called me back and asked if we could talk alone for a minute. I said yes, of course. When the door closed after the group had been herded out by her mother, she reached into a bag and brought out a small present wrapped in brittle white tissue paper swathed liberally with a braided red twine. She handed it to me with liturgical solemnity, deliberately, carefully as if it were rare and precious.

"I made this for you."

I moved to open it, but she stopped me and said, "Later. OK? Your birthday is in a month. Right? Save it for that."

I knew what she was saying: *Wait until I die.*

I started to cry. I wasn't close to this girl. I knew little enough about her, but I was quite overcome and touched by her gesture. This was our first conversation alone in all the time I'd known her. She reached out and took my hand and patted it softly, then kissed it. She leaned back on her bed and closed her eyes, resting. I kissed her on the forehead and thanked her again for the gift. She opened her eyes and smiled, "Thank *you*," she whispered.

I moved toward the door and she suddenly struggled into a sitting position and said, "Please come back soon." I said I would and stepped out of the door. Her mother smiled at me and thanked me for coming and went back into the room. I never saw her again. This was on Thursday. We'd planned to come back on Saturday. She died in the early morning hours on that day.

Her body was sent back to Vermont so we could not even attend her funeral. During the two weeks that remained of the summer, at every gathering the group would order one extra beer, which we would leave untouched—as she would have. A memorial to *MT*. Our friend.

I've come out to the promontory to read under the moonlight. In my hand is one of my few treasures. The book *MT* made. When she said she made it for me, she meant 'made' literally. It was fashioned from soft dyed red leather inlaid with a delicate etched Celtic frame, tooled to enclose a hand-painted medieval illuminated panel showing a unicorn bleeding and a weeping maiden holding the beast's head to her bosom. The pages were made of home-brewed birch bark paper and polished to a high sheen, sewn together and glued carefully into the binding. A rice paper page cover protects an original artwork of flowers and vines creating the title page: *The Book of Gilda Trillim*. In it are original translations from Old French, Latin, and several English and German variants of medieval women mystics. In lovely calligraphy, they are written in inks of red, gold, blue, and black. The preface on the first page is taken from the opening frontispiece of the Beguine heretic Marguerite Porete's book, *The Mirror of Simple Souls*, for which she was burned at the stake:

> You who would read this book,
> If you truly wish to seize it,
> Think about what you say,
> For it is very tricky to comprehend;
> Humility, the keeper of the assets of
> Knowledge
> And the mother of the other Virtues,
> Must overtake you.[3]

Every entry in the book is about the mystery of love. Sometimes it is personified as a being, and others as the mysterious force of God. In every entry there is something about how the women immersed themselves as in a flaming fire that consumed them. The entries are ecstatic and overflowing with passion or longing or exhortation to love. The last piece in the book is a heart-breaking stanza from the Beguine poet Hadewijch's the *Subjugation to Love*:

And I am now forsaken,
By all creatures alive:
This is clearly evident.
If in love
I cannot triumph,
What will become of me?
I am small now; then I would be nothing.
I am disconsolate unless Love furnishes a cure.
I see no deliverance; she must give me
Enough to live on freely.[4]
The last page is inscribed, "With love your *mus timidus.*"

It seems strange to me that all this love was masked from me. Love that would create such work of art as this. Yet to me at the time, she was just an odd little friend who joined us on a summer's adventure. Were it not for her memorable death and this book, I likely would have altogether forgotten her. She would become a creature of memory, one of those bygone souls who withdraws into the fogs of the past, just part of an atmosphere that provides mood to recollection but cannot be brought up explicitly except as a shadow. Someone who when called to mind by a friend or acquaintance by, "Do you remember that odd mousy girl who was in our poetry class?" you might answer, "Kind of. Was she the one with the enormous ears?" "Yes, that's the one. I wonder what ever happened to her?" But all her depth of feeling, her passions, her immeasurable worth and value are masked and lost in the shrouds and mists of a moment passing. Oh, how I wish I could go back and meet her. To know the person this book reveals.

Let me assess. I've tried to discover the depth of things, to find the place in which 'isness' hides in apple seeds. I've explored the connections that make a thing coalesce into a thing. An object. I've wandered through much and after all, end knowing nothing. I don't know what I am. I don't understand what anything is. On my vision quest, I was told that love was the one thing that mattered. Why? Isn't it, as the scientists are claiming, just a brain bathed in certain hormones? A certain tone added to the music of life? Are we not apish machines that click and clack in a mockery of a stopgap motion movie monster over Tokyo? Am I just the spinning of soggy gears and meaty levers? I cannot even come to know myself? When I am asleep my body does things I neither control nor react to, so what do I know?

And yet here I am watching waves cascade one after another in steady regularity tamed by the moon. But the moon does more than draw the white breakers from the ocean: it floods them with light reflected from the sun. It combines with coral reefs, which break and complexify the water into a foamy, roiling turbulence that adds texture to the combination, which, when added to me and my neural tangles, creates in this universe a sense of beauty. A moment of awe. That is something. Not an object. Not a structure although it is conditioned by that matrix. But this beauty? It is more than these elements. It is something that sneaks up from deep evolutionary time, combines with an occasion called now, trysts with matter, dances with consciousness, and into what? Something above all this. An abundance. An overflowing that stretches upward and outward. A grace?

Then Love? I look at the book in my lap. Its beauty exceeds the moonlit play of elements below me. It was born of love. Love known by Christian mystics, drawn to something beyond. And that love flows forward in wave-like ripples that ride the ocean of humanity until it crashes into a young poet and artist who then evaporates into nothingness? But not before she creates a current that pulls me like a riptide into the depths of love and memory. Did those mystics learn it from the Galilean? And his love's origins? Was he the source or does it begin before him? When did love enter the world? What slime-emergent creature first felt its tremblings or even the nascent motions or the first intimations of this thing we call love?

So here I sit. A moment. A moment bathed in light and created by moon, ocean waves, and lava from deep in the depths of the earth. And from a book born of an unrealized love who brought to life fellow travelers from the middle ages, who in turn worshiped a carpenter, who defied an empire by bowing to it, and all blending with a woman who was given a glimpse of creation, or of her mind's conception thereof (is there a difference?), a woman who loved rats and from that love midwifed an emerging music new in the world from sources similar to what her own race must have once passed through. What am I? This moment? This strange blend of past and present, of history and emergent consciousness. Beauty? Love? In me? Overflowing me? Creating me? Defining me?

I pause.

This is where the fragment of a journal entry ends. With 'I pause.' We don't know how this would have ended. The book from *MT* has never been found. Years later she laments a lost treasure in a letter to Babs Lake and most scholars believe that that treasure may have been this book.

Vignette 14 Trillim in New York Notes. Circa Late 1972

The following document and Vignette 15 are the only written records we have of Trillim's stay in New York. She knew composer Monty Smith from high school in Burley, Idaho. Smith was a well-known figure in the Greenwich Village music scene and maintained an extravagant life style under the patronage of the DEA, an organization devoted to the arts and in particular Smith. He was raised Mormon, but had abandoned the Church shortly after leaving Idaho to study music in Los Angeles.

Trillim's trip to New York is shrouded in mystery and much is unknown. But while her Journal mentions almost in passing that she "is going to the Big Apple," she never directly refers to it again. These documents were uncovered by Trillim scholar Sergey Petrov, whose writings on Trillim and Smith's relationship are intriguing and well worth perusing if just for a wealth of arcane information about high school life in Burley in the 1950s.[1]

Document 1: Mary Lassiter Mental Health Hospital. Manhattan, NY. Floor Logbook.

Floor Logbook

For attending staff floor notes only, please refer to patient's chart for full information.

Patient name: Jane Doe #394
Admitting Physician: Dr. Aaron Mossberg, Ph: 212-116-2874
Date: Oct. 13, 1972
Time: 11:40 pm
Baseline: Pulse: 128; Blood Pressure: Sys: 154, D: 94; Wt: 123; Pupils: slightly dilated, responding to light.

Physical Appearance: Patient arrived filthy, with multiple superficial abrasions incl. both knees, elbows, nose, chin, and forehead. Patient is missing R. hand at wrist from previous injury. Face bloody from nasal contusion and one canine knocked out through trauma. Rat bites on hand and arms. Patient not oriented to time or place. Speech confused. Periods of calm punctuated with violent episodes of uncontrolled thrashing noted. No identification.

Reason for Admittance: Psychotic episode. Asks repeatedly for Fatty Lumpkin and Paps. Was found screaming in sewer near the corner of West 4th St. and Perry St. At least some injuries incurred in resisting Fire Department's attempts to extract her from the sewer system.

Treatment: Placed in a straight jacket and retrained in cushioned restraint room 23B. Given 25 mg/mL injection of Thorazine and 600mg Aspirin. Wounds have been cleaned and bandaged, largely superficial except for the tooth. (Arrangements for an oral surgeon have been scheduled for tomorrow afternoon.) She is currently sleeping.

Update: 5:20 am. Awoke asked for water. Did not understand where she was or how she got here. Seems calm.

Vignette 15: Article from *The Greenwich Peeper* by Pseudonymous Author, 'Madam Alley Cat.' October 15, 1972.

Mew, mew, mew Village cool cats! Your one true and lovely pussy has been slinking about on the prowl, putting naughty whiskers where none belong and leaving long luscious stripes skating down the backs of those who won't give her a nibble for her sweet-sweet purr-purr. Stay on Madam Alley Cat's groovy side (you can call her MAC, she loves familiarity and even enjoys the occasional petting party) or find your mug under the tease and tickle of her unsheathed pen! (Still looking for that striped Tom among the big intact males around the trashycans that will win licks from her sticky tongue!)

So what's up in and about the Village? Let us see!

Who is that kibble dish hanging around monsieur violinist Martin du Gard at the NY Phil? Hot, hot redhead, (and MEOW, with that red dress and ruby red slippers she can click click click me to Kansas anytime, the Madam isn't picky. Purr!). But no one knows her name—Until now! For MAC has found fresh sardines in the oily can! What will the Ambassador think when he finds Mrs. Ambassador has developed a new enthusiasm for the symphony? Ah the music is so sweet! Kyllä! (That's Finnish for Ja!)

Now lookee lookee MAC was nosing through the leavings behind 'Serendipity 3,' and whose voice came rogue elephanting through the door? Was that the editor of *Style 180* breaking decibel levels loud enough to discomfit the ears of this streetwise feline whose soft tufted ears have heard the cry of many a frustrated Tom? Yowl! If one day you find yourself that brassy blue-penciler's assistant never, ever forget that grand lady's appointment book. And I hear there is now an opening in the dame's vicinity for a new lackey peon! So you of stout ears, get your résumé polished! Also, anyone need a slightly deaf assistant? I hear there is one available who promises never ever to forget a daybook again!

So now for the undercover, top secret, report of the month. Madam loves to stretch the length of her line to draw out the wild and wacky world of the Village to a depth only a kitty cat can plumb. And we have a woozy doozy this time! What happens when a minimalist novelist and a minimalist composer smash their heads together to wow us with the claim that they have fashioned the best and most wonderful thing ever? Meow! The screeches of 'ittle boyds' mimicking rats? Sound bad? Yup, yup, yup. I've eaten better four-day-old fish livers.

So what is it about the water of yon Burly, Idaho that pushes out stud muffins (or is it spud muffins) and minimalists? Turns out the literary writer of wonky lists, Gilda Trillim is friends with the Village's own spare composer Monty Smith! Both from that art haven Idaho, the state providing a never-ending supply of the French fry equivalents of art. You know greasy and bland but oh so hard to resist. You'll remember him, kittens, as we have crossed paths in the night a time or two. He prowls in a house stacked to the brim with a who's who of the local crowd (including that wack, wack, wacky Japanese Beatle heart thief). He's regaled us with those three-hour pianoforte 'concerts' (and let those cute little quotidian marks guide your ideas about what I think of these little 'gatherings'). Indian gurus wielding a tambura are being dispensed for a shiny dime out of a machine in the corner and the incense never stops smoking in those digs when the gang gets their well-tuned claviers claviering! But one-handed Gilda, meow, yowl, what a weird sour bowl of milk is she. She disappears on a USO tour in Nam and turns up where? Back in the USSR, boys, you don't know how lucky you are boy, back in the US, back in the US, back in the USSR. How she got from the Nam-ish Southeast Asian pisshole to Moscow is anyone's guess, but you can bet that old J. Edger has his peeping

Tom eyes on her (he would like to get his paws on *this* prowler, but he's a fat old paddy cake that can't find his way to this quick running pussy).

It's every kitty cat's dream to be in a room of delicious delectable rats, but does she fricassee their moist and tender bodies? Does she dress them in mint sauce and roast them until slick with paw-licking grease? Oh no, dear reader she does what? She teaches them to sing. So she says. I was there as she talked to the little gang of true believers that gathered to hear the tale (or the tail in a rat's case). No, she does not gobble them up, she gives them the von Trapp family rodent treatment and lays down the do re mi.

Right then and there our own little tyrant Monty Smithy declares that we will recreate the Hanoi Hilton A Cappella Rat Ensemble, "There will be nothing like it!" He's got that right, and we can only hope it stays so. The first problem rises sea serpent-like because at what range do our furry friends warble? Eight octaves above middle C! Whoo, I haven't heard that high a cater-wauling since little Missy Whitepads was doing the humph, humph dance with that bobcat sized orange tomcat that stalks down by the docks!

So his highness calls upon his minion musicians to find the appropriate instruments and zip zap they try and try and worry their little heads, but only instruments high enough to reach rat-squeak assai altissimo also lack the *je ne sais quoi* so lovely in the rat-screech timbre Gilda longs for. Whaah, Whaah, says poor Smithy. But at last a devoted fan (and sometimes lovey dovie, lead singer of a certain local band I will not mention except it starts with 'Enemy' and ends with 'People' and has a very small word that starts with 'o' and another that starts with 't' in the middle). She shows up with birdcalls, wood twisted on wood things that squeak like a rat, or so says our dear one-armed music bandit. Monty the wonder horse runs out to the birdcall/ratcall emporium and buys up more than 200 which give a couple of notes up and down from that high, high, high, high C. He added a few Vietnamese song loans for good measure (they were trying to imitate Vietnamese rats don't you know?).

To make it authentic (and who would even want to participate in an inauthentic rat choir?), the rat goddess arranges ladders and trundle beds hoisted up the wall with clever little pulleys, so that we can crawl up the walls and sit in the corners like well-positioned rat artistes. "Detail. Detail. Detail people. Let's make this real!" Monty would call with all the seriousness of the damned and deranged. It was here, dear reader, that your intrepid reporter almost pulled the plug and fled this downer scene. But no, no, no! How could I live with myself if I did not put my readers front and center and do the hard work of exposing the inanity of art gone mad? So in a fit of determination unbecoming of the Madam, I pulled myself up by my tail and faced the music or rather the cruel blasphemous din.

So on the day of the 'concert' we took our positions. Me sitting as pretty as a tortoiseshell Manx, up on one of the trundle beds. There were six ladders and four beds hauled up to just the right heights to satisfy the most discriminating rat music aficionado. Monty took a position on a ladder all his own, one with a little cushy seat that kept his tush well tended for the duration of our enduring polyphony.

Then with great portent and seriousness her rattiness Queen Gilda handed out the score. Oh my, oh my, my little kittens, such pretentiousness has the Madame not seen since the reign of Queen Lady Ragnar the Gold at the Wagn' Drag-on where said lady sang lustily the body eclectic.

The 'work' was composed by Miss One-arm, but scored by his Holiness himself and brace yourself for the title, as lovely as the music it represents, *Rat Vomit Symphony No. 1 in B8 minor, for Fifty-six Bird Calls and Five Song Loans*. I thought nothing could ever, ever be as awful as that title until I heard the music. The atrocious title my dear ones does not capture the vileness of the music. Rat vomit indeed!

Gilda came forward with … with … I cannot say it without a chuckle tremoring my feline frame, a baton medical-taped to her stumpity stump! Oh, yes there she stood wearing a pair of pink overalls and a ghastly teal T-shirt, her hair was cut Twiggy style, except badly, and on her shoes? Birkenstocks! Of course! The abomination was complete.

She raised her arms and everyone brought a birdcall to their chest, one hand on the handle and the other holding the little wooden bowl mounted like a wheel and axle designed to squeak when twisted back and forth. And so we began. We had practiced a bit so had the basics down, but it took a few minutes to get going and the maestro made us stop and begin again ten or twenty or thirty times. But at last we were on the move. Because rats have no way to hold their notes we did some tricky things to overlap one another's squeaks. "Find the structure in the music, people," Monty pleaded, "it's in the structure you'll find the depth of eternity!" But at last we were rolling. And by rolling I mean we were rolling on a rusty wheel squeaking abominably but with vim and verve and a determination to see the monstrosity through to the end.

To listen to five minutes of this would have been misery. Ten minutes would have been inhumane (I myself would have not even done it to a rat). Thirty minutes? What would you, dear reader, think if it went that long? Surely you would call Geneva and tell them that their lovely conventions were being turned on their head. But, no, even thirty minutes would not have come close to describing the length of that duration. We went, and I kid you not, hand on a stack of catnip, three hours, seventeen minutes, and many seconds each of which we were embedded in the full horror of the sound of wood on wood screeching.

All the while, stumpy Trillim had such an effect of pathos on her face that if you saw her, your heart would break at the power of her thrice-bemoaned countenance. What acting! What fawning. I kept waiting for her to place the back of her one good hand against her forehead and swoon away in a melodramatic syncope. Her look was serious. Oh so serious with an intensity that would have intimidated even the most hardened Soviet politbureaucrat's eyebrows and all. Comical almost beyond my ability to keep from giggling, but I am the master of composure. I am a cat after all.

Magister composer was no better, save *his* reaction rather than affective pain was pure ecstasy. Like Bernini's St. Teresa he looked orgastic, his eyes rolled back into his head and a look of divine bliss blistering his countenance as he twisted the bird call with purpose. Oh when I looked at his face I swear the divine nature rested on it. If by divine nature you mean flatulent silliness.

I must admit dear reader to one moment at about five minutes into the second hour. For just a second. I was caught up in the moment. The spirit of the rats entered into me and I saw a beatific ratty vision of the all. But then at seven minutes into the second hour it was gone and I was back in the world of squeaking inanities. Sadly a good number of the players took on this Trillim inspired method-acting demeanor, a mien that spread throughout our merry band until I was almost ready to deliver fresh wet hairballs to one and all.

At last, at last, when it was over, there was silence. The quiet of the damned when the flames die for a moment and the sulfurous burning pauses. The Queen Mother fell to the floor— overcome with her own vastness. The High King slumped over exhausted. The queen of the rats was weeping. The king sobbing baby-like burbling and whimpering unabashed. She finally staggered to her bebirkenstocked feet and they shook and sobbed in each other's arms. There was not a dry eye in the room—one cannot keep the tears of mirth at bay for that long. Even a cat has its limits. Finally the potentate spoke:

"Never before in the history of the world has the voice of the rats been spoken more powerfully. There will be none here that will easily forget this day! This music is sublime. Not for mundane ears. This we will put away ..." And here his face took a mystical air as he shook the score at us and his eyes wandered to the heavens, "... for it is too sacred for this earth. Too holy to be mocked." (And you can be sure kittens that it would be. Oh how it would be.) "So it will be sealed to come forth when the great god comes to reclaim his kingdom when this song will be sung again by all the rats of the earth with one voice."

So let it be written so let it be done.

Then on cue, the one-armed rat woman fell on the floor weeping and screaming Loudun nun-hysterical. Like an alley cat hopped up on catnip and with its tail on fire and being chased by a pack of greyhounds. She started running around the room looking for things, screaming for Fatty. Then she bolted. Out into the street. We ran after her but lost her. No one has seen her since.

So dear readers shed a tear. Gilda Trillim has left the stage. Will she return? We hope not. We certainly hope not.

Vignette 16: Interview with Reporter Dob Klingford, Published in *The Paris Review.* July 3, 1981

I've been a fan of Gilda Trillim for years. Her minimalist book *A Coven of Pines* is in my top ten list of favorite books ever. As an ex-war correspondent, I think her status as a POW in Southeast Asia first endeared her to me, but then her book's strange beauty soon compelled me to love her writing for its own sake.

When allegations surfaced that she had betrayed her fellow captives by playing the whore to our then enemies, and rumors floated that she was a Russian spy and that she was an 'enemy of the people' as it were, I was stunned. Truth in war, they say is the first casualty, and the same is true when the vivid signs of wear in a public figure's reputation start to show, so I decided to investigate the matter myself.

Tracking down Trillim's whereabouts was no easy romp in the park. She was known to be in southeastern Utah. I had little to go on. I knew that after her father's death, Trillim's mother, Maggie Trillim sold their farm and bought property somewhere in that region of the West. Sleuthing out *where* required visiting the county tax records in nearly every city of that arid region (and is a tale, which surely will win me a Pulitzer Prize for heroics should I ever write it up). The property turned out to be in the La Sal Mountains, east of Moab on the Utah side of the Buckeye Reservoir area, adjacent to the western border of Colorado.

I decided to backpack there, thinking (not incorrectly) that if I came bounding up there in a truck, I would frighten her off. Something about the immediacy of the lone walker I thought would grant me a moment of her time that would be denied someone who could just hop back in the truck and drive away.

The hike was magnificent. I thought should I fail in obtaining the interview, the trek alone was worth the effort. Under a late summer sky, I walked up from a little dying mining settlement called La Sal, a lonely outpost, less a town than a collection of trailers with a post office and a small store. The journey began in the low sagebrush hills foregrounding the magnificent La Sal Mountains, a chain of snowcapped laccoliths that erupt from the canyon lands like the Moai of Easter Island—seemingly placed there to inspire awe by ancient Gods.

It was warmer than I like, but not awful. I followed a gravel road for many miles. My frame pack swayed to a rhythm that I've come to associate with many pleasant memories. The sage turned to scattered Gambel Oak and the land seemed inhabited only by jackrabbits and large drooling cows which would stand and stare stupidly until, after realizing I was not giving up in my resolve to continue down the road, they would bolt in a noisy burst of lumbering motion.

As the road switched from gravel to a two-track dirt track, the scrub oak turned into gorgeous, shady, aspen stands mixed with scattered patches of fragrant Ponderosa pines. Among these I spent a night under stars with the Milky Way burning across the sky like a pale fire. The magnificence of those heavens defies description.

In the morning after an agreeable breakfast of instant coffee and ash biscuits I continued up the road now twisting beneath a dark canopy. I did not hurry—I was within five miles or so, and I didn't want to arrive too early. The presence of the cows never abated and provided an audience that watched me pass with a lazy, hollow gaze.

At last after wandering through a sere meadow of grass harboring large old and stately tan colored pines, I descended a hill beside a small creek that laughingly led me into a narrow valley. Just before the road crossed into Colorado (marked by a barbed wire fence and cattle guard) I came to a small homey cabin sitting serenely under the protection of mature Ponderosa pines. It was rung on all sides by a full porch. The home (for such is a better description than cabin) was walled with tight raw timber boles.

Three women were sitting on the porch rocking contentedly in the morning air all dressed in jeans and T-shirts. All three were easy to identify. Gilda Trillim: dark, unruly, ruddy hair, pretty, stark face, missing hand. Her mother Maggie: much the same in aspect, but heavier, white-haired, strong and fierce—knitting. Babs Lake: athletic, dark hair and complexion, taller than the other two, an SLR camera sitting open on her lap and film being loaded onto the spool—radiating a calm protective air. An ancient white-muzzled black lab was lying under the door mantle.

I waved at them from the road, then strolled the seventy-five yards or so over toward them. As I approached, the old dog raised his head for a second then laid it back down keeping a single eye trained on me. They were calm and unafraid. I was glad I had not come in a truck; they seemed unperturbed by my presence. We chatted a while about the area, about the animals I had seen. I complained about the cows and their effect on the ecosystem, praised the cabin, and complemented their cozy space.

Then Babs asked, "So what brings you this part of the world?"

This was the moment. Now or never.

"I'm looking for Gilda Trillim."

The group froze. Babs reached down and grabbed a .22 rifle that had been laying there unnoticed and laid it across her lap in a calm confident manner. No one said a word, so I continued in a mad-dash-get-it-all-out-there verbal blitz that was at the same time overly formal while simultaneously said in almost a single breath.

"I'm a fan, a big one, and I've read almost everything you've written, and I'm now a freelance reporter and did a lot of work in Nam and more recently covering the literary scene and looking behind the scenes at writers and poets and their lives because I myself love the written word and anyway with all the idiots out there saying bad things about Gilda … er … Miss Trillim, I wanted to set the record straight and tell her side of the story, so I backpacked all the way out from La Sal hoping to do an interview and clean this mess up that I don't believe anyway, the mess that is, but people do, and well I just want to know 'cause I, having been in Nam and all, know things aren't as they seem and you, well, haven't said much about what happened over there, and well, there are crazy stories."

Babs looked at Gilda, who gave her a slight nod that I don't think I was supposed to notice. She went into the cabin and I was afraid she might be going after ammo. But she came back out with a kitchen chair and sat it down and signaled with her eyes that I should take it. I did. A little breathless. I almost tipped it over in my anxiousness.

We talked all the rest of the afternoon. All three women were engaging and lively conversationalists. Topics ranged from the life of the frisky squirrels found abundantly in the trees, to the writings of Hildegard von Bingen. For dinner Maggie cooked up a pile of Swedish pancakes, served with fresh butter, homemade blackberry jam, and tall glasses of milk. We had gotten lost in conversation since I arrived and other than some peanuts we had eaten nothing so the meal was rare ambrosia. I fear I embarrassed myself by the sheer quantity that found its way past my lips. They invited me to pitch my tent or sleep under the stars outside their cabin and after another long conversation we retired. But not before Gilda agreed to an interview.

"I cannot promise to tell you anything," she said, "but if I like the question I'll answer it." It was more than I had dared hope.

The following is a cleaned up version of three days of conversation. I agreed to allow Gilda to edit this final version for content and so it is published with her approval. She could be both frustratingly elusive and intensely profound. And sometimes banal to the point I could not keep my eyes open. Still it left me with the feeling that there is much we will never know about this author. However, she is neither the monster claimed by some, nor the fool championed by others—yet there is something otherworldly about her that draws me to believing she sees things others do not.

I recorded the conversations on my cassette tape recorder and they were transcribed by my assistant Mary Dent.

DK: Tell me about your life here. How did you come to settle in these mountains? What is your day-to-day life like?

GT: After Vietnam I drifted quite a bit preferring to be alone. I found the cheerfulness of others unbearable and I wanted to sort things out.

DK: Excuse me, sort what things out?

GT: The nature of things. What are we? Why are we here and how did we come to be. The usual questions. What are these relationships that all things share—living and non-living?

DK: OK.

GT: I went through a bad spell after a trip to visit an old friend in New York. My friend Babs came to my rescue. … Let me back up. My father had died a few years ago and she and my mother had conceived this plan to buy some property near Atlantic City, Wyoming and move in with me there, but they had trouble finding a place isolated enough, but then found this lovely spot here where we had vacationed a few times when I was young. So about three years ago my mother sold our farm and bought eighty acres up here and a place down in Moab for the winters.

DK: And this is where you write? What is your typical day like?

GT: Right before dawn we arise. Babs and I go for a walk around the lake …

DK: How far?

GT: About four miles, give or take. There is a path around the lake that winds its way around the marsh that gathers around the southern shore. There is an owl's nest near the eastern side of the lake and we often stop and converse with the owl—inquiring about her hunt. About once a week we stop to gather owl pellets, if any are to be had, and dissect them and write down in a logbook what she has been eating.

When we return mother usually has made a light breakfast often of either mush with raisins or biscuits. Then I sit at this table and write.

<Note DK: The table is an old solid oak table. On it lay words written in pencil and cut from an artist's drawing pad and cut into strips and arranged in combinations and patterns.>

DK: Is this how you write by choosing, cutting out the words and then arranging them into your books?

GT: Yes. Mostly. The patterns seem to arrange themselves, with me acting more as mere facilitator.

DK: OK, so how long do you write and arrange?

GT: About three or four hours.

DK: What do the others do?

GT: Mother often paints. Babs writes about the land here. She is working on a book of short stories and a book of essays. Sometimes she fishes or draws. We all read a great deal.

DK: What sort of books do you read?

GT: It's all over the map. We all like the classics. Babs adores Kurt Vonnegut and Ray Bradbury. Mother likes Nancy Drew and Hardy Boys. I like Thoreau and Emerson. But we often read each other's latest discovery. Our only trip down to Moab is often to visit the library.

DK: It sounds wonderful.

GT: It is. At night Babs has a large ten inch Dobsonian she pulls out …

DK: Dobsonian?

GT: A large telescope. She ground the mirror herself. We call it the 'beast.' We'll pull it out tonight if the clouds retreat.

DK: I'd like that.

GT: After a few hours or so of watching the stars, or knitting, or talking about the day, mother reads us the scriptures and we go to bed.

DK: Mormon scriptures?

GT: Yes, *The Book of Mormon* or Bible usually.

DK. And in winter you relocate to Moab?

GT: Yes.

DK: OK. To move on I'm going to read you something that I think you will find painful. But I think it is important to clear this up. This is from one of your fellow prisoners, Silke Peeters. She has been fairly vocal in her condemnation of you.

GT: I know.

DK: I should tell you I don't believe her. Or at least I don't want to.

GT: It doesn't matter to me if anyone believes her or not. What she says is not true.

DK: OK, but let me read what she said and we can go from there.

GT: If we must.

DK: She says in this translation of an interview in the German magazine, *Der Stern*:

She arrived with two others. The rest of us had been there about three months. We noticed she got special treatment from the very beginning and we suspected almost immediately that there was something odd going on. Our cells were in a long cement block building. Her cell was near one end, so that she could come and go without being seen by the rest of us. It was also the largest and had the best ventilation. While we would spend every day laboring in the fields doing backbreaking work she always stayed behind fucking the guards and giving sexual favors to the camp officers in horrible and unspeakable ways. She was paid well for it. While we were nearly starving she was well fed until in the end she was as fat as a pig. There was a squeaky mattress in her cell and on rainy days when we all stayed behind because it was too muddy to work, she would still be working the bedroll with whatever Cong wished it. She had no shame. Although she spent the day nibbling on delicacies and the fine food the officers ate, she would still line up with us and take a portion of what little food we were offered. One year there was a terrible famine and several prisoners died. We were like bones walking. All except Gilda, who was as plump as a Christmas goose. She claimed she was eating rats, as were many of us, but they gave little nutrition and were wily and hard to catch. An obvious lie.

When the Russians arrived they were so enamored with her sexual tricks they demanded of the Vietcong that she be allowed to go with them. She did not even hesitate. No one was sorry to see her go. She was a constant reminder that there are those in war who lose all their morals and turn into a corrupt and fetid shadow of what humans are supposed to be. She was a whore and now that she is some big deal novelist I find my mind even more disturbed about the attention she is getting. I find it disgusting that anyone can praise the work of such a vile creature.

GT: Sad. None of it's true of course.

DK: Why do you think she is lying about you?

GT: I don't think she is lying. I think she is mistaken. I did not work in the field because my missing hand kept me from handling tools. I suspect that because I was not there helping with the labor, resentment built and these are stories that came to them as a way to feed these resentments. My last year there I was treated very badly by my fellow prisoners. In the morning they would often be grouped together and some of the more vulgar soldiers grab their crotch and yell things like, "Hey, Trillim how about a piece of real meat rather than Gook sausages?" or "I'd offer you mine but I know you only eat Cong cock." The major would tell them to knock it off but he did it in a voice that let everyone know including me that I deserved it, but he was of a more chivalrous bent, and as such was against their lower standards. I laughed because I did not know what to do. After they left I would cry and wish myself dead.

DK: What did you do during the day?

GT: I sat in my cell.

DK: And did you grow fat?

GT: By camp standards I did not lose as much as they did. To them I likely did appear fat, but I was much thinner than you now see me. But I found a source of food that they did not enjoy.

DK: So you never slept with any of the guards?

<<Here she became very uncomfortable, agitated, and asked to be excused. She literally ran from the room. She did not return for several minutes, but when she returned she seemed composed. >>

GT: Where were we?

DK: I asked if you slept with your captors.

GT: No.

DK: OK. Did you have a mattress in your cell while they slept in straw?

GT: I slept as they did on a bamboo mat.

DK: If you did not work in the fields how did you spend your days?

GT: Largely bored almost out of existence.

DK: You've intimated that you had some life-changing experience. There are rumors from your stay in New York that you claimed that you trained rats.

GT: I will not say anything about that.

DK: Won't you tell me what happened?

GT: No. It was holy. Sacred.

DK: Shouldn't it be shared then? At least to dispel the claims by Silke Peeters?

GT: No, I will not share them.

DK: We could all use more stories of encounters with the sacred. Don't you think?

GT: The holy must be experienced. I stood alone. A single

individual in awe of what had unfolded into the world. To try to share it would cheapen it. Only two things could happen. One, you might believe me and take my experience and embrace it. Appropriate it. But you could only do so intellectually. It could only become another fact in the world. You might make rituals of it, or art, but eventually it would become codified, institutionalized, there would be authorized and unauthorized forms, sects.

DK: Wait. Are you saying that your experience was so profound that in hearing it I might start a new religion based on it?

GT: Maybe. But not likely. Let me give you the second scenario, which I think is what would actually happen. If I were to tell you, you would not believe me. You would strip it of awe and wonder. You would fossilize it. Solidify it into a mere supposed fact of a world that is subject to analysis, such that it might be accepted or rejected. But this happening was born into a world into which it will not easily fit, therefore by your lights it would have to be rejected. You would strip it of possibility and of actuality. Your only response could be to mock it. To ignore it. To declare me mad or simply a liar. All my experiences then would have to be reinterpreted to fit in this sterile world.

What scares me most is perhaps even I could be convinced by your dismissal. Maybe I could be brought to forget the wonder born in those soggy afternoons in a prison in Southeast Asia. Memory is a fickle thing. What if I tell the world and teams of psychologists and philosophers all agree that I am mad and proclaim it with such force and conviction that I cannot bear the weight of their wagging fingers at my story's impossibility? What if under their therapeutic eye they lead me away from my experience and clothe me in the garments of their skepticism? They might declare my memories the imaginations of a mind oppressed with the terror of my captivity. They might say it is a brain breaking under the strain of torture, malnutrition, degradation, filth, disease. Which is more likely, that Gilda Trillim lost her mind in a place where anyone would lose their mind, or that Gilda Trillim experienced a thing of such beauty and magnificence and breathtaking awe that it cannot be understood by the mortal mind? No, I will not tell you. To tell you will be to make it impossible. I know what I experienced and to lose that would be to lose everything. Do not cast pearls before swine and all that.

DK: So when others are presented with Peeters's story they must believe either your fellow prisoner's detailed accounts or believe you were engaged in activities so sacred and awesome and holy that in a filthy cinderblock prison, suffering the most humiliating and awful of conditions, that to tell them of it would strip it of meaning? Should we just trust you on this?

GT: Trust me? Heavens no. All I can do is encourage you to enter into the world with open and daring eyes and see how the wonder and grandeur of this world manifests itself to you. To trust me would be absurd.

DK: What is behind these manifestations? Is it God?

GT: Who cares? I see a thousand experiences that get co-opted as explanations for a thousand gods. I don't know what is behind them. I cannot even guess. Is it a person? Is it a force? Is it a mystery? Well certainly that, but of what kind? I don't care a lick for these metaphysics, proofs, and formal arguments. I like the way Wittgenstein said it, I'm paraphrasing, but it was along the lines: "There are many things in the world that cannot be said in words, of these things we must remain silent." I cannot tell you what happened because there are no words to describe them adequately. You would have to experience it yourself. If I used libraries upon libraries of words and descriptions, I would still be without the means to instantiate within you the awe, wonder, and beauty that attended the experience. Maybe poetry could draw it forth, but if so it would be by creating the experience in you anew, not by describing it. Scripture does this. I think that is what ritual does too. It does not describe, but instantiates. If done right. It draws forth the possible. It enrighteousizes and sanctifies the memory of the experiential event. Allows the holy to reaffirm its original presence and establish its sanction.

DK: There are hints that it had something to do with rats?

GT: (laughing) You won't give up will you. Next topic.

DK: Last night while we were sitting on the porch talking about the night sky, your mother said at a comment you made about evolution, "Oh she's an atheist." You countered, "Mom, I am as Mormon as you are." Tell me about your Mormonism.

GT: As I said above. I'm not interested in figuring out God. There are those who pencil in long lists of their attributes. ...

DK: (interrupting) Their?

GT: Mormons believe in a father and mother.

DK: OK.

GT: So anyway, there's the standard tags we hang on our God concepts: omniscient, omnipotent, omnipresent, full of love, on and on. We even make lists of things they are not. It's all nonsense. I don't care. I don't feel like I need to know *about* the Gods. I know them. My mother thinks I need to embrace claims about them, like that they have bodies, or they know everything, and are timeless. Not me. To me whatever they are, they are. I just know them through encounters. Claiming that I have to know *about* them before I know them is like saying I have to be able to know what your liver is like to genuinely know you. That I have to get inside your intestine and visit the inside of your digestive track to know the real you. He may be the lovely Caucasian bearded fellow my mother believes in or an advanced inter-dimensional space alien who has been around the block a few times. It doesn't matter. I know them. I've experienced something. I think Joseph Smith experienced them too and gave us some rituals that remember that event. But the thing we really need to draw from them is that we too can encounter the Gods. Rituals remind us to seek similar things. I love so much about my faith. I love that it insists that we find our own experiences with God. Or at least it used to.

DK: You attend church in Moab in the winter?

GT: Yes. I don't think they like me and don't welcome me much. But my Mom needs it and I suppose so do I.

DK: Let me ask you about your books.

GT: OK.

DK: Your books all embrace a technique where you make lists of nouns, adjectives, and verbs. How should we read them?

GT: Any way you want. The world is made of objects and connections of objects all the way down. There is nothing more. Nothing less. Relationships of relationships all the way down. My books are explorations of that realization.

DK: I'm a huge fan. I use them as a meditative device ...

GT: I cannot think of a better use.

DK:... but they are cheered as works of genius or panned as pure nonsense. How do you handle the critics' harsh dismissals?

GT: I just don't care.

DK: You don't care about God or critics. You are a brave woman.

GT: <<laughs>> Well, it's not like I'm trying to sell the film rights.

DK: So let me just ask some random questions I know people are curious about.

GT: Oh boy.

DK: How did you lose your hand?

GT: I was in South America and took a drug to participate in a vision quest. While my mind was roaming the universe, I fell into a fire and burned it off.

DK: Really? Wow that must have been some vision.

GT: The world is not ready for it <<She laughs as she says it in a mystical voice indicating she's not serious>>. I've written it up for *Look Magazine*. That is all I want to say about it. But in that vision I lost my hand. It's a bother mostly. Sometimes I ask myself that if the cost of my vision was my hand, was it worth it? No. Not really. I miss badminton. I miss the feel of my fingers in someone's hair. I miss playing the piano. I miss picking my nose with accuracy <<laughing>>, but we don't get to make these choices do we? We take what we are handed, or dehanded in this case <<laughs>>, and build our world from them. Right? What else can we do?

DK: Is there anyone special in your life? I know you are not married, but have you found your soul mate?

GT: Answering that would steal my mystique, wouldn't it? Besides, soul mates are a dime a dozen. Since shoveling shit is the main task in life, the real gift is finding someone who will muck out the stables with you.

The conversation roamed all over and held more profundity, and pathos, but this is what Gilda agreed to allow for publication and I honor her choices. Let me just finish with this. Gilda Trillim is one of the most intriguing people I've ever met. I will continue to read her books, and anything she writes. On my backpack home I pondered our days of conversations and am still thinking about them. And I want to close with this.

After our interviews I stayed two more days. On the morning before I left, I went fishing with the three women. Babs and Maggie had waded into the shallows and were fly-fishing, without much success despite the fish rising to midges all around them.

Suddenly, Gilda began pointing to things and naming them, randomly, haphazardly, without rhyme or reason. The particulars began to mount as she pointed at and named them or named something of which they were apart, e.g., "Knot from dead bole, part of a pine; antennal segment, part of the sensory organ of a Cerambycid beetle; #5 weight line, part of a fly-fishing pole; cloud, part of a system of atmospheric moisture; Soil fragment, part of a dirt clod; … " on and on she went. I thought she would tire, but she went for nearly half an hour.

Suddenly, she turned to me and asked, "How long do you think I could go on with this?"

I gave her a long incredulous look and said, "Well, forever by the look of things."

She laughed, put the long shaft of a seedy grass stalk in her mouth and leaned back onto her back and staring into the high mountain blue sky. She placed her hand and arm behind her head as a pillow and smiling said, "Oh, I could go on longer than that."

Vignette 17: Gilda Writes an Event. Circa Summer 1983

This erotic bit of prose was found folded into a copy of *The Sandpiper's Daughter*. It is unknown whether this was about actual events or was an excerpt from a creative work.

My hand on your naked shoulder drinks its warmth. Although it is dark and the night is moonless, I know it is freckled—the memory becomes part of the seduction.

My hand drifts onto your shoulder blade soft and firm then to the middle of your back—it is damp and I feel small imperfections as if it were a Braille message embossed there. Carefully, softly, I decipher each bump, each pimple. I slide my hand over your vertebrae, one by one, larger landforms of your body's topology become manifest, no less and no more precious than the smaller stipples that I still explore while attending to these new hills and valleys.

I feel you move closer to me. Snuggling. I feel your hand moving over my back matching my motions pulling me closer, pressing us together. My handless arm pulls you tight to me. My lips find your neck. I withdraw my hand from your back for a moment to pull the hair away from your nape. Your hand has reached between the shallow line that rises to meet my lumbar. Your finger runs up and down that separation, promising, teasing. I return the favor. I press against you harder, pulling you in with my spirit hand in a tight embrace. We are on grass like crickets rubbing their legs along their abdomen creating vibrations meant to draw others into this dance. This dance we too find ourselves moving in, ancient rhythms acknowledging the pull and push that drives us forward.

We slide to our knees. Our thighs and pelvises press together. We kneel face to face. A motion of prayer. Of supplication. A strain of longing makes purpose of our inhaled breath, our exhale communicates desire. You half whisper, half sigh—love from deep lung vowels held long. Then need and selfishness takes our quickening breath away. We kiss. Long. Wet. We fall to the side and my arm acts like a pillow for your head and we continue to kiss. Our hands are asking questions, querying, seeking elucidation, seeking signs and wonders. Flesh inquiring after flesh. Hunting among the tender softness of your skin on my skin.

Then.

There it is.

You find it.

My eyes cannot focus and urges, swift and necessary, contract muscles in ways for which I have no conscious control. I am no longer human. I am the cricket, the grass, the coyote that just barked striving, striving, striving forward from a shallow chaos to a deeper one.

Then again.

And again.

We slow and rest pausing as I try to bring you into the primal abandonment. I know you well and I don't think you will mind if I transmogrify your ears a size larger, and point your nose just a little sharper as you whisper in imagined Latin from Ovid:

Dicite "io Paean!" et "io" bis dicite "Paean!"

Decidit in casses praeda petita meos![1]

We are wet. You are resting on me, face in my neck. Buttocks forming a lovely white hill against the low sky, while I, facing the sky trace a satellite with my eyes as it dashes across a black sky splashed with stars.

We arise. You brush off my back—we've lain down on a cow pie. Hard to avoid. We laugh because it doesn't matter. We dress in silence. And walk back to where the others are waiting for us to return from a night walk.

Vignette 18: Letter from Trillim to Babs Lake from Nairobi, Kenya where Gilda was Teaching a Short Course in Writing. August 12, 1988

Gilda was invited to teach a short month-long course in writing at Nairobi University. It was funded by the National Endowment for the Humanities as part of a cultural exchange program.

Dear Babs,

It must be still Saturday there. You've driven down from the mountain with my mother and picked up a few things at City Market. Most of it common supplies like wheat, Bisquick, frozen fruit and vegetables, and peanut butter. But you've also picked up some exotic delicacies for Wednesday's Gourmet Crockpot Night. Which recipe have you pulled from your book? Will it be the Poulet a la Grecque you've been threatening to make? Or perhaps the Asparagus Mushroom Strata you've been promising my mother? (Now's your chance with me, 'Asparagus-hating-Gilda,' out of the picture.) You've just had a lunch at the Sundowner, likely the grilled trout, or the shrimp salad. You've stopped at the Post Office to see if I'd written. Now you head to the library to drop off the old books and browse the stacks until you find something that strikes your fancy. How I wish I was there.

Life in Nairobi this last week has been hectic. I'm still not sure why they invited me here. It seems strange. All of the other authors they've brought in through the endowment have been big names with more mainstream literary sensibilities. I can't help but wonder why me? Apparently I am a favorite of the Chair of the English Department, but will the students have heard of me?

Other than the heat, which wears me out and oppresses from the moment I step out of the door of my hotel, things have been delightful. My class has been enthusiastically attended. The university is lovely and I must admit I find the students as engaging, curious, and possessed of that rare intelligence that marks a thirst for learning found in climes that I know better. The classrooms where I teach are not air-conditioned and the rows of ceiling fans are no match for the late afternoon sun when everyone is so sleepy (including their teacher) that no one can push through the stifling warmth without a sloppy languor creeping into every attempt at sensible engagement.

Veal cutlets served at lunch do not seem to help my teaching either, but I do what I can to get my message across. 'Which is?' you might ask. You'll remember how uncertain I've always been about teaching. I really don't have any idea how I do what I do when I write so how could I teach it? My writing is organic and waddles out of me like toads from medieval mud by spontaneous generation. Can I teach them anything when I have no idea how I engage with the creative process? I realize that my writing emerges from the dust of my beginnings, framed and fashioned by the culture in which I grew up. I could at least encourage that. I can teach them to let their own culture flower into something that forms fruit.

Everywhere I turn I find stories that astonish and transform me. If the rest of the world could read what these students have lived through, the tracks of a thousand tears would trace a line from millions of eyes down the cheeks of as many faces that would given time, make a pool of such pathos that it would drown hate forever. Maudlin I know, but even so. There it is.

Yet, what's been most surprising is the common ground we've found in our discussions of religion. My students are of a mixed lot. Many Protestants, a good number of Catholics, a couple of Muslims, an annoyingly vocal atheist, and three who embrace traditional African religions.

Old habits die hard I suppose and too often I find myself going off topic and expressing my feelings on religion. I love that you have held onto your Jewish faith despite not believing in God. But poor me I don't know if I believe or not. It's neither that I do believe or don't, so here I sit and spin in a whirlpool that I wish would take me down or let me out, but on I spin, turning round and round swimming away from the yawning gapping center hole yet never moving toward the edge where I long for some sense of freedom.

Unicorns, I think, are a more common beast than me and my lonely faith and my hunger to be a Mormon, yet convinced that underneath it all there are more questions than answers. I've been thinking about something my mother said before I left. Something that will not leave me alone and gnaws at my innards like an unrelenting worm.

"Before you go, I want you to get a blessing from the Bishop," she whispered desperately to me the weekend before I left.

"A what? Rather than protect me it will likely cause a lightning strike." I acted shocked and put out. I hate when she does things like this to me. She knows my Mormonism is not hers and there is no way I was going to let this stranger declare a blessing on my head.

"Blessings have never hurt anyone," she snapped at me.

"Stop, Mom. I don't want one," I bit back.

"Look," she said, "I know you're an atheist, but it would be a comfort to me."

Atheist. That's what my mother thinks I am. But does it work? Does that fit? No. Atheism is a claim about what is not, theism is a claim of what is. I'm not making any claims. I stand in awe at what unfolds. Atheism is just creationism in disguise. It assumes some universe just pops into existence in all its complexity and now is just sitting here—a grand object jutting out of space-time that happens to have things like shoelaces, kangaroos, planets with rings, soap bubbles, old tomato cans, coffee plants, geckos, and maple seeds flitting on the breeze. Because time is an illusion, in their view, time and space are just a manifest glob sitting in this weird universe. It is worse than creationism in that nothing causes it. It just leaps out of nothing for the hell of it. This complex object we call the universe just is this strange manifold floating endlessly through existence.

Conversely, theism is just atheism in disguise. There's this thing sitting there in the middle of nothing contemplating itself in some sort of timeless la-la land, bored and lonely and then up and decides to create time and potato chips. In both these two extremes, there is always something that just happens to be there, in one a universe, in the other a God. Each pointing their finger at the other and declaring that their neighbor has no evidence for *their* beliefs. A childish game ensues with theists pointing to the atheists screaming: Unmoved mover! Natural Theology! Ontological Arguments! God Exists! God Exists! While the atheists wag their finger at the theists and say: material world is all we see! Is all that is! Is all that can be! Show me God working in the world! No Causal efficacy! No God is necessary! If God is not necessary God is not! QED! Neither one not seeing they are the same doggerel verse on two sides of the same limerick.

Kick them both up the side of the head! Why do they think they can figure this out? I think about that poem you shared with me, *What the Ant Knew*:

Every day, at a certain time
(with some variation)
when the sun was shining,
the informative sky would
darken only for a moment
then brighten again.

No one asked why,
(except her,

she was curious
for an ant)
her tiny brain spinning
around and around
trying to work out why
the darkness came
and where it went.

She would often pause
in her task, whether
it was in gathering
some bit of food,
or attacking her neighbors,
or swarming en masse
some marauding beetle,
she would consider
this puzzling aspect of her world.

The more she thought about it,
the less obvious it became
what could be afoot?
She realized
that perhaps she needed
a change in perspective.
So despite her wet-programming,
or perhaps because of it,
her tiny neural mass
click-clacked her away from
the colony.

Up up up she climbed,
until from a high place
she could survey the world.

She kenned the time of day
from the polarization
of the sun's light,
and at the appointed time
she watched.

It came,
a white blur,
pulling with it the darkness
she knew so well,
past the place where
her colony robotted
so far below.

Her sight was poor
(her senses more
attuned to olfactory needs),
so she moved her head
a tiny bit and waited
for the next day
when it happened again.
And again.

And again.
In her tiny memory,
each day, she stored
a bit of sensation,
a modicum of perception.

Each day she moved
her head
ever so slightly,
seeing at different angles
the busy white blur

the dragged the shadow
sliding with it.
Day by day.

Until one day she saw it
clearly,
fully,
white, square and holy.
So she went home
to gather food again,
to attack her neighbors,
and swarm en masse
a wandering beetle,
but this time when
the darkness
passed over
she knew something
the others did not.[1]

You told me once that the ant was watching the arrival of the
postman's truck. That the darkening was the shadow cast as he
delivered mail at nearly the same time every day. It knew nothing
of the societal network that formed the complex relations tangled
in the mail system. Or of the postman's fear of his wife's cancer
and the invention of a new treatment that gave him hope. It knew
nothing of the road or the machines that built it, or of the lumber
operation that milled the post to which the mailbox was affixed.

Ostensibly, we stand at the top of a great chain of being
hugging the knees of angels while we play at the foot of the
shepherds. But is it so tough to imagine that we are more like that
ant than the Olympians we fancy ourselves?

Umbrage must be taken against our arrogance. I dismiss all
knowledge about gods. Remember my vision? The vast ball of
existence that just sat there filling up all that is? That still makes

sense to me. I don't want to say that that is what I believe, because I don't. I did learn things through it. Not about ontology. No I learned something about my consciousness. About deep things within me. But I like the idea that we emerged from randomness, from chaos. Like in the opening lines of Genesis where God is brooding over the face of the waters, without form or void. That's something like what I encountered there at the edge of all beginnings before it exploded into an infinity of space, time and objects. I like that idea, but I cannot bring myself to think I'm right about the nature of existence. Too often we clutch too firmly what came to us accidentally and are we unwilling to explore new horizons. So I abandon the project of certainty. I wash my hands of surety.

A testimony? Like given in my Moab Ward? Sure why not? Would you like to hear it? OK. I have had encounters with something deeper than me. I sense it likes me. That it knows me. It wishes me well. It once, as I sat on the edge of insanity visited me as rats I loved died around me. It visited me in music of such beauty it kept me sane. Or maybe it didn't, but sane or not it was there for me. More or less. What it is, I make no claims about.

Realistically I know that my vision came in the midst of extreme duress and every psychiatrist worth his couch would wager on me having a bad trip freak out. But I was there and I had an encounter. I can't bring myself to disbelieve in it as thoroughly as I should. As hard as I've tried to make myself into a raving madwoman it doesn't work. My memories are too clear. My mental states too apparent. Its reality is remarkable.

Everyone who I've told, including you and my mom, have smiled and patted me on the head and looked for other explanations. You, I understand. You, an ultra reformed Jew situated in a firmly materialist universe, have no room for Heavenly Mothers or guiding shepherdesses. As you know I don't expect you to change your mind and I've encouraged you to just processe it however you feel comfortable. Our relationship is based on the joy we take in one another's company, similar interests, and shared experiences, not upon some metaphysical alignment or agreement on ontological commitments.

Enter my mother though. She has told me many times that she knows that Joseph Smith encountered God in a grove of trees. Her faith is founded on a boy who had an experience, not much different than mine (although his God did not have much style and not even close to having as fabulous shoes as mine did). Experience grounds all of the axial religions: Abraham, Jesus, Paul, Mohammad, St. Theresa, Hildegard von Bingen, Pascal, on and on, these encounters with something beyond this world become an access point to that something-beyond. Indeed, all of Mormon faith is about seeking an encounter with the divine. So why when I have one is it not authorized—I can't see any case of an encounter that was sanctioned by whatever religious community happened to be dominant at the time. It is only on the lonely road, the cave, the cell, in the desert, on the floor while a prisoner of war lies surrounded by an ensemble of singing rats that these seem to occur. And they are always personal, reluctantly shared, reinterpreted, but at the time it was just a one-on-one, 'I Am is here.'

Vacuous as it sounds even to my ears, I believe Joseph Smith when he says he saw a pillar of light descending over his head and two personages standing in a blinding white light. I trust his encounter was as real as mine. I sense big things afoot, as if the universe wanted to take these apes somewhere magnificent. Some place more beautiful and wondrous. I cannot guess what it is; I am an ant over which a shadow falls. I could give it a name. I could assign it attributes, or declare negative attributes of what it was not. I could call upon it for help in times of trouble, but not knowing what it is does not make its felt and sensed presence less real.

Encounters need not be interpretable to be meaningful. I remember my father when I was in my last summer before I left for college, became enamored with a set of books called, "The Lectures on Faith." He would lead us in discussions about them in Family Home Evening. He was obsessed with the idea that you could not really have faith in God without understanding his character, perfections, and attributes. Somehow the more we knew about these things the more we would trust him and have faith that he was leading us on to something good.

Ridiculous. What good would it be for the ant to discover that the postal truck was manufactured in Detroit? What would that add to the shadow that passes over her world every morning at ten o'clock? The shadow and the ant meet, perhaps by accident. Might it not be that bigger things are afoot such that the ant can never fathom their depth? Maybe my encounter on the floor of a Vietnamese lodge or Joseph's amid the hardwoods he was felling were the aftermath of the ebb and flow of events rocketing past of so massive or monstrously vast events that these encounters are nothing save something like the air whipped up in the fleeting vortices of a car passing an ant colony. Our brush with these higher passings is something like the shadow of the postman is to the formican denizens of the concrete cracks below the mailbox.

Yet. Yet that is not how it felt. Is it? I encountered most of all, love. The encounter was with love. That is my only claim.

That.

Heft.

I.

Noticed. And it.

Gripped me through and through. Emptied me. Grasped me to a core that I've not been able to wrestle from any object (and you know how desperately I've tried to find that nucleus and in every attempt was proved inadequate). Love ground me to existence and revealed something underlying all surfaces. Love seems more than adequate to unveil masked things, including things secreted in me. Love does that.

As always I am your,

Gilda

P.S. Hi Mom. I know you snuck and read this so I just want to say you taught me much about love. It infuses all that I am. Thank you.

Vignette 19: Trillim's Reflections on Bodies. Journal Entry. La Sals, September 6, 1988

This event has been used often to argue that Trillim was mentally unstable and prone to visions. Based on this event, literary critic Asaka Iguchi and psychological historian J'Kahla Khornezh have argued that there are clear indications of undiagnosed schizophrenia in Gilda Trillim's writings and especially in accounts such as the following.[1] This will come as a blow to these researchers because of the evidence I present in this portion of the thesis. This finding alone does not answer the question of whether she was mad, of course. However it does remove a rather prominent arrow from their quivers.

This entry also gives a sense of the depth of Gilda's Mormonism and its central tenet on the importance of embodiment (see for example, Faulconer's treatise[2] on the subject). Here she reflects on the centrality of the body for spirituality. A recurring theme for Trillim in much of her work. This is the most explicit treatment of that idea among all her writings.

The aspens are shimmering in the morning air, their pale green underside, the dark emerald top flipping back and forth creating a jitterbug that enlivens the already delightful sunlight streaming into our little valley. The carefree stream that falls from the western La Sals into Buckeye makes a lovely splashing sound and drowns out any other noise. I'm following the little rivulet up to a beaver dam that I like to watch.

I come to the dam, then skirt it and approach from the side, trying to creep closer to the pond where I take a position from which I can survey the giant rodents' work below me. I sit on a fallen aspen that they (I'm sure) have provided for my comfort by falling it and not dragging it away for their construction projects. Delightfully kind of them. I take out my sketchpad and try to draw the scene below me. It's a small pond, maybe an acre, and roundish, surrounded by aspens on one side and Ponderosa pine and scrub oak on the other.

I have two friends here. One is a strange otherworldly creation of my mind. The other is real. The fantasy apparition has appeared twice, both near sundown. The first time, I'd been relaxing by the pond drawing. I had just finished a sketch and set back to enjoy the magic that falls upon the place when the sun gets low, the shadows lengthen, and the stark lemon sun starts to sneak behind the La Sals. I fell into a late afternoon drowsy slumber; I awoke to find a small young woman standing on the other side of the water looking at me. By 'small' I mean strangely so, perhaps three and a half feet tall, but proportioned like an adult, not a child or a dwarf. She was a wild thing. Her hair was fierce and untamed, not long or short. She was dressed in a soft leather kirtle, but with a fey, otherworldly, shimmering purple shift beneath. A deerskin was draped across her shoulders like a cloak. On her feet were loose, well-fitting leather moccasins. Most strange of all she wore a silver tiara with a gorgeous star sapphire centered over her forehead. It was in that bit of detail that gave away that she was the creation of my own mind. I looked at her for a second and she looked at me and flipped me off; raising her middle finger with a look on her face that sent a chill down my spine. I rubbed my eyes with my fists and opened my eyes again and sure enough she was gone. I'd heard of this effect occurring when people awake suddenly and the mind continues in a dream state. I went to the other side of the pond and looked for a sign that she had been real, but it had been unusually dry that season and there were no tracks of any kind.

However, I saw her again. Or I think I did. This time she was buck-naked with a small bow in her hand. I came upon her while I was hiking up near Taylor Flats in late summer. I saw her down a sheer embankment following a small stream through some thick dark aspens. I had taken a small cattle trail off of the main road and as I rounded a corner I looked down the draw and saw her as clear as anything. She looked up at me and leapt away, her white butt flashing as she fled. Babs thinks it was a mule deer with its white bottom doing the same. It's true the mind can play tricks, but it seemed so real to me! I suppose that scores of Bigfoot sightings are bears or elk in which people are sure they saw the monster instead[3].

Today I see my other friend. My real one. Or rather her manifestation flying below the water creating a moving chevron traced out in the tiny waves that mark her passing. It surfaces, its brown back and flat black tail exposed. It's the female. I've named her Beth because I'm unimaginative and have decided to give them all names that start with 'B.' I watch her gliding along the surface. She dives again, and heads directly for the lodge in the center of the pond—a large dome of piled sticks that serve as a nursery and sleeping berth.

She has a wondrous beaver body. What would that be like? To swim, to have teeth that can gnaw through the trunk of an aspen, to have the strength to pull a felled tree a hundred yards and then swim it into place for a dam of one's own construction and design—and to be driven so to do? To feel compelled to cut another tree, to pull it to just the right place in the dam? What would having such a body be like? One that could swim in icy winter water? One with webbed feet that would give purchase to those motions that propelled it through the pond like a proper water dweller. Like a fish. Bodies are such remarkable things. We need them. They define us and our place in the universe. They allow us to be who we are. I love my body. Do beavers love theirs?

The bodies of my rats were essential to their singing. Their claws grasped minute protuberances, each chosen by their relationship to how it allowed them to position their bodies on the wall. Their angle, given in relation to Earth's gravity, was facilitated by tiny imperfections in the surface of the wall that determined, for example, how spread out their legs were, how hunched they had to hold their back to keep from losing balance and tumbling to the floor. The little holds fixed just how akimbo each limb had to be positioned in relation to the others— sometimes their front legs were pulled far forward and perhaps one back leg was pulled in close to the body while another was held at a distance at an odd unnatural angle (where 'odd' here is in reference to their normal gait while scurrying through a field or up a tree). These body positions, held in reference to multiple forces, (e.g., the topology of the wall, gravitational fields, frictional forces determined by the humidity, or the growth of some odd mold, algae, or lichen, or the pattern of air flow or circulation, or what sorts of things adhered to their claws like slimes or muds, etc.) must have affected their song. Perhaps their bodies being stretched too far, in some cases, their lungs held less capacity and influenced how long they could hold a note, or by being contorted in some strange way it conditioned the timbre or quality of their musical expression. As such, each concert was a unique moment in the universe's existence. Never to be repeated. All because they, like us, are embodied. All their muscles, neurology, the keratin mesh molding their claws, their whiskers sending messages to their brains adding nuance to its position and place in the universe, their tails providing the balance their body needs to move properly, all combine to create the music.

And their bodies do not just exist in relation to the physical world as given, but stand apropos of other bodies that add another layer of positioning with which they must engage. A given rat finds itself not just in physical fields of force, but social ones as well—how far must I arrange myself from my enemies? How close to my friends? Does a rat notice the quality of their song in the context of another's? Does this influence how they want to place themselves on the wall? As in, 'I sound so much better above so and so, and to the right and below of that person?' Who's to say rats, highly social creatures indeed, are not placing themselves to their best advantage in creating beauty in concert with their neighbors?

It is in the bodies of rats that all this music is integrated, and defined, and this rarified materialized manifest bubbles into the world as something new and wondrous. Bodies. What wondrous things they are and what a poorer world this would be if we were but some kind of ghost or spirit. It seems to me that this is where the freedom of expression found so abundantly in the universe flowers and fruits. For it is only in such a feeling thing, integrating across myriad fields, that the interest in placing oneself in relation to other existences emanates and springs new into the universe, creating novelty. Or so I believe.

Babs is ringing the lunch bell. My mother has promised to make toasted cheese sandwiches for lunch, which I often make when it is my turn to craft our noontime repast, but somehow my mother's are superior in every way. A work of art. My mother, cheddar cheese, butter, bread, and a searing skillet, are without question one of the universe's most pleasing creations.

Vignette 20: Fragment from *Travel Magazine* Article: "Dreams of an Ancient Kingdom: Remembering Old Siam" by Rose Butler. Published Jan 15, 1989

..After leaving Wat Pa Udom Somphon, where we spent three days meditating with one of Somdet Phra Maha Ghosanandaays's students, we traveled to Wat Phra That Choeng Chum. This is a seventeenth-century temple built on the site of an eleventh-century Khmer ruin. Built over the footprints of four previous incarnations of the Buddha. We came to see the praying rats. According to our local guide about a year ago the rats arrived and began to gather, once a day, on the walls of the temple and offer prayers by chirping wildly for several hours before departing into the forest.

We arrived just as the rats began to crawl into the temple. The rodents were massive beasts of a Southeast Asian variety that put our black and brown American city rats to shame. It took verve and strong resolve to stay in a room filling with such loathsome creatures, but we kept our courage and waited with them as they formed small groups on the walls. As if on cue, they begin to squeak out their outlandish mousy prayers. Gathered in packs each cluster seemed to be taking turns offering what blessings were being pronounced in their peculiar high-pitched rat language. We listened to these for almost an hour and when we finally left they showed no sign of giving up. Our guide explained that the monks believe that they are announcing a new incarnation of the Enlightened One. Who can say they are wrong? It was an eerie and otherworldly experience. And I wondered what they were really doing (please forgive my doubting the monk's interpretation). Have they been trained by the monks to draw in the tourists and other pilgrims? It is hard to say, but I can offer without hesitation that it was decidedly worth the detour to hear these marvelous creatures shout their barbaric yawp to the world.

After that we returned to Sakon Nakhon for a fabulous meal at Apha, then back to our hotel for a sound night sleep before flying back to Chiang Mai.

Vignette 21: Gilda's Write-Up for Her Mother's Funeral. It Was Not Used there for Unknown Reasons. July 13, 1989

The impact of Gilda's thought, writing, and life are best under-stood in light of her relationship with her family and especially her mother. Her sense of spirituality was deeply conditioned by the way she was raised and how it influenced her view of the world and her place in it. It is well understood that the other western writer with whom she is often compared and contrasted, Wallace Stegner, was deeply influenced by his relationship with his father. Richard W. Italian writes, "Perhaps as much as any major writer of the West, Stegner drew heavily on his own family history to represent the spiritual values he was beginning to hold. He employed the divergent and conflicting attitudes of his parents to illustrate tentative conclusions about his own journey. Pen portraits of George and Hilda Stegner appeared in his novels, stories, essays, and autobiographical works."[1]

This could as easily be said about Trillim, and I think research on understanding Gilda's work and her relationship to her family is an area where future study needs to focus.

This piece though makes explicit this connection. This write up was to be read at her mother's funeral, but for unknown reasons was not. It may have been that her largely Mormon extended family was uncomfortable with the idea of a woman giving blessings, even though the practice was well established in the early centuries of the church.[2]

Just a week before she died my mother blessed me.

Her sister had given her a box of letters, notebooks, and other odds and ends that her own mother had secreted in several old cigar boxes. One was a small diary about the size of a deck of playing cards. It had a blue cover and the pages inside were ruled with delicate lines of the same color. Its entries listed people her mother had laid hands on and given a blessing with the date of the blessings, the person administered to, and a small sentence or two on what the blessing contained. Like this:

July 15, 1901. Agnes Blomquist. That her knee's swelling would go down that she might continue to serve the Lord.

August 25, 1901. Sister Calamine, Pres. Davison's wife. That her breasts would flow with milk that her baby might be healthy and strong. **

September 11, 1902. Mathilda Linford. That the fever might abate and she might rise up to care for her husband and tend her children. **

September 20, 1902. Bertha Tanner. That her back may knit itself back together from her fall from her horse's saddle.

December 15, 1911. Dotty Franklin. That the unease of her mind abate and she find calm and joy in her current troubles.

March 8, 1919. Alissa Blick. That the polio not take her life and she find the strength to recover from this afflicting disease and should her legs remain ever bent that she might learn to love her affliction and serve others so affected. **

The entries were all for women and a few young children. Stars seemed to indicate that the blessing had been efficacious. All in all, there were 213 blessings from 1898–1919. My mother had forgotten, and I never knew, that women within the Church had once given blessings. She remembered her own mother giving her blessings when she was a little girl, but the practice had somehow disappeared from the Church.

This book deeply affected my mother. She often carried the book with her into the woods and she would read it over and over sitting on a log near the lake. A few days before she died, she decided to write a book of poetry based on each entry, somewhat in the spirit of *Spoon River*, a book she adored. She only wrote two.

She laid on hands without a drop of guile,

On Katie Tidwell's burning braid.

The girl lay in fever wild,
Beyond the doctor's clever aid.

But lo, through power deep and mild,
The destroyer was at last unmade.

When she showed it to me, I was in a sour mood and suffering severe cramps and just said, "I've seen you do better." Although it was true, it was unkind and unnecessary. She looked at me disapprovingly and walked away. A few days later she brought this to me saying, "This is likely no better, but want your opinion."

There is little doubt that she
associated with the stars—

my grandmother's grandmother
one of the Lord's humble beggars.

Who crossed over cold Wyoming
dust, an act of faith,

she, like the heavens knew well
her course and pace.

Considering now the same starry
orbs that she once knew

I wonder how the texture of
the trail affected the view—

the smell of the campfire;

the rain on the sage;

small mice rustling through
unguarded forage;

the graceful pop of a
slow burning fire, sending

reluctant sparks skyward
to the stars appending;

the shake and whinny
of a nervous horse,

the quieting whisper
of calming support.

And when sorrow troubled
this earthly frame?

To the fevered sickbed
the gifted women came,

to ease the burning of a
chilled, fevered child;

by giving a blessing
calming and mild.

With graceful hands
they laid hands on head;

A mother in Zion's
command "rise from your bed."

The landscape has changed
I, just a sixteenth her genes,

look also to the sky—where light
from the city now intervenes

only the brightest stars I see—
recalling the hand that holds them,

in majesty and power, was not as baffling
to root as it now seems to stem.

I burst out crying. I hugged her and told her it was beautiful. She
was pleased and I was blubbering away like a sentimental mush.

"Mom. There are no city lights out here," I said, taking her by
the hands and kissing her.

"Artistic license," she said, tears mounting in her eyes. And
now I find myself doing so again as I write these words because
this was the last thing she would ever write. I now find it
beautiful beyond description.

Two days later I was feeling upset because of something I read
in a travel magazine. I was anxious and visited by old ghosts that
stripped sleep away and reunited me with fears I thought slain
and buried. My mother noticed and asked if anything was wrong.
I spoke my worries and she asked if I would like a blessing.
Something about this touched me more deeply than I thought
possible; I stared at her for a long time trying to understand what
this meant. It was such a rewrite of the way I knew my mother
had been in the past when in everything she had bowed to
priesthood authority. To offer to give me a blessing? I could not
imagine what she was saying. Finally I nodded.

She was nervous. I was nervous. A chair was pulled from the
kitchen table and placed in the center of the meager living space
of our cabin. It sat there alone, waiting while we stood staring at

it. Uncertain how to proceed. How many times as a child had a seat been placed thus and my father stood behind it? We would sit down, back straight. Anticipating. Then in silence we would feel his rugged hands stationed on our head and blessings rich and powerful spoken from sources as deep as the universe.

My mother looked at me and indicated the chair with her eyes. I gave a slight nod and bravely mounted the seat. My mother stood behind the chair and like my father used to in times of need and placed her hands upon my head. She spoke, and I felt that same rich spirit that used to attend such blessings. The words flowed from her dulcet and luscious voice with that same cadence I knew from a childhood of priesthood blessings:

Gilda Trillim, by the power of being a woman and mother, and by the authority granted me of God, I lay my hands upon your head to give you a mother's blessing. Gilda, you have wandered far and wide in this world and seen things that are terrifying and full of beauty. Our Heavenly Father and Mother know you. They feel the depth of your soul and even though you do not know them as you once did, still they watch over you. They love you.

Your heart is troubled by the things you have heard. Fear not. God is working wonders in this world and you have assisted in drawing forth the beauty and wonder that is to be. Again, I say unto you, fear not. Look again into the teachings that your mother and father have taught you. Gilda they love you.

You must go and see the things that have troubled you. Be brave. Angels are with you. They will bear you up in these times of need. And need them you will, for your Mother cannot always be with you. I bless you with the health you will need to complete your life's work. I bless you that your mind and heart will be strengthened for the tasks ahead. I call upon you to be a savior on Mount Zion—to be a redeemer of things great and small. I seal these blessings upon you in the Holy and Sacred Name of Jesus Christ. Amen.

She is gone now. Three days later Babs and I had morning

coffee, but my mother did not appear as she usually does for her cup of Postum. We did not worry because sometimes any of us might sleep a little longer if we had stayed up watching the stars or stayed up late reading. But at 10 am, I wanted to check because sleeping this late was highly unusual.

I peeked into the room. The sun was coming in from the south-facing window. The pane was open a crack and the air seemed virginal—that invigorating freshness I always imagined came fresh-breathed from the Ponderosa pines and Gambel oaks that pressed close around the cabin. My mother was tucked into her covers, a patchwork quilt she had made many decades ago of red gingham and light blue patches. Her eyes were closed and her white hair as perfect as when she went to bed. Her face was relaxed giving her a weighty seriousness rather than the smile that usually played about her lips. She was perfect. Completed. I collapsed in tears in the face of such holiness.

Vignette 22. Babs Lake's November 3, 1996, Letter to Her Mother

The last entry of this thesis will be a look at Gilda's death. More has been written on this event than any other aspect of her life. The controversy is fierce, with different factions taking multiple sides, launching volleys at their enemies and erecting towers to defend their particular theories. I cannot do justice to the many divergent views on her demise. I am convinced that dissertations will be written for centuries to come about her end.

We have spent some time in this thesis examining her life from different sides and I will now try to outline the two main schools of thought that interpret her life from opposite poles. Of course there are branches, nuances, and forks off of these two threads, but most fall into one of the two camps.

In the first, call it *A*, Gilda was mentally ill. Psychotic and profoundly disturbed. A few speculate she was bipolar.[1] In Vietnam she was a camp whore. The rat story was cover for deep psychological trauma, or an outright lie. Her death was nothing but an orchestrated Christ-complex. Researchers of this persuasion see her death as a manic episode in a life that demanded constant construction from the ground up of a narrative that began in her imprisonment and continued to grow and develop in the years after. To them the surrounding detailed story was largely a mythology perpetuated by Lake's refusal to face the truth of Gilda's madness. In other versions, Lake was an actual accomplice in Trillim's deceptions. This faction also tends to discount Trillim's creative work. Although this is not universal. A preponderance of the *A* school does not recognize the literary worth of her strange minimalist novels. They see them as mere "word lists," as critic Melvin Steward claims, "with no more meaning than what my wife intends when she hands me a note detailing what groceries I should pick up on my way back from the university."[2] Margery Tobkin says, "Whatever meaning people take from her novels, is nothing more than what they put into her work. Trillim is like a funhouse mirror that distorts and returns again what is put into it. It reflects nothing that was not there in the first place."[3] This group is the most dominant faction in American and Western European Trillim studies. This perspective is overtly naturalistic. Its advocates do not hold with any of the mystical elements that Gilda's story demands if taken at face value. This group has also produced a number of psycho-analytic interpretations of Gilda's writings, casting them with a Freudian or Lacanian spin to try to offer interpretations on what she was doing in her outrageous claims and stories (for examples see Sandra Lightfoot's excellent review[4]). I have read many of these and find them fascinating and in some ways compelling. Their views are constructed carefully. They pay attention to intriguing details in her life that seem to make a strong case for a troubled and unstable personality disorder that, after Vietnam, descended to a clearly manifest mental illness. They are all grounded in thoroughly naturalistic interpretations of the events in her life.

The second faction, *B*, believes that Gilda must be taken on her own terms. Her words are those of a sincere seeker, neither mentally ill nor a charlatan creating an elaborate hoax. I must admit that I am of this persuasion. Having spent a great deal of time poring over her journals, reading her letters, and seeking to understand her views, I find a deep sincerity in her voice. She never shies away from painting herself as imperfect or off kilter, and seems to expose her deepest questions with curiosity and with an authenticity that strikes me as genuine. She *was* troubled. That is clear. But did it lead to the kind of psychosis that the *A* group promotes? I don't think so. Indeed, I think the *A* machine exists solely because her account has no place in their Umwelt. It is a kind of naturalistic heresy that brokers no explanation in the tick-tock world of matter in motion. A rat choir breaks all the rules of parsimony. It tramples on Popperian science. It bulldozes over materialistic regularities like so many sandcastles before a rising tide. What do we make of Gilda and her rats? Those who look for alternative explanations jump through a maze of hoops to ignore the simplicity of her story and construe madness as the best explanation for what she relates. With no other corroboration for this view in any other aspect of her life, they must assume madness from the story itself. They then spend much time spinning why it manifests itself in no other way, while those who believe her story get to have a consistent and compelling Gilda at every stage.

I must admit accepting her story requires a bit of creative framing. And there's the rub. One can keep naturalism, but then one loses the parsimony and is required to construct a shaky house around the multiple events in which she is acting more or less as any of us would. Yet by accepting her 'as is' one enters into a strange *Twilight Zone*-like world where the foundation of one's understanding about how the universe works requires a new framework. Neither option is appealing. I suppose that's why the two groups continue to contend—either way the evidence is just not there to render a verdict. One requires a complete rewriting of naturalistic metaphysics, the other a complete contextualization of the reported events and the addition of multiple ad hoc hypotheses: madness, bouts of sanity, conspiracies among actors, e.g., Babs Lake, Gilda, travel magazines accounts of praying rats that one must argue correlate only loosely with Gilda's story, the creation of a rat music, and in the end, explaining her novels as meaningless lists, while at the same time sensing a profound artistic ability in her paintings, poetry, and other written works. Both groups are forced to give up precious things.

Neither option seems like a good one. Perhaps someone will offer a tertian quid, but for now I find it easier to swallow the Trillim I know from her texts and paintings than the one constructed by those who don't want to believe her own narrative.

Now on to her death.

Trillim's Death

In March of 1996, it appears Gilda may have been diagnosed with a serious disease. She had been spending summers in the La Sals; however, after her mother died in 1989, she started spending winters in Wisconsin with Babs's family. These years are poorly documented. Gilda became less interested in keeping a detailed journal and focused on her books. Whatever the disease was, there is no direct reference to it in her writings. My interviews with Babs's aged parents suggest it may have been a type of cancer. We do know she went to Grand Junction, Colorado for two days. This was unusual. The hospital there had a fire that destroyed most of the records in 1999, so we don't have direct evidence once again that she was there, but there is enough circumstantial evidence that it appears likely. This evidence has been carefully examined in Karen Franks's 2008 study on this issue.[5] It was during this time that Trillim wrote her starkest and darkest works.

While most scholars buy the story that Trillim had some form of cancer or degenerative disease, I will offer my interpretation after examining Babs's description of her last days. That spring Gilda began to sell off many of the things she loved: her home in Moab and many of her possessions. She also deeded her cabin near Buckeye to Babs. Following this, she and Babs flew to Thailand with apparent intentions for it to be an extended visit. Some speculate it might have been some sort of treatment with alternative medicine not available in the US.

Now, as most of the details have been hashed over and over again, I'll let the full tale of Gilda's demise be told through Babs Lake's letter from Bangkok to her mother, dated November 3, 1996.

Dear Mom,

My heart is breaking into so many pieces. When I called you last week with the horrible news of Gilda's death, you offered to fly out here to be with me. I told you I was OK. I'm not. Please don't come, though, I'm coming home soon—I've put the details at the end of this. I feel so lost in this foreign land. And without Gilda I'm not coping well. I should come home sooner but it will be a few days—I need to understand what happened. I need to watch to see if the rats come back. I need to understand their song. To hear what Gilda heard. To understand how they remember her. I know this sounds crazy. It sounds crazy to me too.

The day before she left she seemed more chipper and light-hearted than I'd seen her in ages. She made jokes and appeared almost giddy with excitement. She was like a little girl. Of course, she wanted to come here ever since she read about the singing rats many years ago, but her excitement seemed beyond even this. I should have realized something was up, but I was just so pleased with her mood I didn't want anything to spoil it, especially with some ill-founded suspicion that she was masking what she really was going through.

Mom we don't drink a lot, but that night Gilda kept plying me with Lao-Lao a local Saki. She was making toasts and tossing them down. I now suspect she was not drinking at all, but knocking me out so she could make a clean getaway. It worked.

It was almost noon before I could crawl out of bed. My head felt like someone had split it open with an oak beam and filled it with cotton. Even the smallest noises sounded like a jackhammer going off in the room. I sat on a chair trying to gather my wits, asking for Gilda, but getting no reply. When I realized she was not in the hotel room I didn't think anything of it—I just assumed that she had gone out for some supplies, or for a quick snack. About three o'clock, I started to get a little worried. I took a long hot shower and dressed. It was now nearly four. I was just looking for the room keycard to go out and see if I could find her

when I noticed that she had left a note on the writing desk. This
is what she said,

Dearest Babs,
You are on the bed snoring. You look lovely.

I must go see the rats myself. I can't explain, but this is
something I must do alone. Please don't take offense. It's not that
I don't want you there, it's just that ... I can't explain. Just trust
me. I'll be back in three days. Just go to the Chatuchak Market
and shop to your heart's content. I'm fine. Really. I feel better than
I have in months. I have to do this alone.

Love,
Gilda

I called the concierge and he confirmed that Gilda had arranged
for a 6 am flight to Sakon Nakhon and had taken the shuttle to the
airport very early that morning. The next flight was not until the
same time the next day. I hung up not knowing what to do. Gilda
has traveled the world. I knew she could handle herself. I felt
hurt that she wanted to do this alone, but I understood. But I was
overwhelmed with terror for her because I was afraid that seeing
the rats again would trigger some terrible anxiety or flashback to
the awful things she suffered, and that would send her over the
edge. If that happened she would need me there. I had to be with
her. But what if I flew out there and could not find her? I didn't
know where she was staying. I paced back and forth in indecision
for a long time. When I finally made up my mind it was nearly
time to go to the airport. I left a quick note in case Gilda returned
before I did and fled the hotel.

It was the longest flight of my life. Every minute was agony.
When I arrived I did not know what to do. I'd brought nothing
but my small book bag filled with some necessities. I stared at the
wall of taxi drivers, hawkers, and pickpockets (I supposed)
waiting outside the barrier separating the small baggage claim

area from the outside world and burst into tears. I sat on the ground and just bawled. A kind Thai gentleman in an extremely expensive business suit who had just picked up his bag off of a luggage cart stopped and squatted beside me and said in nearly flawless English, "Can I be of any help?"

I don't remember what I said, but I know I spilled my guts, fears, and terror out in one very, very long sentence. He listened patiently then said, "Here is what you will do. I will share a taxi with you to the Dusit Hotel. It is very nice and they speak English very well. You will check in there. There I will arrange for a driver to take you to the Wat where you think your friend may be. He will wait all day until you are ready to return."

He helped me up and I waied and cried and he waied back with a big smile. He was as good as his word. I soon found myself riding in the back of a taxi to the Wat Phra That Choeng Chum where Gilda believed the singing rats would be found. I was so anxious I could not enjoy the ride. The forested landscape only reminded me that this must be very similar to the place Gilda had been held captive for so many years and left me wondering what effect this might have had on Gilda when she arrived.

We pulled up to the Wat and oh, Mom, there she was like a miracle shining in the sun, her floral dress catching the breeze. I walked over hesitantly, afraid I was in for a lecture or worse for having followed her, but when she saw me her eyes lit up and she hugged me and said strangely, "I knew you would find me."

All I could answer was, "Of course. I'll always find you."

"I know. That's why I called you here. I needed you to be with me for this."

"You did not call me here. You tried to run away from me!"

"No. I called you to me by running away."

"I never understand you."

"Come. See this."

She took me by the hand and led me into the Wat.

It was filled with large rats. They were everywhere. Gilda told

242

me the stories of her experience with rats in Vietnam, but the raw reality was beyond anything I expected or that I can even now describe.

Involuntarily, I let out a scream and backed out of the ruin saying, "Eww!"

I have known Gilda for many years and I would have bet my vinyl record collection against a jellyroll that I had seen every face she could muster, but the amalgamation of horror and reproach that contorted her face made me step back in fright.

However her anger quickly faded and she said, "Oh Babs. These are my friends."

We went back into the temple together and we watched the rats scurrying about, eating grain provided by the monks, getting into occasional tussles over some scrap or some favored position in some hierarchy visible only to them. Every once in a while they would sing, which would delight the visitors thereby. But it was not like Gilda's or the travel magazine's version. They did not take up special positions. Instead a few would start squeaking, and this would spread like a wave to the others, who would offer a few chirps and it would ripple through the rats and it would die down again. It all seemed rather accidental, despite how unusual and otherworldly. When it had gone quiet again, whatever people remained would clap with delight. Every time this happened, I looked at Gilda. She would frown and seem confused as she watched this display. Tourists were passing in and out, but we remained. As the afternoon stretched into evening and these visitors thinned then finally abated, Gilda suddenly raised her arms in dramatic fashion like a conductor calling an orchestra to attention, her eyes fixed on the rats milling about the temple, and her posture full of intent. Yet they did not so much as look at her. She made the same motions again, then again. She looked at me and in a panic said, "I don't understand. Yesterday they let me lead them in song just like I used to." She tried again several times, but to no avail.

"Perhaps it's me?" I said.

She did not answer but a look of hope graced her brow for a second.

Forgive me, mother, but for the first time I wondered if there was something wrong with her mind. I worried that she may be slipping into madness, but then if it was madness it must have been a long one because she often told of her time with the rats. She seemed so normal in every respect. And now so broken in retrospect.

We took a cab back to her hotel and picked up her things and then came back to mine, which had a much larger room. She seemed so strange and withdrawn. Her face was white and pale. I was frightened and I suggested we get something to eat, but she said she wasn't hungry.

She got a strange look on her face and said almost in a whisper, "I'm dying." I chided her and told her she had a long time yet. That she was just sad the rats had not sung and that I was sure they would sing tomorrow.

She smiled sadly and said, "Babs whatever happens just know it is for the best." Now I was crying and telling her in no uncertain terms that she should quit talking like this. That we were going back to Bangkok and that this had been a bad idea from the start and that we even ought to go back to the States. She became quiet and subdued like she was literally detaching from the world. She reached into her bag and pulled out a copy of her mother's scriptures—an enormously thick work that contained the entirety of the Mormon canon: *Bible, Book of Mormon, Doctrine and Covenants,* and *The Pearl of Great Price.* She opened it up and asked me to read something to her. It was from the New Testament.

I refused and pushed the scriptures back into her hands. I told her that I'd had enough of this seriousness and that we were going to go get something to eat: "You can't do this to me now. You are acting really really weird."

She finally consented and we went out into the night. We stopped and had some fish head soup in a coconut broth and Thai steamed rice. I'm not sure she had eaten since she arrived and I knew this would do her a world of good. In Thailand it is the tradition when you begin a meal to first take a small bite of rice to show gratitude for the gift of this vital grain. Gilda picked up a bit of rice with her chopsticks and raised it to her lips then paused and offered it to me instead. I took it gladly then I offered her a similar offering from my plate. For some reason this made her silly with delight. The mood shifted to one of strange gaiety. The food was delicious; we were laughing and telling jokes. Some people in the karaoke bar next door were singing rounds of Elton John songs, songs that both Gilda and I loved, and we found ourselves singing along; *Tiny Dancer*, *Daniel*, and a few others. The singers varied, but for the most part, and despite heavily accented English, they were quite good. When finally they sang *Candle in the Wind*, with Gilda and me adding our poor harmonies, I looked up and I found Gilda crying. I noticed I was too. She reached over and took my hand, then took her napkin and pressed it against my eyes.

"You remember this night, OK?"

She said it with such pathos and so emphatically that I could do nothing but nod and add, "I won't forget. But you remember it too."

She finally smiled, her teary eyes lit from the bright lights surrounding the restaurant and said, "Of course."

We walked through the bustle of the town arm-in-arm and came to a place offering foot massages. The funny thing was she insisted we go get one. She had to talk me into it, as I was not really too keen on the idea of having a stranger playing with my feet. But for Gilda's sake I followed her through the red door emblazoned with a golden dragon. She went first so I could watch. They soaked her feet in a bowl of steaming water then washed them with soap and dried them with a thick white towel.

After, they took a delightfully strange smelling oil, the odor of which I have nothing to compare. It seemed neither floral nor pungent like eucalyptus, but it was not unpleasant. Just different. They rubbed her feet for about fifteen minutes. Next it was my turn. I sat on the chair and placed my feet in the warm water. It felt amazing. When it was time to wash them however, Gilda insisted that she be the one to wash my feet. I protested, but she was very insistent and given how worried I was about her and because she seemed to be having so much fun I let her do it. The Thai woman who was going to rub my feet protested but a 10,000 baht bill from Gilda backed her off quickly.

Gilda took off her skirt and wrapped the big towel around her and knelt on the wet cement floor. It was not an especially dirty floor but the soap and water of a thousand customer's feet lingered there and the possibility of an infection or a fungal disease was all I could think about. I was protesting but she quieted me and washed my feet with the soap, dried them, and then rubbed both of my feet with the fragrant oil. I tried to relax and it did feel good, but I was worried about Gilda, nervous, and not thrilled with her doing this. Frankly I was glad when it was over. But it took a while because she was determined to give me the full treatment.

As she massaged my feet she told me a story of when she was in Norway living in the old farmhouse up on one of the fjords. She said she was thinking about the connections between things both animated and unanimated. One day, she said, she was gazing up the steep sides of the cliffs that framed that little hamlet, looking at the trees, the rocks, the water, the beauty of the white snow, the houses, and all the things, all the objects linked to varying degrees, some tightly bound like the trees in the soil, or some loosely—the road she stood on, the water of the sea that lapped the sides of the pier at the end of the road. Then she looked up from the floor and said, "We never really realize all our connections do we? And we never even realize what we are? Or how time structures all the connections that frame and define us." It struck me as strange and irrelevant. Here we were in the tropics and she is talking about Norway and connections between things. She looked up from my feet and smiled and said as if she were reading my mind, "It's just that the rats will need rituals. Something to sing about. Something to ground their practice and performance. They need a memory."

"I'm not following," I said this curtly. I wanted to understand what she was saying but it really was making no sense.

She smiled up at me, "I know. I'll be quiet." Then she continued to rub my oiled feet. Looking back, I wonder why these were her last thoughts. Why did she make this her last real conversation with me?

When it was over she replaced my shoes, replaced her skirt, took me by the arm, and led me back out into the street. The events of the day were starting to wear on me. The lack of sleep. The panicked flight from Bangkok. The strange arrival. The events at the temple. Gilda's bizarre and upsetting behavior had all worn me to a frazzle and I started to feel panicky and anxious. I told her so and she agreed it was time to return to the hotel and rest.

I made her take a shower because she had knelt in that filthy foot washing water and she did not argue. I was sitting on the bed watching CNN-International on the TV, but she came over with those scriptures in her hand and handed them to me, "Now will you read me something?" I agreed and she opened it to Luke: 22: 19–20, which reads:

19 And he took bread, and gave thanks, and brake it, and gave unto them, saying, This is my body which is given for you: this do in remembrance of me.

20 Likewise also the cup after supper, saying, This cup is the new testament in my blood, which is shed for you.

"What does remembrance here mean?" she asked formally. Socratically.

"Gilda, what is this about?"

"I'm dying. I'm emptied out."

"No you are not."

"You know I am."

"Well you're not dying this minute."

She didn't answer, but flipped to an opened section of the scriptures and handed me the book. I refused, "Look, let's get some sleep. Things will look much better in the morning. I'm so tired." And I was. The events of the last 48 hours had been too much for me. She gave me a long sweet hug and kiss on the top of my head as if she were tucking in a child. "Go to sleep. We'll see what the morning brings."

Oh, Mom if I could just go back to the moment, I would have held onto her with all my strength and never let her go. But instead I fell asleep. I knew she was distraught. I knew she was worried about dying, but I fell asleep anyway. I was so tired.

About three in the morning I awoke with a start and knew something was wrong. Gilda was gone again. I never for a second doubted where she had gone. I jumped into my clothes, ran out of the hotel and flagged down a taxi and commanded them to get me to the rat Wat as fast as they could drive.

Dear, dear, mom, when I arrived all was in chaos. There were police cars with lights flashing scattered everywhere and a crowd of people had gathered from the village. I tried to find out what was going on but no one spoke English. I kept asking and asking until I found a young monk, about twenty, who spoke passable English. He said, "Rats attack some person. Very bad." I frantically dragged him with me to the temple. There was a crowd of policemen and monks all hovering over a large spot of blood and next to it one of Gilda's shoes and a good number of dead rats. I screamed and passed out.

I awoke to the young monk patting my cheek and repeating, "Miss. Miss." I awoke to the horror that Gilda was gone. This is what happened? I got this from the young monk who translated for me from what another monk told him.

He said that shortly after midnight Gilda arrived and woke up the monk caretaker who directs the temple. She demanded he open the gate and let her into the shrine. He refused, but she was insistent, acting like it was life or death and finally he relented after she paid an extra fee for the late hour (a bribe). He said she came into the place and asked that he leave. He saw no reason not to, so he departed. He checked about an hour later and she was listening to the rats sing as they did every so often. He thought nothing of it and only stayed a minute and left again. He slept for a bit. He came back after another hour and she was lying on her back, her arms outstretched letting the rats run over her. She looked up at him and angrily pointed to the door, yelling for him to get out. Which he did. When he returned, he came upon a scene of grizzly horror. Hundreds of rats had nearly eaten her up. As he stood frozen at the sight, he said a rat would run over, take a large bite, be it bone or flesh, then run back to where it had been sitting on the wall, but there were many many rats each snatching a morsel and running back to their original position. He grabbed a broom and tried to drive them off but they attacked him and he ran for help. He called the police and rang the village bell that alerts people to a fire. Many people came at the sound of the alarm, but by the time they arrived Gilda had been wholly devoured by the rats. They managed to kill a good number before the rats fled from the temple.

Oh, mom, when I called you that night, I know I was a wreck but I think you can see why. Gilda is gone. I cannot get my head around it. Somehow I think she intended this. That she thought she was dying and that somehow she induced the rats to do as they did to her beloved friend Fatty Lumpkin. Or worse in a moment of insanity she believed she was the shepherdess of rats and had to die for them like Jesus and that is why she had me read the scriptures she did the night before. I have looked at where she was going to have me read, and it is these verses from

John 15 which were marked with a red pencil:

11 These things have I spoken unto you, that my joy might remain in you, and that your joy might be full.

12 This is my commandment, That ye love one another, as I have loved you.

13 Greater love hath no man than this, that a man lay down his life for his friends.

And then this one from John 17:

11 And now I am no more in the world, but these are in the world, and I come to thee. Holy Father, keep through thine own name those whom thou hast given me, that they may be one, as we are.

Except she has crossed out "Holy Father" with just "Mother."

I'm sick Mom. I did not see her madness. I should have. I knew she thought her death was imminent, but maybe I just did not want to believe it. Maybe I was blind to what she really knew. I'm so, so sad and broken. I've got the only thing that survives her being devoured—her bloody shoe. I'm going to bury it near the cabin in the La Sals. What I don't know is if she died while blessing the rats, for that is what I believe she was doing laying on the floor with her arms outstretched, or if she took her own life first. It's all lost in events that cannot be recovered by anyone's memory. Only Gilda and the rats know what happened. Did she intend this? How wicked of her! How mean. How cruel to leave me behind like this! Mom, I'm so mad. I'm so hurt. It makes no sense. We had such a wonderful night? What has she done?

Mom. I'm so heartbroken. I'm crying all the time and did not stop for a second as I wrote this. That is why it looks like it has been submerged in water and dried. Because it has been.

I'll leave for the States next week; I've already made arrangements. I'm sending this by Federal Express. I fly into Chicago at 2:25 on DL 2348 from LA. I love you Mom. I'm a wreck, but I'm OK. I'll make it. Don't worry, I'm not going to follow her into the darkness. I'm just never going to get over this. Ever.

Love,
Babs

Vignette 23. A Small Fragment of a Text Supposedly from Gilda, Found in a Romance Novel, Discovered 2002

The following is a scrap of text claimed to be from Trillim herself[1]. It was found written in the back of a paperback book, *Glynda* by Susannah Leigh, at the Dusit Hotel where they kept a shelf of books for the guests to take or leave. The provenance is suspect: Trillim scholar Anthony Donatello claims to have found it shortly after her death, however, no researcher has been as lucky as Donatello at finding these sorts of treasures and some have suspected that his luck is just too good. He insists that it is a matter of his doggedness rather than fraud that accounts for his success and some of his finds are above suspicion. Handwriting analysis supports the claim of authenticity. However, detractors, mostly of the naturalistic camp, want it to be a fake as it does not fit their understanding and the fragment plays into the framework of those who take Gilda at her word, perhaps a little too readily. Here is the fragment:

It has all come together. Babs is here. And the descendants of my beloved friends have gathered to sing to me and to offer up sweet remembrances. Last night upon my arrival the singers in fur of rich browns and golds took up their positions along the wall and I led them as I have so many times. Their song was of that same beauty I remember. But these cannot be the same rats I knew. No. They must be 60 or 70 generations removed, maybe much more, yet they took my direction for the song when I gestured to them from some instinctual memory as willingly as did their progenitors. Or have they practiced deep within the forest for many rat years the tones and songs learned so long ago? Most glorious of all, something of my mother was present whether brought out from my memories or from something eternal I cannot say, but she was there. After the song, I laid down and stretched forth my arms and again the rats received my blessing after licking my stump. Over the years I had begun to doubt. No more. No more. We are objects in relation, and relations of relations. Objects of processes and processes of objects. We are both one and many. Many and one. I stand in an infinity of connections to things that define and are defined by me. Oh rats. My lovely fellow beasty objects. How love structures and frames everything.

Vignette 24: Gilda's Final Note Written Two Months after Her Mother's Death. Given to Me by Babs Lake, 2013

So now to the new material I've obtained that makes this thesis a unique contribution to Trillim Studies. Babs Lake has refused all interviews. During the summer she still lives in the La Sals in the cabin Gilda gifted her. For the last several years I've made a pilgrimage to visit the now aged Babs. She is always cordial. She will talk about a vast array of subjects, from the ecology of the great laccoliths that dominate the horizon to the latest bestsellers. She will berate me and my family for keeping sheep and the damage they do to the mountain. However, there are two areas that cannot be broached: Gilda Trillim and rats. Despite their unlikely occurrence in these Gambel oak and Ponderosa pine-dominated landscapes she keeps a number of rattraps set on the porch and around the cabin. If you bring up the subject of these vermin her eyes flash with destruction and she will hold up a finger and warn you, "Do not mention such things in this house!" It is clear she means it. When you bring up Gilda, her eyes will mist over and her lips will tighten and she will nod several times and then leave the room. She will come back and beg forgiveness and say she cannot yet talk about it despite the many years that have passed since. Until now.

Gilda's life has been well analyzed and this sketch I've written to introduce her is a mere outline, just a pencil tracing, I fear. The debate about her life goes on. But I will add something that rounds out the account of her death. On my last visit to Lake, she seemed weaker than I had ever seen her, even just a month or so ago. I had previously left her with the manuscript of this work up until the last Vignette, hoping to get her comments on it and check it for accuracy. We were sitting at the kitchen table having a cup of peppermint tea, which she claims calms her stomach.

The manuscript was before her and she laid her hand on the pile and told me there was much in there she had never seen and felt blessed to have had a chance to read it and thanked me heartily for putting it together.

She then got up and wobbled over to the bookcase. She took down a volume of Montaigne's essays and from within drew out a few pages of hand-written notes. They were of course from Gilda.

"Take these. They are yours."

I have not submitted them to other scholars to establish their provenance. I did not enter them in the slow machinery of scholarly preservation and analysis. They are mine. Perhaps my only treasure. Do not fear. Upon my death they have been marked for deposit in the University of Michigan's Trillim Collection, where they can be dissected and their atoms extracted for isotopic signatures and surfaces scanned for pollen traces so their geographical history can be revealed and they can be placed on a couch and psychoanalyzed by whatever theory is current in five or fifty or five hundred years. For the moment, however, I will hold them as an artifact of someone I've spent much of my later life chasing. A physical connection to Gilda Trillim. But I do put here her words from that document, which, at least for me, offer a final insight into her final act. A messiah complex? Perhaps. She was clearly re-enacting Christ's final moments in her own. The washing of the disciples' feet vis-à-vis the foot massage for Babs. The scriptures she wanted read by her best friend. Several elements combine to suggest she was preparing to be a Christ figure. But is that not what Jesus did? In his final moments wasn't he playing out a script set out in the Old Testament on which acts were expected of the Jewish messiah? Maybe all messiahs must enact a theatrical play.

Was she mad? A fraud or charlatan manipulating even those who loved her best to achieve some macabre end to satisfy an over-imaginative ego? Whose martyrdom sealed the fame and longevity of her work? Perhaps all of these.

My own take is that she did become a redeemer of sorts. Not for humans, but for the rats. For after all this, one of the few things I can state with confidence is this: she loved them. This is rarely commented on by those who study her life. They tend to look at motivations of power or madness or attempts to manipulate others to achieve unstated and dimly guessed goals that she was supposed to have harbored. However, the one truth I can't seem to let go of is that she loved those rats.

She saw in them something important and wondrous that brooked nothing but attention and devotion. That they saved her (and I do frankly state that I believe her account as given), and she them. She loved them and cared for them. She followed them like a mother does her children no matter what their distance both in time and place. She delighted that they held onto what she taught them in song and apparently even passed it on to their descendants. Moreover, it is clear that she believed that the rats were becoming something. That this song of theirs that emerged newborn into the world was the manifestation of a new chapter in Earth's history—that it would continue to grow and spread among these strange creatures into something novel and important. I sense Gilda believed her South American vision. Or at least aspects of it. At least that there were things in the universe—she called them shepherds and shepherdesses—that loved complexly. That were devoted to watching and delighting in what emerged. Somehow, that inspired her to do the same—to be a shepherdess of the rats. She died for that emergence, as any great redeemer will. Or so I've come to believe.

This is what was written on the paper given me by Lake.

How strange to find myself here. Mother's gone and I always told myself that I came to these meetings for her. She's been gone now nearly two months and yet I still attend. Around me the deacons with tussled hair and wrinkled white shirts have passed the bread and the water, blessed with ritual exactness (repeated twice today at the insistence of the Bishop).

The Sacrament. The Lord's Supper. What is this? I take the small cup between my thumb and forefinger. I look at the clear water, cool in a white cardstock cup. My gaze descends all the way to the bottom of the cup. I stare. Peering in, it's as if I'm looking into the benthos of a small pale white pond. The individual fibers that make up the paper of the cup are magnified and by attending even more closely, enlarge to fill my field of vision. The young man standing beside the row shifts impatiently, hinting that I should drink it up and return the tray to him, but I don't want to drink it. I want to imbibe it with my eyes. With my heart. With my mind. I keep the cup and hand him the tray. I look back into the water. And I discover I know it! Not the water as H_2O, but as symbol. As an offering. I know it through and through. How strange. Unlike the apple seeds, I sense in the cup's liquid a purity. A revealed totality of essence. I sense it through and through. Not as a noun-ed thing. Neither the fullness of the thing it represents—a remembrance of sacrificial blood. But a symbol whose presence is a given fullness. A grace. White cupped water. A symbol. Nothing seems hidden or withdrawn. It is pure expression. A pointer. And as pointer, pure. To what does it gesture? Events thousands of years ago. Events that have since created networks and networks within networks full and rich, but all somehow condensing in this cup, and through it into me and shooting from me, binding me in complexity and relations running in and through all of time. I've spent my life trying to understand one thing in fullness and am I offered it in a paper cup? Isn't this Logos? The word made flesh and made word again? I look at the water, its surface tremorring in tiny wavelets dancing across, distorting all that lies below it, yet not affecting its givenness. Its grace. I think, wasn't it a single word that God spoke that brought the universe into existence? An utterance, a sound, like the water in the cup that contains the fullness in symbol from which all things emanate? And in this don't we see the purity of this word, which appears as is? Apparent, it offers itself as is. I am that I am. And now it all comes home. Finally I see it. The one thing whose appearance is the thing in itself. Essence in this water. Apparent and graspable in its univocal simplicity. Representing the word made flesh, a word spoken in the beginning from which all things emerge, and returning here in this cup. In my hand.

I looked and looked at an apple seed. I never found it. I looked at all the things connected to it and never located it. Yet here in my hand in clear water is a symbol that I know and from which all things are connected. Nets upon nets tangle and weave around me. The word. The Om. Maybe a remnant of the one thing that fractured through an event of stochastic eruption. A pointer to everything else.

And there it is. I laugh. A deacon looks at me reprovingly. I fall to silence but the smile does not leave my mouth. How strange that these connections established by a few dirty itinerant men and women at the dinner of a dying and doomed and betrayed man have bubbled forward from a tiny tick of land held as vassal by the Roman Empire. From there the threads wind through the Middle Ages, through renaissances and holocausts thick and many, to a small Mormon congregation in Moab, Utah. From that launch point a ritual meal is re-enacted and remembered and has become the word of a god entering the world. A shepherd god. Gods who cry and laugh and sing and dance. Male and female gods. Gods of a wild and strange biology evolved from chaos, then finding and helping what emergences and intelligences that appear. Gods willing to die. Are such possible then?

Who can say?

But this I can say. I came from somewhere. The reasons given that the bread passed my lips came from somewhere else, but they join and combine in me into a richer reality than either of us alone. Is this what a shepherd does? See the nascent potentials and enlivens and encourages them and allows them to flower into what they will? Fly above the void and the face of the deep and see in the chaos embryonic stirrings that might in complexity emerge into newness?

Why? That I know. I know it well. It is for love. What else could engender such sacrifices to achieve the redemptive power necessary to midwife these possibilities, these potentials, these capacities, into existence?

My rats. My beloved rats. I cannot think of them without my heart swelling to nearly the point of exploding asunder like a nuclear bomb at the bigness of the grace they offered me and in turn received from me in their song. Grace. Love. Those things I found in them. What future inheres in that event we shared? How might a shepherdess nurture that moment, like this Son of God, whose flesh I weekly partake, and in whose symbols I find instantiated essences pure? Did he in his act of redemption set in motion the reverberations we feel to this day? If humans pass away like all species do eventually, will the song of my rats continue? Can this be repeated if someone loves them enough to die for them?

The note ends here.

My Thesis

The stars are out bright against a black moonless sky. A pack of coyotes yaps not far away. Stanislaw does not even raise his head to their calls. If they were silently moving among the sheep he would know and be as alert as a prizefighter. Their chatter indicates they are about other things.

I stretch and walk down the two-track road which runs from where the trailer is parked. Little mounds of white sheep appear in the distance as the meadow rises to the line of trees maybe a half-mile away. I did not hear him wake up, but Stanislaw has joined me. He walks observant and silent, content to plod behind in case he is needed.

The air is calm, cool. I breathe it in.

Sitting under this sky, I think about Gilda. About whether she was mad. After reading the above, my advisors asked that I end this with a conclusion as to that question. But what can I say? I do not know what madness is or would look like when everything Gilda did points to a keen and clever mind embracing a universe that makes little sense.

So conclusions? I am convinced like many that Gilda was dying of some ailment. Cancer perhaps—Babs, the only one who knows, refuses to say. I believe she went to Thailand ostensibly for a cure (that is the pretense she told Babs, I believe). But *she* went there to see the rats she had read about in the travel magazine. That is all I can conclude. Did she want to die at their hand? How could she know they would remember the rituals enacted at Fatty Lumpkin's death? I doubt she did. Things transpired as they will. An emergence.

I am convinced that the rats were descendants of her choir. The night after Gilda's death the rats were never seen again. Had they been, I'm sure they would have been killed as a danger to tourists, but they evaporated into the forest and no sign of their existence was ever found.

Was she mad then? If she was, then we all are. She pulled a world into existence and in that world she created a new thing. Something extraordinary that had never before existed.

I like to imagine the rats singing on. Remembering in their ratty way Gilda Trillim. Although I doubt that they will remember that name, perhaps she will exist as a tone-poem remembered and sung for millions of murid generations and in so doing, create a new niche wherein novelty can continue to evolve stippled with fresh complexities that brighten and make new this particular plane structured so that new creations can unfold.

Notes & References

Introduction

1. Based on a paper delivered to the Association of Mormon Letters, March 2019.
2. With the advent of modern computer technology there has been a revival of the French School with its attempt to take the power set of the words in the novel with the constraint that each subset includes at least one of the types of words (objects, attribute, etc.). While there have been some interesting readings using these techniques, (see e.g., Guimond, G. G. and Y. Meunier. "Badiou, Set Theory, and Trillim: The Ecstasy of the Void. *Author & Text* 34 [1998]: 234–41) my own feeling is that these have largely failed.
3. See Levant, S. and M. Gregson. "Emergence of Meaning and the Unnecessary Inclusion of Conjunctions: Linkages, Networks, and Ecological Relationships in Trillim." *Feminist Studies* 6 (1999): 24–56.

Vignette 1

1. I'd like to thank the staff at the Church History Library for helping me with access to Arnfinnur Skáldskapur's journal and family letters. Also thanks to the (still in existence) Redbearded Horseshoers, for access to the minutes of early meetings.
2. The dresses he changed can still be seen in the Astral Room at the Redbearded Horseshoers' Lodge in Salt Lake City.
3. Jorge Luis Borges, discussion published in the Columbia Forum and later quoted in *Worldwide Laws of Life: 200 Eternal Spiritual Principles* by John M. Templeton (Philadelphia: Templeton Foundation Press, 1998. 141).

Vignette 2

1. Smithy, J. G., H. Z. Chang, and R. Gallacci. "Trillim, the 1957 Uber Cup, and the Hidden Influence of Merleau-Ponty." *The Gilda Trillim Quarterly* 7 (2012): 126–38.

Vignette 3

1. I used this as the reference although it is unknown to me which one Trillim actually used, but this is the same translation: Proust, Marcel. *Swann's Way—Remembrance Of Things Past.* Vol. 1. Trans. C. K. Scott Moncrieff. New York: Henry Holt And Company, 1922. Accessed November 11, 2012 (The Project Gutenberg): http://www.gutenberg.org/files/7178/7178-h/7178-h.htm.
2. Leopold, Aldo. "Thinking Like a Mountain." In *A Sand County Almanac: With Other Essays on Conservation from Round River.* New York: Ballantine Books, 1970.

Vignette 5

1. It is unknown what this apparent fight or falling out is about.
2. Scovell, E. J. *River Steamer.* Manchester, UK: Carcanet Press, 1956.

Vignette 6

1. Steig, W. *Abel's Island.* Farrar, Straus and Giroux (BYR), 1976.

Vignette 7

1. Hankski, F. "Dating Trillim's Note on Melancholia." *The Gilda Trillim Quarterly* 2 (2007): 123–25

Vignette 8

1. Obviously this must be the German philosopher Martin Heidegger (1889–1976). Her use of the word Nazi may reflect some familiarity of his work as interpreted by the French Existentialists of this time period (indicating she was more

familiar with what she was reading than Babs seemed to be aware).

Vignette 9

1. Recipe repeated from Millar, J. "Black Cake: (A Recipe from Emily Dickinson, for Emily Dickinson)." *Collapse* 7 (July 2011): 411. Not Trillim's original unknown source.

Vignette 10

1. Trillim, Gilda. "Adventures of Mind, Tragedy of Body." *Look Magazine* (July 1967): 11.
2. Blinova, P. "Drugs and Madness: Trillim and the Argument for a Flashback." *International Journal of Historical Psychology and Behavioral Science* 6 (2001): 109–17.

Vignette 11

1. De Azevedo, L. and C. L. Pearson. *My Turn On Earth: A Family Musical Play.* Embryo Records. 1977.
2. A sonnet.
3. A sonnet.
4. Satan starts with a series of couplets.
5. A villanelle
6. A sestina.
7. An Italian sonnet.
8. A set of limericks.
9. An Elizabethan sonnet.
10. A pantoun

Vignette 12

1. *The Paris Review* 101, (Winter 1986). "Gilda Trillim Interview." *The Art of Fiction.* No. 94b.
2. These words come from Gilda Trillim's unpublished papers. They are located in the Archive, and the story of how I found them is well worth telling, but not here.

3. Gilda Trillim's unpublished papers.

4. Some scholars, in particular Jan Sillitoe of Princeton University and Ping Hsu of the University of Beijing have formally discounted Gilda's story of rats feeding her, and have argued at several academic conferences that this is exactly what she was doing, and her stories started as avoidance of what she had had to do to survive and became so embedded in her consciousness that she came to believe the story. However they are a minority. Especially in light of the eye witness account of the Soviet delegation's report on Gilda's relationship with the rats contained in the files at the Russian Academy of Science.

5. Gilda Trillim's unpublished papers.

6. Larson, S. "The King Follett Discourse: A Newly Amalgamated Text." *BYU Studies* 18 (1978): 2.

Vignette 13

1. There are those who wonder if there is a real object behind the phenomenological experience of the possible object. Berkley held that all was the mind of God generating all sensual experience and that all was just a perception of an object He wanted us to experience. There is no refuting that possibility that 'thought' is all that is real. I may be the only real mind in the word. I cannot refute that, but that is not the way to bet. Yes, it's nothing but a wager that objects exist, but one I am willing to make and accept without further proof— Kit.

2. Note: I don't know Trillim's actual reference but this is contained in: Sweet, D. *Heraclitus: Translation and Analysis.* New York: University Press of America, 1995. 123.

3. Appears to be an original translation. Compare to Porete, M. *The Mirror of Simple Souls/Marguerite Porete.* Trans. and Intro. Ellen L. Babinsky. Pref. Robert E. Lerner. The Classics of Western Spirituality. Yahweh, NJ: Paulist Press, 1993. 79.

4. Appears to be an original translation. (Compare to Hadewijch.) *Hadewijch: The Complete Works*. Trans. and Intro. Mother Columba Hart, O.S.B. Pref. Paul Mommaers. Mahwah, NJ: Paulist Press, 1980. 195.

Vignette 14

1. Petrov. S. "Gilda Trillim and Monty Smith: Minimalist Connections." *Western Culture* 13 (1998): 320–33.

Vignette 17

1. Ovid. Not sure of Gilda's reference. I reference Ovid. *The Art of Love and Other Poems*. Loeb Classical Library. Cambridge, MA: Harvard University Press, 1979. 66.

Vignette 18

1. SLP. "What the Ant Knew." *Silver Blade* 15 (16 Sep. 2012).

Vignette 19

1. Iguchi, A. and K. Khornezh. E. "Elves in the La Sals: More Evidence of Undiagnosed Schizophrenia in Gilda Trillim." *Literature and Mental Illness* 29 (1999): 343–62.

2. J. Faulconer. "Divine Embodiment and Transcendence: Propaedeutic Thoughts and Questions." *Element* 1, (spring 2001).

3. This person (or strange; creature, as many believe it to be) is not unknown among those who have spent significant time in the La Sal Mountains. The Hispanic herders who worked for my father call her *la pequeña elfa*. Some of the cowboys call her 'Littlefoot.' And now I must confess. I have seen her too. I'll explain momentarily. After reading Gilda's account, I started asking around to see if anyone else had seen the woman Trillim describes. Most were loath to admit they had encountered this individual and among those who did, most of the accounts were reports of fleeting glimpses, usually in

the late afternoon.

I wanted to put some rigor into my explorations because I thought if I could interview this strange person, it would add much to the Trillim story, especially if she could corroborate the account of their meeting. While many think she is some sort of supernatural entity, I, of course, do not.

I began to formally chart where these reported encounters had taken place, thinking I might be able to triangulate back to the place where she lived (I was convinced that she lived up here in the mountains). She has been seen over much of the La Sals but only in the densest aspen forests, typically in roadless areas. I was able to locate eight accounts of encounters made by those who snatched a clear enough glimpse to claim to have gotten a good look at her. I also obtained accounts of sixteen fleeting glimpses that had enough detail to warrant further consideration.

Gilda's encounter is typical. Sometimes the strange woman is described as naked. Sometimes as wearing clothes similar to what she was wearing when Gilda saw her. Part of the problem is that the woman has become the fare of starlit campfire stories. A number of people have heard the story of the fey woman and repeat them corrupting the genuine narratives. When this occurs, the 'I thought I saw her' accounts start to outnumber actual detailed reports. I believe this is what happened with Bigfoot in the northwest. This creates a difficulty because people who have heard the legend of an elf creature and have been primed to *see* an elf, start to let their memories of a glimpse of an unexplained movement in late afternoon light augment their experience with memories of the stories they have heard. They add details and amendments resembling popular accounts to the original experience. These often enough start looking like archetypal fairies from fairytales complete with wings, or pixie skirts, or other Tinkerbelle accoutrements.

However, the eight solid accounts are worth noting in that

until I enquired, in all but two cases the men (they were all men) who repeated them to me had never mentioned the encounter to anyone else before. I have deposited these accounts in the archives of the Utah Folklore Association at Utah State University. I give only two in this work. I include my own as well.

The first was from a hand who worked for my father. He says this happened in 2008 in June up near Minor's Basin.

"Yeah, well I was riding a four-wheeler down a back logging road because there were some fences your pa wanted me to mend. I parked it and had to walk the line for a couple of miles into some dense aspen most of the morning. I came to a little clearing and decided to have some lunch. I pulled out my sandwich and a RedBull I had and then laid down to rest, propping my pack up against a tree to use as a pillow. I must have nodded off but when I woke up I see what I thought was a little girl looking at me, but it wasn't a little girl because she had tits like a full-grown woman and they were bared for all the world to see. She was just standing there and when I opened my eyes she looked for just a moment and then ran like a deer into the deep forest. It took me a minute to come to and to be honest I was pretty sure I was dreaming. But it seemed pretty real and I've never seen nothing like it before."

The second encounter was from a Mexican ranch supervisor who worked for my father (I've translated this from his Spanish).

"It was during the muzzleloader hunt about the end of September 2012. I was up high in the Beaver Basin. I was on Slayer, up that road that runs up by the flanks of Waas. I was alone up there, largely because a big Pine had come down on the road and no one had cleared it away yet. It was blocking ATVs, motorcycles and trucks, but the horse had no trouble going around it. I was plodding through some light snow when I spotted a three-point standing broadside in the road looking at me. Slayer came to a halt and I slipped out of the saddle. I had the rifle out and moved forward real slow and took the shot. I thought it was dead on behind the front leg, but it was high and the gutshot beast busted up hill. I followed on foot, it being too rocky for the horse. The wounded animal was leaving a blood trail wet and clear. It was losing a lot of blood. I knew it could not get far so I reloaded the gun with three pellets, put in a bullet, reprimed, and started following it up the hill. It was crazy steep. I found the buck sitting in some underbrush breathing hard. I finished it with a good heart shot. Now I was glad that it had run uphill 'cause it was going to be easier to drag him down to the horse instead of up. I had my elbow length rubber gloves because they were talking then that some of the deer had Mad Deer Disease so I put those on and gutted it and grabbed it by the horns and started pulling it down the hill. It was pretty overgrown so about half way down to the road I stopped to rest.

I was sitting on a boulder, when I look up and see what I thought was a little girl standing there. She was in a buckskin dress of sorts and wearing a crown-like thing on her head. I'd heard of this elf in stories and knew a guy who had seen her. I said ¡hola! and she asked me in Spanish if I was going to pay the tribute for the deer off her mountain. I asked what it was and she said a small piece of the hindquarter. I was actually pretty scared. This girl was like a woman but smaller, but she had devil eyes, and so I told her to take what she would like. She was fast and just stabbed a long-bladed knife right into the butt and carved out a piece. Said ¡gracias! and then took off up the hill. She was a rabbit."

One can see from the map that the encounters (more certain encounters are in blue, and less in red) run along a line running roughly from the Buckeye Lake (near the yellow pin marking Trillim's cabin) to the Mt. Waas area.

In the region near the most sightings, I set up a deer stand high up in a pine. I used logging shoes and climbing equipment to set it up and then I waited high above the forest floor.

I waited three days on the first attempt. Sitting in my deer stand, eating, reading, and watching. I nearly went batty. Long into the night I would stare through my night vision scope, looking at the trail below me. I saw deer, bear, and cows in abundance. About two weeks later I tried again. This time I was successful. Sort of. I didn't find her, she found me. I fell asleep (so many of the accounts report sleep preceding her appearance) and when I awoke she was looking at me, squatting on a branch of the pine in which I was concealed. She was dressed in camo pants and a black T-shirt—quite unexpected given the reports I'd heard. Like finding a leprechaun dressed in jeans. She was small. Maybe four feet high and lithe as a dancer. She looked older than I expected, maybe even some graying on the edges of her dark brown hair. Her eyes were clear but there was a bit of age about them. I would put her perhaps as old as thirty-five or even forty. This quite surprised me as I expected more a young girl as the reports tended to suggest.

I made no move, but looked her in the eyes. Then I smiled. She did not smile back, but said, "¿Sabes que facillo sería matarte?" (Do you know how easy it would be to kill you?) I didn't know what to say, but nodded. Then in American English she said, "Stop looking for me." Then added in Spanish, ¿Entiende?" She then climbed quickly down the tree, making an almost fifteen-foot drop at the end from the lowest branches of the Ponderosa to the ground. I finally had enough clarity of thought to shout after her, "Did you ever meet Gilda Trillim?" It was a stupid thing to say, since she had only met her twice in brief, random encounter. How would she know who Trillim was? But as if in answer, she turned and smiled at me and flipped me off, just as she had Gilda. Then she turned away and began moving as if she meant to sprint away. I called out almost in desperation, "Do you have a name?" This stopped her. She turned her head up, almost in amusement, and said, "Estrellas. My name is de las estrellas." Her Spanish and English were both flawless. The name translates as 'From the stars.'

Since then I have given up the search. I felt a genuine threat in her first declaration to me. I took it seriously. There are human laws, but there are also mountain laws. Someone who does not want to be found must be allowed that right. But these things I believe about her. She is educated. Her diction is very good and there was a wryness about her that spoke of intelligence and mischief. No one has ever seen her in the winter, so I believe she spends her winters elsewhere. But something in her look when she raised her middle finger led me to believe it was a dog whistle, signaling me that she knew who I meant. She was letting me know Gilda was known even to her.

Most important in this she was a real person. A number of scholars, most notably, Gillian Weaver of the University of Idaho, have argued that Gilda was going mad and these hallucinations were signs of some sort of mental collapse that might explain the strange turn her life took toward the end. She was not mad—unless I am as well.

Vignette 20

1. Etulain, R. W. "Wallace Stegner and Western Spirituality." *Literature and Belief* 21 (2001): 255–71.
2. Stapley, J. A. and K. Wright. "Female Ritual Healing in Mormonism." *Journal of Mormon History* 37 (2011): 1–85.

Vignette 22

1. Friedman, K. T. and G. N. Glick. "Wild Fluctuations: Was Gilda Trillim Bipolar? A Look at New Evidence." *The Journal of Historical Psychological Research* 45 (2007): 344–51.
2. Steward, M. "Empress Trillim is Wearing No Clothes." *The New York Review of Books* 58.16 (2011): 34–36.
3. Tobkin. M. "Trillim, McCarthy, and Stegner: One of These Western Writers Has Crashed the Party." *Quarterly West* 57 (2004): 28–35.
4. Lightfoot, S. *A Comparison of Jungian, Freudian, and Lacanian*

Perspectives on Trillim's Life and Work. PhD Dissertation. University of North Carolina Chapel Hill. 2011.
5. Franks, K. "Was Gilda Trillim Dying? A Re-examination." *Journal of American Studies* 41 (2007): 321–29

Vignette 23
1. Donatello, A. "A Fragment from Trillim's Last Day." Trillim Archives Catalog #1497. 1999.

Roundfire

FICTION

Put simply, we publish great stories. Whether it's literary or popular, a gentle tale or a pulsating thriller, the connecting theme in all Roundfire fiction titles is that once you pick them up you won't want to put them down.
If you have enjoyed this book, why not tell other readers by posting a review on your preferred book site. Recent bestsellers from Roundfire are:

The Bookseller's Sonnets
Andi Rosenthal

The Bookseller's Sonnets intertwines three love stories with a tale of religious identity and mystery spanning five hundred years and three countries.
Paperback: 978-1-84694-342-3 ebook: 978-184694-626-4

Birds of the Nile
An Egyptian Adventure
N.E. David

Ex-diplomat Michael Blake wanted a quiet birding trip up the Nile – he wasn't expecting a revolution.
Paperback: 978-1-78279-158-4 ebook: 978-1-78279-157-7

Blood Profit$
The Lithium Conspiracy
J. Victor Tomaszek, James N. Patrick, Sr.

The blood of the many for the profits of the few... *Blood Profit$*
will take you into the cigar-smoke-filled room where American
policy and laws are really made.
Paperback: 978-1-78279-483-7 ebook: 978-1-78279-277-2

The Burden
A Family Saga
N.E. David

Frank will do anything to keep his mother and father apart. But
he's carrying baggage – and it might just weigh him down ...
Paperback: 978-1-78279-936-8 ebook: 978-1-78279-937-5

The Cause
Roderick Vincent

The second American Revolution will be a fire lit from an
internal spark.
Paperback: 978-1-78279-763-0 ebook: 978-1-78279-762-3

Don't Drink and Fly
The Story of Bernice O'Hanlon: Part One
Cathie Devitt

Bernice is a witch living in Glasgow. She loses her way in her
life and wanders off the beaten track looking for the garden of
enlightenment.
Paperback: 978-1-78279-016-7 ebook: 978-1-78279-015-0

Gag
Melissa Unger

One rainy afternoon in a Brooklyn diner, Peter Howland
punctures an egg with his fork. Repulsed, Peter pushes the plate
away and never eats again.
Paperback: 978-1-78279-564-3 ebook: 978-1-78279-563-6

The Master Yeshua
The Undiscovered Gospel of Joseph
Joyce Luck

Jesus is not who you think he is. The year is 75 CE. Joseph ben
Jude is frail and ailing, but he has a prophecy to fulfil ...
Paperback: 978-1-78279-974-0 ebook: 978-1-78279-975-7

On the Far Side, There's a Boy
Paula Coston

Martine Haslett, a thirty-something 1980s woman, plays hard on
the fringes of the London drag club scene until one night which
prompts her to sign up to a charity. She writes to a young Sri
Lankan boy, with consequences far and long.
Paperback: 978-1-78279-574-2 ebook: 978-1-78279-573-5

Tuareg
Alberto Vazquez-Figueroa

With over 5 million copies sold worldwide, *Tuareg* is a
classic adventure story from best-selling author
Alberto Vazquez-Figueroa, about honour, revenge and a
clash of cultures.
Paperback: 978-1-84694-192-4

Readers of ebooks can buy or view any of these bestsellers by clicking on the live link in the title. Most titles are published in paperback and as an ebook. Paperbacks are available in traditional bookshops. Both print and ebook formats are available online.

Find more titles and sign up to our readers' newsletter at
http://www.johnhuntpublishing.com/fiction

Follow us on Facebook at
https://www.facebook.com/JHPfiction
and Twitter at https://twitter.com/JHPFiction